OVERSOUL SEVEN IS:

Lydia—A twentieth-century American poet, scheduled to be born again—three centuries before her death. She refused her destiny until she had plumbed the mystery of the gods.

Josef—A painter in seventeenth-century Sweden. A "dream" saved him from a frozen death, that he might live to solve the riddle of his genius—and guide his baby daughter, the incarnation of Lydia's passionate and seeking soul.

Will—A proud and desperate young man who held the universe hostage as he questioned the value of his own life.

Jeffery—A modern-day psychologist, imprisoned within his five senses—until he became the unwitting scribe of the spirit that freed him.

Books by Jane Roberts

How to Develop Your ESP Power
The Education of Oversoul Seven
The Further Education of Oversoul Seven

Published by POCKET BOOKS

Most Pocket Books are available at special quantity discounts for bulk purchases for sales promotions, premiums or fund raising. Special books or book excerpts can also be created to fit specific needs.

For details write the office of the Vice President of Special Markets, Pocket Books, 1230 Avenue of the Americas, New York, New York 10020.

JANE ROBERTS

THE FURTHER EDUCATION OF OVERSOUL SEVEN

PUBLISHED BY POCKET BOOKS NEW YORK

POCKET BOOKS, a division of Simon & Schuster, Inc.
1230 Avenue of the Americas, New York, N.Y. 10020

Copyright © 1979 by Jane Roberts

Published by arrangement with Prentice-Hall
Library of Congress Catalog Card Number: 78-26860

ISBN: 0-671-83263-8

First Pocket Books printing January, 1984

10 9 8 7 6 5 4 3 2 1

POCKET and colophon are registered trademarks
of Simon & Schuster, Inc.

Printed in the U.S.A.

Dedicated
to
The Gods
Behind
the Divine
Camouflage

Contents

CONTENTS

CONTENTS

This Book
Is
Written
in
the Time of
Jeffery

(Circa late 1970s A.D.)

THE FURTHER
EDUCATION OF
OVERSOUL
SEVEN

Prologue One

Cyprus said, "This is how the book will
begin:

> Lydia was
> Nicknamed
> Tweety,
> Because Bianka
> Said she was
> Tiny and skinny
> As a newborn
> Bird."

"Wait a second," Oversoul Seven said. "I think your
tenses are wrong. Even though Lydia died in the twentieth
century, and is reborn in the seventeenth, shouldn't you say,

'Lydia *will be* called Tweety,' because she hasn't experienced that life yet? Or is, 'Lydia *was called* Tweety' correct, because people think that the seventeenth century happened first? Or—"

They both burst out laughing.

Cyprus said, "You'll just have to wait and see. That is, though all time is simultaneous, I'll have to wait until writing the book catches up with my experience."

Prologue Two
(Some Time Later)

"You *are* going to write this book, aren't you?" Oversoul Seven asked, somewhat anxiously.

"In a manner of speaking," Cyprus said. "I think the first part will be called, 'The Odyssey of Jeffy-boy, Ram-Ram, and Queen Alice.'"

"Who on Earth are they?" Oversoul Seven asked. "And what do they have to do with Tweety and her new life, and my further education?"

Cyprus smiled. "That's something you'll have to learn for yourself. Real education always involves surprises. But pay attention, now. The odyssey of Jeffy-boy, Ram-Ram, and Queen Alice is about to begin. Of course, Jeffy-boy doesn't realize what's happening yet."

Chapter One

Journal of a Surprised Psychologist (Jeffery W. Blodgett)

These notes contain a record of my . . . what?

Dream activities? Hardly the word for them. No, to be correct, this manuscript is a chronicle of journeys embarked upon, strange as it sounds, when my physical body sleeps. There are several points to be made and I will make them here, with my first long entry. To be honest, I write that last statement with painful acceptance of general limitations that I for one no longer accept. For I know beyond all doubt, as you will see, that there is no past, present, or future in usual terms. Granting that, from now on I'll keep this journal as up to date as possible, and I have the oddest sensation that something important is about to happen even before I have time to sketch in what has occurred thus far.

Theoretically, these notes could be discovered in the past, even before I write them in my present. For that matter, they could come to light in some reality of which I know nothing. They could even emerge (as I know now) as automatic writing on the part of some stranger who lets down the conscious barriers of his mind; appearing as . . . psychological apports of a kind. Even as I may appear a wanderer in your dreams. Or you, in mine.

It seems that I've come alive only in these past few months, yet when these events first began, I was staggered. Even now, at times, I doubt my sanity. Yet what has happened so far has given me glimpses into the undersides of reality, and these only make the topsides that much more miraculous.

For the record, let me state that I've taken no drugs of any kind. Nothing that I know of initiated the adventure in which I'm now involved. These notes, written in the daytime, represent my attempt to relate my activities in dimensions of which most people are completely unaware.

So far I've managed to return to normal daytime living, but I have no guarantee that this will always be the case, particularly since I've encountered difficulties at times of a certain undefinable nature. Again—so far—I've retained my normal conscious stance in the reality accepted by everyone else. But I do grow aware of a precarious balance.

As long as I write these notes and read those that I've written before, then I'll know that I've returned safely from those equally valid realms. If I decide not to return, then I'll record my decision here, so that anyone interested will know that my exodus was voluntary, not the result of coercion, or worse, error or carelessness on my part. Particularly if my ex-wife, Sarah, ever reads these notes, I wouldn't want her to imagine me trying to claw my way back from an underside of reality that she could not understand.

Perhaps I should mention here that I'm a psychologist. My degrees alone will at least ensure that these notes get a reading. (B.A. at Cornell, master's and doctorate in behavioral psychology at Harvard.) To those who still recognize such ludicrous badges of erudition I say, "Hear me out. By your own standards, I have a right to your recognition." To those who think that degrees are primarily signs of ritualized ignorance I say, "I'm on your side." But I spent many years acquiring such status, and I may as well take advantage of it in that academia to which I no longer belong.

I should also tell you that I'm thirty-six years old, and still partially distrust that part of me over thirty. My ex-wife lives on the other side of the continent, remarried practically if not legally, and pregnant with her first child. I was trying to make up my mind as to whether or not I wanted to grow a human being in this crazy garden of existence. Sarah, apparently, got tired of waiting, and took up with another, more willing package of seed. So I was living alone when these events began.

I'm convinced that I'm involved in work of the utmost importance. I'm also aware that my attitude has all the earmarks of egomania, or a good deal of them. But I'm not suffering from any kind of Messiah complex. For one thing, I'm tired of examining myself for signs of schizophrenia, particularly since I've discovered that what I used to regard as my normal state of consciousness represents only the surface ripples of my identity. For another thing, I'm using my own personality as a psychological guinea pig in my adventures, and part of my work necessitates playing around with different states of awareness.

I hereby admit to those anticipated criticisms that my colleagues will make against me: that I'm not maintaining suitable objectivity or conforming to the "scientific method." I'm even turning my back on the electroencephalograph and the now respectable "dream laboratories," as they're called, though they have their place. Where I go, I must go utterly alone. No one can tell me what methods are useful or dangerous. The ordinary assumptions of daily life serve me not at all. Yet I will not turn back. The hope of great personal accomplishment—and knowledge—far outweighs the hazards, those that I have discovered and those that may still wait.

So after this lengthy introduction—psychologists are notoriously long-winded—I'll record the events that led me to this pass. The first episode seems so insignificant, by contrast with my later activities, that my initial astonishment now seems almost amusing. Yet the first hole in physical reality opened for me that night. The first crack appeared in the ordinary existence that I'd always known.

I was living in one of the wild stacks of modern apartments connected with the state university in a town in upstate New York. Each cube dwelling had its own entrance. The buildings had just been completed, and each terrace looked out on piles of rocks, dirt, and mudholes. The apartment itself reminded me of a Skinner box, complete with artificial environment, air conditioners, soundproofing, humidifiers; everything to make life sanitary and dull.

I couldn't get to sleep that night, so I got out of bed and went into the living room. For a few moments I stood on the terrace. There were no stairs connecting it to the ground, and I was on the seventh floor. Across the way identical terraces stuck out, hanging flimsily out over the snow-covered debris below.

It was 2 A.M. when I came back inside, after having been on the terrace for perhaps five minutes. I checked the clock and threw myself down on the couch. Immediately I fell into a deep sleep and dreamed that two men were talking to me. They wore ordinary clothing, suits of some innocuous nature. We were discussing the failure of behavioral psychology to uncover any but the most surface qualities of human personality. I disagreed with their indictment. At this point, a terrific noise awakened me. I sprang to a sitting position, fully alert—and I must admit, instantly alarmed.

To my astonishment, the two men still stood there. I recalled the dream clearly and recognized the two of them as my dream images. Blinking furiously, I rubbed my eyes.

7

"The wind knocked over the empty geranium pot on the patio. Don't bother yourself," the first man said.

I didn't speak. Quite deliberately I looked around. Everything was as it should be. The room was solid and real, except that the men couldn't possibly be in it. The sensory clues in that respect made no sense. There was one dim light lit, and I could see the men as clearly as I saw the couch, or desk, or anything else. I would have thought them intruders, burglars, if I hadn't remembered them from my dream.

As reasonably as I could, I said, "Look. You're dream images. I can't possibly be talking to you because I'm wide awake. Unless I'm still asleep and don't realize it."

"You've been overworking. Is that it?" The first man smiled in a way I found curiously comforting; and like an idiot I nodded my head vigorously and said, "Yes, that must be it. I *am* still asleep and dreaming."

But the second man laughed, and didn't seem as well-disposed toward me as the first. "Interesting hypothesis," he said. "Suppose I insist that you're a dream image of mine instead?"

I scowled, but even then I noted my own reactions. This second man was somewhat younger than I, and I resented his manner of knowing, or pretending to know, more about the situation than I did. To make it worse, the other man then grinned indulgently and said, "On the other hand, you may both be images in a dream of *mine*."

By now I knew that I was, indeed, fully awake. And I was frightened. For a moment I suspected that both of the men were lunatics who had somehow gained entry—intruders, in fact—and that I'd only confused them with earlier dream images. I pinched my arm. My reflexes were normal. My critical faculties were operating. Yet I could make no sense of the situation at all.

The younger man said, "Now that we've provided you with suitable stimuli to your curiosity, we'll enjoy watching your further reactions."

With this, I sprang up from the couch. Two things happened at once. Before my startled eyes, the two intruders began to disappear as if space itself was eating away at their edges. Then a severe, shattering click came at the base of my neck. The next thing I knew, I was back on the couch, thrown there in some fashion that utterly escaped me. The room was just as it had been, but the men were gone. Moreover, there was nothing to prove that they'd ever been there. Something else: I remembered opening my eyes, though I don't recall ever closing them. As soon as the men vanished, I ran to the French doors and threw them open. The geranium pot was in pieces on the patio floor.

As the days passed, I convinced myself that the whole affair had been some kind of dream-within-a-dream. Only one thing bothered me: my certainty that I had jumped up from the couch the moment the men's images were vanishing, while the next minute I was back on the couch, with my eyes *closed*. If it were only a dream, why would I have thought my eyes opened or closed? I mean, usually in dreams you see what you see, and that's the end of it, or so I thought at the time. The clicking at the back of my neck was also difficult to explain away, but I decided it was caused by some spasmodic jerking of my muscles.

I didn't tell anyone about the experience. Indeed, I managed to put it out of my mind so well that I might have forgotten it entirely if it hadn't been followed by an even more bizarre event. This next, more alarming, episode happened about a week later, and there was no way I could assign it to dream activity.

As far as I can recall, this was the sequence of events. I was at my desk, concentrating on a student's paper. It was devoted to a discussion of some experiments we'd done on the frontal lobes of rats. Then, without transition, I was caught up in an experience of frightful intensity. First, my body felt as if it was expanding, yet growing lighter in weight. The process continued until I felt impossibly light. Miles of space seemed to exist between my ears.

I became aware of the cells of my body in the oddest fashion. Each seemed to possess an alertness, a mini-personality—eager, responsive, and individualistic—and most of all, each initiated action and didn't just respond to stimuli. I had some crazy idea that my consciousness had dropped back to its components, when suddenly I felt . . . loose, or unfixed. There was that same clicking sensation in the back of my neck again, and to my horror I found myself quite literally suspended in the air, outside the terrace, about five feet away from the railing, with nothing but some sixty feet of space between me and the ground.

At any instant I expected to go crashing down. But nothing happened. I yelled for help, though there was no one in sight. It was late afternoon; I'd come home early to work on the student's report, but most people in the building were still in classes or meetings. In complete disbelief, I hung there, telling myself that I couldn't possibly be where I was, and wondering why I wasn't falling. It seemed that nothing was *ever* going to happen; no one would come to discover me, and I'd be left there for all eternity, like a fish on an invisible line, waiting to be pulled back in. Then, just as suddenly, I was back inside the living room, but still in the air, floating.

Next, I changed position and got the next-worst fright of my life, for I was staring down at my own body. There "I" sat, eyes closed but pen in hand, as if I'd taken a catnap while reading. I looked down at the top of my head; each hair springing up merrily like red grass from my scalp. My shoulders were slumped. The familiarity and unfamiliarity, so intermixed, quite transfixed me. My body looked so weirdly forlorn that a heartrending pity for it rushed through me.

But how could I be outside my body, looking down at it? I'd hardly thought of the question when I was drawn back into my usual form so quickly that I closed my eyes, imagining the worst kind of crash landing. I'm not sure what happened next, except that the clicking sound came again, and with it a sound like a soft explosion. Almost beyond panic, I opened my eyes to see my fingers holding the pen. I was back in my body. But if I had just opened my eyes, what eyes had I closed just before I plunged back in?

Dazed, I looked out the window to where I'd hung just a few moments earlier and I had the disquieting fear that I might see myself, still dangling there.

That night I knew I had to talk to someone. Only one person came to mind—Ramrod Brail—an older colleague who'd dabbled in fields like hypnosis and parapsychology. Now I wonder what would have happened if I'd chosen someone else to confide in instead. Certainly in the next weeks I wished more than once that I'd never made that phone call.

Chapter Two

Ram-Ram's Experiment

Thirty-six can sound pretty ancient if you're in your early twenties, or incredibly young if you're over fifty. To Ramrod Brail I was a mere youngster—although, because of my educational background, one to be taken seriously. He came over as soon as I called him, his curiosity aroused by the few hints of my experience that I tossed out over the telephone. I had called him for several reasons. Quite frankly, I was shaken not only by my experience itself but by its implications. Also I wanted to discuss the whole affair with someone perceptive but levelheaded, and someone who wouldn't blab all over campus.

Ram-Ram, as the students and younger professors called him affectionately, was what best can be called a faded campus flower, past retirement age and still teaching in an honorary position. He'd made a name in several specialized fields, from industrial psychology to hypnotic research. It was because of this latter unconventional interest of his that I thought he might be helpful.

His quick nervous cough told me he was outside the door even before he knocked. He held a cigarette in one hand and a half-finished drink in the other. Without preamble, he said, "Mmm. Not on pot or acid or anything, are you, Jeffy-boy?"

"Look, I don't like to be called Jeffy-boy," I answered irritably. "And no, I'm not high on anything."

He ignored my first remark and said, "No, I suppose you aren't; it's not your style; but I want to know where we stand. Now suppose you tell me, slowly, exactly what's been going on here. You weren't too clear on the phone."

I showed him to a chair and explained both episodes. He seemed excited, which surprised me somewhat. All the while he sat, chain-smoking, his eyes seldom leaving my face. I paid little attention to his kindly-old-psychologist's smile. I'd seen him use it too many times. He *is* kind, but not nearly as kind as he looks, and he's exceptionally shrewd, or he was until lately.

At one point in particular he interrupted me. "Yes, yes, yes," he said. "That click you felt at the base of your neck. Explain that part again." He spoke with exaggerated nonchalance, or so it seemed to me. I wondered if he was on to something, or thought he was. I repeated what I'd told him, and as he didn't stop me, I continued with my story.

Then he stood up impatiently, moving around in a kind of slow frenzy. "Yes, yes, yes," he said, more to himself than to me. "And what do we tell our young man here?" As he muttered this last, he swung around to face me. "We greatly need some good experimental work in this field. They're doing it all wrong," he said.

"Who? What field?"

"You really wouldn't know what I'm talking about, of course, being a hard-line behaviorist. You are, aren't you?

13

Never mind." He sat down heavily, too heavily in my wicker chair for a man his size. The chair creaked and groaned, but held. "Now, this is it," he said. "I have a proposal to make. First, you have no insight at all, yourself, into the experiences you just told me about?"

"I have no explanation, if that's what you mean. Some odd quirk of perception? Complete hallucination brought about by a belated response to my wife's leaving me? Who knows?"

"Exactly," Ram-Ram said. "So?"

"So? So—nothing. If I didn't hallucinate, then I was really out of my body, and I can't buy that. I hoped that with your background, you might have some alternate explanations."

"Suppose you *were* out of your body?" he asked. "I'm not for the moment saying that you were, but have you considered the possibility seriously?"

"Why, not really," I answered, surprised. "I'm the first one to admit that behaviorism hasn't solved all our problems, or begun to, but it's offered sufficient evidence that our consciousness is the result of our physical mechanism and the way we use it. In those terms, there's no 'me' to get out of my body. I wouldn't have any perceiving organs." I paced about, rather angry and defensive. All of this was too obvious to me at the time to argue about.

"Now, hold on," Ram-Ram said. "Look. You *felt* that you were out of your body. You felt that you were hanging out in the air there, and later you looked down at your own body. Since all this was so vivid and unmistakable then, what convinced you that it was not *in fact* happening?"

"At the time, I thought it *was* happening, of course," I said, more mildly.

"Then what later convinced you that it hadn't?"

By now my exasperation was rising again. "Good common sense, I suppose. People just don't hang out in thin air without support . . . without falling—"

"You deny the evidence of your own experience, then?"

Ram-Ram smiled his famous mischievous-little-boy-psychologist grin and said, "That would be *true* insanity, you know."

"I don't deny having the experience or I wouldn't have called you," I shouted.

"Now, look here and listen to me." He smiled honestly and fully for the first time that evening. "You're a nice young man. Several times you've carried my garbage down those monstrous stairs to that modern trash heap of a mess below. A man like that can't be all bad. But it seems that in the past you've managed to be very prosaic, as a rule, which is why all of this surprises me.

"Look here. The various schools of psychology don't do a very good job of communicating with each other, ironically enough. You may not even consider parapsychology a legitimate field of endeavor, for all I know, yet some new men are doing some evocative experiments along certain lines—"

"Oh, come on," I said. "I've come across a few of those reports, mostly in pseudoscientific magazines or drug literature. The popular occult craze has even taken over the movies. Then there's the old Rhine experiments. It's all fringe stuff."

But Ram-Ram went on stubbornly: "They're investigating OOBs, or out-of-body states. So far psychics are being used primarily, or other laymen who profess to experience the phenomenon at will, or think they can. But to date, no gifted psychologist has worked it from both ends. What's needed is a psychologist who can project his consciousness out of his body and objectively study the experience from both an in-body and out-of-body context. No mystic mumbo jumbo . . . no—"

"Uh huh," I said.

"Now"—he waved his fat little hand in the air—"I'm not for the moment suggesting that you take on that role—"

"Good," I said. "And good night, Dr. Frankenstein."

15

With clownish grand eloquence, I bowed and pretended to usher him out. It occurred to me, though, that his best days were over; that I'd been mistaken to call him; and that perhaps his reputation had been exaggerated.

He looked genuinely hurt, so I grinned and fixed us each a drink. I'm making no excuses for my attitude at the time, however; then I was convinced of the rightness of my position and it was one shared by many of my colleagues, of whatever age. I just didn't want to hurt Ram-Ram's feelings.

"I *thought* I saw two men. And I *thought* I was out of my body," I said more gently. "I'm sure that there's some logical explanation. Instead, you take the experience at face value—something, frankly, that just didn't occur to me. I can accept both episodes as hallucinations, though the idea does make me uneasy. But not as facts."

"Yes, yes, yes, certainly," Ram-Ram said. "But wouldn't it be ironical if man were independent of his body after all? And if psychology denied the one characteristic of human nature that could free us of the fear of extinction? What energy would be released if it were proven that man's consciousness *is* separate from the body!"

I didn't answer immediately. It was a painful moment for me anyhow: any psychologist worth his salt should know better, I thought, than to mix psychology and religion. Ram-Ram's voice drifted off. He eyed me slyly.

"The fairy tale of all fairy tales," I said.

"You think that I'm an old man, nearing his end, grabbing at any straw to convince himself of the impossible. Quite all right, and a natural enough deduction," he said.

I started to deny it, guiltily, and he said again, "No. It's all right. In your place, I should think the same thing, I suppose. And yet"— he stood up, giving me a quick, shrewd and yet haughty glance. "And yet if I'd had the experiences that you've just had, and I was your age, I'd be daring enough, curious enough, to investigate them. I wouldn't be quite so willing to deny the evidence of my own senses, and I'd ponder more on the meaning of such experiences to me personally and as a psychologist."

I started to interrupt, but Ram-Ram's kindly-old-psychologist's mask was gone again and he went on, rather brusquely. "I'm quite aware of my reputation on campus with the younger professors. Poor old Ram-Ram, senile old coot, with all of his brilliant work behind him. You're surprised? Of course I know my nickname. We gave nicknames to elderly professors too, and usually there was some intuitive truth in them, as there most likely is in my case. But despite the youth cult, man's mind is not necessarily obsolete in those nameless decades past, say, sixty. Instead, its activities may even accelerate in the oddest fashion.

"But the thing is, you called me because you hoped that I'd somehow confirm your idea that the whole thing was hallucinatory, a sort of self-hypnosis that still didn't involve any mental instability. You wanted to shove both experiences under the rug, because they didn't conform to your beliefs about reality. But I refuse to be a partner to that. Your experiences are valid, psychologically speaking, and maybe factually as well. I propose some experiments, then, instead of this verbal pussyfooting around."

"That's unfair," I objected. "You're trying to cast me in the role of callow youth, and I'm too old for that; and moral coward, which I resent. I'm as curious and open-minded as anyone else."

"Hell, isn't it?" He smiled, apparently delighted at my discomfort. "But tell me, what do you do when you're just past thirty and discover that the world is half mad? Go along and play the game, or try to discover what's wrong?"

"We *are* trying to find out what's wrong!"

"By examining rats instead of people? By losing yourselves in statistical analyses of test data and ignoring the subjective realities of the human mind?"

"Oh, come on, now. Those are pretty pat objections to behaviorism, and you know it." He was laughing at me openly, so I said: "All right. What do you have in mind?" I shrugged and gave up for the moment. Clearly he wasn't going to leave until he'd had his say.

He began slowly and deliberately enough. "First, examine both episodes with an open mind. If you decide that hallucinatory effects were involved, then try to discover more about hallucinations. If you aren't sure, pursue the matter further. If you still aren't satisfied, then I suggest some definite experiments, and I have several books I'd like you to read. I'd expect you to keep complete records, of course, with copies for me."

Ram-Ram was growing more excited by the minute. I stared at him. "Why don't you try all this yourself?" I asked, on the spur of the moment.

"I have," he said. "Years ago, with no notable results. But you're quite gifted in that respect, I think. Call it an old psychologist's intuition, if you will. But if you could visit a definite place and correctly report what you saw while out of your body, we'd at least have a start.

"Some other young psychologists have attempted such experiments, but either they dropped out of the establishment entirely or otherwise messed themselves up with the scientific community through drug use and lifestyle generally. So the way is open for someone like you, within the system, to begin some serious experimentation—"

I looked at him as if he'd *completely* lost his wits. "Look, if I *did* get out of my body, I don't know how I did it, much less how to change my location—or get back where I started." As I spoke, I remembered how I'd felt, dangling out the window, and to shake off a sudden uneasiness, I laughed. "Besides, suppose I got out of my body and couldn't get back inside?"

The glow faded from his eyes. "Yes, there's always that possibility, but I don't think it's a practical danger."

I said in amazement, "But I was only joking."

"Were you?" he asked quite soberly. "Actually there *are* tales of people facing just such difficulties."

"What? The whole idea is preposterous." I nearly shouted.

"Is it? Old wives' tales?" Ram-Ram shook his head. "Maybe, maybe not."

"No 'maybe' about it. It's nonsense," I said. "And as for the experiments, what you're actually talking about is my taking a trip without drugs."

"And without props," he said. "Yes, I'm trying to get you hooked on something else entirely. I'm trying to get you to do something that I tried and failed at. I've told you my motives; that's only fair. There are a few things that I'm holding back, but if you decide to go along with me on this, then I'll take you into my full confidence. But if—and this is a big if—if you can get out of your body with any predictability, then we may really be able to prove something."

I said slowly, "And you'd have a revolutionary paper to deliver, no more resting on your laurels—"

"Exactly." He didn't look at all guilty. In fact, he looked quite pleased with himself.

So I went on. "I'd be your prize subject, and still be acting as a psychologist since I'd be studying the subjective mechanisms. And your reputation would ensure publication of our results."

He was positively beaming.

I said, "I've had some doubts about behaviorism, I admit it. But, look: studying the effects of psychedelic drugs is accepted now. It's almost old hat. Encounter groups are on the rise, and some psychologists are getting interested in various methods of 'mind control.' But what you're talking about smacks of the occult and God knows what else. Do you honestly believe that there's that much to learn about human consciousness? I have to admit that I'm prejudiced in the other direction—that perception is the result of brain activity and nothing more."

"All the better," Ram-Ram said. "Your notes will make that obvious, too; and in the scientific community, that will serve us well. You weren't a believer of any kind to begin

19

with. Don't you see? That's what we'll say, and it will be true. But we must conduct this work—if we do it—in complete secrecy. If it's known that we tried and failed, we'll be considered idiots. And your career won't be worth two cents. First, if you agree, I want you to study OOB methods."

"Methods? You mean there are do-it-yourself manuals for that too?" For some reason, the thought sent me into bouts of uncontrollable laughter; probably just my nervous reaction to the whole night's events, but the mental images aroused by Ram-Ram's remark were hilarious. In the meantime, *his* expression went from amusement to outright irritation, which only made me laugh louder.

Our discussion ended shortly after I regained my composure. Ram-Ram went into his own apartment and returned with an armful of books which he left with me. When I was alone, I leafed through them, noticing idly that they were library books, taken out a week earlier. At the time I attached no significance to this. Nor did I question my choice of confidant. If I'd known what was going to happen, I'd have kept Ram-Ram there all night, questioning him. As it was, I didn't realize until months later how cagey he'd been.

Chapter Three

A Book Out of Nowhere and an Interview in a Mental Institution

You can imagine my feelings three days later when I learned that Ram-Ram had been admitted to a psychiatric clinic under his own cognizance and labeled a schizophrenic. In the oddest way, this relieved my mind; I wouldn't have to regard what he'd said to me that night with any seriousness; and while I felt sorry for him, I also felt absurdly free.

Yet as I looked back at our meeting and remembered his strange excitement, I wondered: Did our interview and my own bizarre experiences set him off? Even so, he must have been predisposed toward that particular illness for some time, I thought. Yet it seemed that I should have been alert enough to spot the symptoms. So, somewhat guiltily, I decided to visit him as soon as possible.

It was nearly a week before the opportunity presented

itself. For one thing, my academic load was considerable then, and despite my resolution I kept putting the visit off. All kinds of excuses came to mind until I took myself in hand and realized that I felt illogically responsible for Ram-Ram's condition. I was reacting quite mechanically, feeling guilt for no reason, as I'd been programmed to do by my background both as a private person and as a member of our society.

So the very next day I made my duty call, and met Ram-Ram's new friend for the first time—Queen Alice, as she's called, a kooky old lady about Ram-Ram's age who's taken him in hand. Or he's taken her in hand. But the interview was most unsettling and peculiar. I say this because it almost seemed as if Ram-Ram was checking on *my* state of mind, instead of the other way around.

"Dr. Brail?" I said, striding, I hoped, with a strong, positive, reassuring step into the common room.

"Ah, Jeffy-boy, step into my parlor," he said, with the sweetest of guileless smiles. Other patients made way. Ram-Ram was playing the role of kindly old psychologist, this time to perfection, and the other patients surrounded him like supporting actors, showing him deference while Ram-Ram kept smiling like some ancient pied piper.

He indicated one corner of the room where an old table stood; a beat-up conference table about which chairs were cocked at crazy angles. Then he smiled again and sat down as if I were a patient of whom he was particularly fond. His whole manner indicated that this was his office or its equivalent. He wore his own clothes rather than any hospital-like garb, and he treated the table as if it were his desk, ignoring the piles of torn magazines which he shoved aside.

I was taken aback, yet willing enough to go along with the pretense, considering Ram-Ram's condition, when he gestured to a woman who came up beside us, and said, "Dear Queen Alice, do sit down with us. You'll be interested in Jeffy-boy, here."

As Ram-Ram spoke, the other patients began to mill

about, make noises, cough, sneeze—or in other ways seem to indicate that they were involved in their own concerns and wouldn't eavesdrop. At the same time, their motions also seemed sly and aimless. I had no idea how to react to them, being more used to dealing with laboratory rats than people.

I pulled myself together, smiled jovially, and said, "Well, now, how are we feeling?"

"Fine, fine," Ram-Ram answered, with no indication that anything at all was wrong. "I'm continuing our research at this end, and Queen Alice, here, has become my assistant."

"I'm very glad to meet you," I replied nervously, and I had to turn to look at the woman as Ram-Ram's attitude so clearly demanded. I didn't want to ruffle him, but I didn't particularly want to deal with anyone else either. Queen Alice's white hair made a wiry bush about her face. She was wearing dungarees and a shirt, and for some reason her attire upset my sense of propriety—an attitude that even then I understood was unfair and ridiculous. "Queen Alice?" I said gently, with just a hint of a smile, I suppose.

"Another nickname of sorts, or rather, a title of deference," Ram-Ram said. "It really denotes the fact that she's out of her time. She's living in the wrong century."

"A dreadful inconvenience," Queen Alice added. "And so few understand. Oh, some do, I'm not saying that. But no, I'm not a queen. I have no pretensions of *earthly* royalty . . . I presume you're a gentleman of your century?"

"Oh yes, he is that, indeed," Ram-Ram said with obvious relish and an almost sarcastic chuckle. And the entire affair was just too much for me. I was about to make some excuse and leave when Ram-Ram leaned forward with a sudden, almost gay attitude of conspiracy and said quickly, "We haven't all the time in the world, you know, so I want to fill you in on what I've learned so far."

Tolerantly enough, I put off my departure and said, "Go ahead," for I hoped that I could learn just how irrational he actually was. And certainly my curiosity was more than aroused. This was my first encounter with schizophrenia in a human. We'd induced similar symptoms in rats through the use of disorientation conditioning, but this was something else.

So while I tried to look sympathetic and personally involved, I kept track of Ram-Ram's reactions at the same time. He acted feverish as he started speaking, gesticulating quickly, urgently, his small brown eyes not leaving my face for what seemed like an eternity. He wouldn't let me look away, and kept punctuating his sentences with excited exclamations of "You see? You see?"

So I was forced to say, "Yes, yes," and sit there while he stared at me with the greatest intentness—a most uncomfortable spot to be in, I might add—and a very curious situation indeed.

"These people here, in their way, are quite sane," he said. "A fact that I've often suspected about such patients. They are not—I repeat, *not*—insane. You see?"

"Yes, of course," I answered, not wanting to upset him further.

"But beyond that, listen. This is important. Queen Alice hears voices. They speak to her at various times, delivering what seems to be the most astonishing information. Once I heard them, too, though not as clearly as she does, and I'm not really certain that they *were* the same voices. I believe this information to be a kind of garbled divine dialogue. Do you follow me?"

His eyes still hadn't left my face. I tried to hide my almost overwhelming dejection that a fine mind could deteriorate so in such a brief time. Lacking practical experience or not, I knew enough to recognize the classic symptoms of his disease.

"You see? You see?" he said impatiently. His normal clothes and appearance contrasted so sharply with the wildness of his manner that I was ready to leap from my chair in consternation when he reached out and grabbed my arm

24

forcibly. "Have you begun your out-of-body experiments yet?" he asked, in a hoarse whisper.

"No."

"Well, you must. At once. It's vital." This time he shouted.

"Yes. I will. Tonight," I said, as soothingly as possible, but having no intention, of course, of doing any such thing.

"He doesn't believe in my voices at all," Queen Alice said suddenly. I spun around to look at her, having forgotten her presence entirely. She stood up, frowning, staring at me with the uncompromising clarity that children and the mad both sometimes assume.

I didn't know what to do or say. Certainly I didn't want to upset either of them. Just then, a tall clownish-looking man came up to us. He walked bent over, but quickly, on the balls of his feet. He took a magazine from the table and winked at me sympathetically. "Don't let it bother you none," he said. "None of us hears the voices either like Queen Alice does. Maybe you'll be able to hear them later on yourself. You never can tell." He winked encouragingly and went back to his chair.

I just stared after him. This . . . *patient* wanted me to understand that I was in the same boat as all of them—he was trying to comfort *me*. I rose to leave. As I did, again the other patients began to mill about. Queen Alice squared her scrawny shoulders and asked suddenly, "Who do you think you are? I mean, who do you imagine yourself to be?"

"Nobody," I said.

"That's too bad," she answered, and with the craziest smile, Ram-Ram said, "That's his trouble." Without another word, I left.

Actually I was more shaken than I wanted to admit. Obviously the conversation in my apartment *had* set Ram-Ram off, I thought, for now he supposed that we were conducting some esoteric experiment together, in which Queen Alice's voices were also involved. I shook my head: "The poor old coot." Yet as I returned home, I could feel

25

my mood swing about in the most unusual fashion from definite disquiet to an almost lethargic passivity. From this latter I was then struck by a sudden exuberance in which it seemed that everything would work out well, and, indeed, that none of my problems or Ram-Ram's were important at all.

I'd been working too hard, I thought. Obviously the two experiences that led me to call Ram-Ram were perfectly natural results of exhaustion. I decided to take some vitamin C. Then my exhilaration quickened. The idea came to me that there was something I must write down at once. Almost without thinking, I inserted some paper into my old type-writer.

I recall being surprised beyond measure at the first sight of what I'd written. For there at the top of the page the following words appeared as if in a title:

The Further Education of Oversoul Seven

I stared. The further education of *what?* What had possessed me to write such a nonsense phrase? Yet even as I puzzled over the sentence, excitement seized me. Suddenly assured and full of confidence, I began typing as fast as my hands would go. The words seemed to slip through my brain from someplace else, and onto the paper, yet I had no idea where the material was coming from. Moreover, a story of sorts seemed to be developing.

I was aware of the words perhaps a second before my fingers actually typed them, and to my amazement, the pace actually quickened. I didn't even have time to read what was on one sheet of paper before, urgently, the next sentence appeared. Two hours passed. Finally I stopped, dazed, lit a cigarette, and almost immediately felt again that strong compulsion to type. *Was* it a compulsion? It was certainly far more than an impulse, yet I was sure that I could resist it if I chose. Instead, I decided on the spot to go along as an experiment of sorts, to see what would happen.

What happened was the beginning of a book with the rather improbable title given earlier. Except for a short break, I typed steadily for four hours. I had no idea of the quality of the material, but its imaginative fantasy struck me as highly uncharacteristic of my own personality. Outside of dry academic papers, I've never done any writing in my adult life.

The rest of the evening I spent trying to trace my own subjective states before and during the experience. This time I didn't make the mistake of calling anyone, but I was more frightened than I'd been earlier. Now I was faced with the physical evidence before me—a stack of writing produced by me in a way that I could not understand. Where had it come from? Would I be seized by the same compulsion again? And could I really resist if I wanted to, or was I only fooling myself?

Even those questions became unimportant as another, more terrifying thought came to me: If Ram-Ram was considered mad because he sometimes heard voices, where did *this* put *me?* Was it possible that schizophrenia was actually caused by some as yet undiscovered virus, and had been passed on by Ram-Ram to me? Impossible, I thought. Yet such an explanation would at least place the entire affair in the realm of the real and reasonable. I knew it was silly, but I took another vitamin C, remembering that large dosages were supposed to combat infections. I also comforted myself that no auditory or visual hallucinations had been involved.

As it happened, the episode was followed by another, and still another. I'm recording these odd chapters here, with no changes. As you read on, you'll see the strange way in which *Oversoul Seven* began to take over the ordinary details of my life.

Chapter Four

Gods Wanted (or Chapter One of Jeffery's "Further Education of Oversoul Seven")

The interviews had been going on for centuries, or for only moments, according to your point of view. Oversoul Seven frowned, put an *Out To Lunch* sign on the door, and said to his teacher, Cyprus, "Everyone wants to be a god. I never saw anything like it. I don't trust any of the applicants either; they're all too anxious." For the present, Oversoul Seven looked like a guru, because that was what the earth applicants expected. He caught a glimpse of himself in the mirror over the waiting-room coffee table, and smiled despite himself. "I do sort of look like Christ, too, don't you think?"

Cyprus was thinking so fast that she kept changing form constantly. She paused long enough to say, "If Lydia is all ready to be born again, then I really don't see why you're going to all this trouble on her behalf at a time like this.

You'll be graded on how smoothly you help Lydia begin her new life, and if the affair is vital to her, it also makes up your own most important work for this semester. So I don't see where this search for the gods fits in at all."

"How do you think I feel, getting sidetracked like this? But my earth peoples' education has really hit a snag, just because of their god concepts. The earth gods are just senile. Too bad and all, but what can you do? When you toss gods into time, well, they get tinged by it just like anyone else. It just, uh, takes longer. And even though Lydia *is* one of my personalities, she has to discover the answers for herself."

"I hope *you* remember that, Seven," Cyprus said. "And I also hope you remember that you're dealing with subjective realities this semester. I suppose the *Out To Lunch* sign has something to do with earth customs? Even so, I'm not sure that I approve of the setting you've created for the interviews."

Seven said broodingly, "Well, it's the replica of a doctor's waiting room that Lydia visited in her twentieth-century life. I'm trying to use earth symbolism as much as possible to give her a sense of security between lives; she gets awfully skittish. I was pleased with this environment— physician of the soul, that sort of thing."

Cyprus said, "That kind of venture *can* get quite complicated." She paused, giving Seven time to comment, and when he didn't, but just blushed guiltily, Cyprus disappeared. Her voice, coming from nowhere in particular, said, "Apparently you have no real problems with Lydia, though— at least nothing that you can't handle—so you can carry on quite well alone. Just so Lydia gets born on time."

"All *right,* come back," Seven yelled, symbolically speaking, because actually the entire conversation thus far took place soundlessly, and wordlessly as well.

"There *is* one little problem," Seven said, blushing again as Cyprus reappeared, this time looking very stern. She materialized as a mixture of man and woman or woman and man; and of age and youth or youth and age; one aspect or another of her image being emphasized as she reacted to Seven's words.

"Uh," he said hesitantly, "actually Lydia refuses to be born until she searches for the gods. She wants to know if they really exist or not before she takes on another life. All in all, she's been very stubborn about the whole thing."

Cyprus's face turned ancient and glowering. "And? What's the rest of it?" she asked.

Oversoul Seven sighed deeply and tried his best to look only slightly (not deeply) concerned. "Well, Lydia's mother-to-be in her next life is Bianka, as you know—Josef's wife. And she's approaching labor right now in seventeenth-century Denmark. Remember, Lydia decided to go backward in time for her next life—in her terms, of course. I mean, *we* know that all time is simultaneous, but—" His voice drifted off miserably.

Cyprus felt so sorry for her pupil that she turned immediately into the image of a kindly old physician, and Seven's spirits momentarily lifted.

"Actually the problem is mainly one of time, using earth terms," he said. "I mean, in *those* terms, a woman's labor pains can't be put off forever. And there *is* always the chance that I can change Lydia's mind."

Cyprus disappeared again, this time because her reactions were so quicksilver fast and contradictory that she couldn't get any one image to express them. She said, "Are you trying to tell me that Bianka, Lydia's mother-to-be, is nearly ready to deliver a baby, and Lydia wants to go on some kind of misguided pilgrimage to the gods first?"

"Uh, I'm not positive, but if I have the time sequences right, then Bianka is expecting to deliver a baby in twenty-four hours or so," Seven said very quietly.

Silence.

"Of course, with probabilities, there's variations of all

kinds," he added. "Any time from three hours to forty-eight, I imagine."

Cyprus said, "Or, granting probabilities, Lydia *could* decide not to be reborn as Tweety at all." This time Cyprus's voice rang, echoed, thundered. Vowels and syllables turned into images and went flying through the air, catching the sunlight and turning into multicolored prisms. Only these prisms also *sounded,* so that the vowels and syllables fragmented, splintered, and registered in so many different scales at once that Oversoul Seven shouted out and covered his guru ears.

When the commotion ceased he said glumly, "You didn't have to do that—" and with belated dignity: "I understand your concern."

"Oh, Seven!" Cyprus said. She'd changed back to the image she often used in such discussions with Seven: that of a young woman with ancient knowledge—or that of an ancient woman with young appearance, according to his (or her) point of view. "You're Lydia's *oversoul,* after all. How could you let her do such a thing?"

"She gets me confused," Seven protested. "In her last life, she didn't believe in me at all. Then once she realized that she *had* a soul—after death—she wanted truth handed to her on a silver platter, if you'll forgive my earth vernacular. On her own, she decided to be born as Tweety, Josef and Bianka's daughter. But if you ask me, she's carrying this free will business too far. Now she's not sure she even wants to be born again at all, unless she—"

Seven broke off. In his dismay, he'd forgotten to maintain the hallucinatory doctor's office; or his own image, for that matter. He and Cyprus were two points of light in the middle of nowhere. Quickly Seven re-established the environment, hoping that Cyprus hadn't noticed, but she just smiled wanly. Since she didn't comment, Seven continued as if nothing had happened.

"It's hard on the father-to-be, too. In fact, I had a little

31

trouble with Josef. First he wanted to be an artist, free, with no responsibilities. Then he wants a wife and children—"

"And *now*," Cyprus interrupted, "with his wife about to go into labor, he doesn't know if he wants to be a father at all."

"You've been checking up on me," Seven protested. "You knew about this all of the time!"

"And Lydia wants the world to stop while she tracks down the gods. Is that it?" Cyprus asked. Vowels and syllables started to glitter in the air again, spinning down to the red velvet couch in the corner and landing on the dark leather chairs.

"Now don't start that again," Seven cried, but it was too late. The sounds went flying all about, some tinkling like crystal, some booming like thunder as they fell apart into fragments of light-and-sound; linked. They fell onto the lush rug, twirling in the pile. And ignoring the entire display— indeed, only half aware of it—Cyprus said, "Looking for the gods can be a very tricky, serious, and funny affair all at once. Now, listen to me. Remember that Lydia and Josef are both your personalities, so they have some of your characteristics. Lydia says that she really doesn't believe in any gods, which is why she wants to find them so badly, of course. And—"

"She's coming," Oversoul Seven cried. "Please don't tell her that we discussed all this. She has the most exaggerated sense of privacy—"

"All right. But *your* beliefs about the gods are important too, Seven. Don't forget that," Cyprus cautioned. She made the vowels and syllables disappear, and Lydia walked into the room.

She looked to be in her early twenties. She gave her long black hair a decisive toss, snapped her fingers, and said, "A doctor's office. Physician of the soul and all that stuff, I bet."

Oversoul Seven grinned and said, "I thought it applied."

"It does," she answered. "Physical doctors aren't very

competent, and physicians of the soul probably aren't any better." She smiled, though, and took a hallucinatory cigarette from her dungaree pocket. Seven lit it for her and said to Cyprus, "What did I tell you? She's . . . difficult."

Lydia had met Cyprus on several occasions. She gave her a grin of welcome and shrugged her shoulders. Seven ignored the flippancy; or almost. He frowned slightly and said, "Anyhow, Lydia is going to advise me about earth conditions, in case we find any new gods to insert into time."

Cyprus turned into a young woman, more or less. That is, she tried to relate to Lydia by adopting a similar image. Her thoughts went so fast again, though, that to Lydia it looked as if she appeared and disappeared in the most confusing fashion.

Lydia puffed nervously on her hallucinatory cigarette and said, "If I'm going to be born again, then first I want to find out about the gods—or God, or whatever. When I'm in a physical life, I get sidetracked, so I'm taking the opportunity now, while I can. Otherwise, I don't know. The gods never did much good as far as I can see—if there *are* gods. But I thought that if we found a decent one, we could—well, insert him in time. Or *her*. Earth could do with a woman god for a change, if you ask me."

Oversoul Seven smiled brilliantly at Cyprus and said, "See, the gods can be inserted just after Lydia's time in her last life. She knows all about that period. Even her prejudices are still fresh in her mind."

"I suppose that's considered an asset?" Cyprus asked. "And if I were you, I'd forget about inserting any new gods in time—*if* you find any willing to undertake such a venture. I should tell you, Seven, that there *are* a few things you've forgotten on purpose for this semester's work. Your own entire range of knowledge on certain subjects isn't available to you, because otherwise you might be tempted to overdirect your personalities."

There was something about Cyprus's speech that wrin-

33

kled the edges of Oversoul Seven's momentary smugness. He almost panicked, but instead he went on, quite bravely he thought: "Lydia knows what people expect of the gods. Of course, we'll have to check out the old gods first. But if we find any new ones, they'll have to know earth customs. Earth people keep their sexes separate, for example, as you know. In each life they stick to one sex or the other—"

"Or the *other?* So there are only two?"

Cyprus's words went thundering through all of Oversoul Seven's experience, scattering images everywhere. The millions of sexual variations of plant, mineral, and animal planetary life glittered before his mental eyes; the endless convoluted yet sparkling couplings and transcouplings by which life multiplied and refreshed itself. He knew it. He knew it all, but at some level he had forgotten. Or else he pretended not to know—for a reason. But for that moment, Seven stepped out of his own vision into that immeasurably vaster one, and he felt as if he possessed a thousand heads, all of them reeling. And in the very back of his mind, he wondered uneasily what he'd forgotten about the gods.

Cyprus was still saying, incredulously, "Only two?" when Seven regained himself. This time he took on his fourteen-year-old male image and stood there, head bowed, fresh new cheeks puffed out—pouting—and said, "Cyprus, that wasn't fair at all."

Now Cyprus looked far older than Lydia, older than anyone ever in the strangest fashion, even while her features hadn't really changed in any usually observable way. She wanted to smile at Oversoul Seven and Lydia; she wanted to reassure them. Yet looking at them through her knowledge put them so far away that she could barely perceive them. She sorted through times and places, sometimes growing weary, until finally she found them again—Oversoul Seven first—drawn to him by that rambunctious energy of his, which now was turned into grave inquiry.

"Where were you?" he asked, telling himself that he should know better than to ask the question at all.

"I never know what's going on," Lydia protested. She sat down on the hallucinatory red couch, her fingers flashing nervously through the magazines. "I have the worst feeling that this search for the gods may end up in some completely different fashion than we suppose."

But as a fourteen-year-old boy, Oversoul Seven felt himself drawn toward some ancient childhood, falling back into some newness that was (and is) the center of each tiniest spark of being. And he knew that godmaking was a children's game; but the only one worth playing.

As he thought *that,* Cyprus disappeared, as did the physician's office with its fine velvet couch. He and Lydia were on their own. Seven felt a momentary flash of dismay— there were so many things he'd wanted to ask Cyprus first— but it was too late for questions. He looked around, expectantly. The environment was changing, doubtlessly because of Lydia's beliefs, and Seven wished fervently that he had a better idea of just what her beliefs about the gods *really* were.

Chapter Five

*The Beginning of the Search
and
a Demon in the Foothills*

Lydia was feeling petulant. "I thought that after death, you were supposed to know all about God, or whatever," she said. "And even though I didn't believe that I had a soul when I was physical, I thought that souls—if they existed—would at least know the answers. Instead, here I am, helping my oversoul go tracking down the gods. After all I've been through, I'm not certain of anything."

"Shush. Will you be quiet?" Seven cried, exasperated. "We're in someone else's territory. I can tell."

Lydia grabbed a cigarette from the pocket of a hastily hallucinated trench coat and looked around nervously. "What do you mean, someone else's territory?" She squinted; things *were* changing. There were walls and walls of shadow that weren't there before. And they were advancing. To test her perceptions, Lydia stood still. And sure enough, the walls seemed to come closer, stealthily.

"On earth, it would be like an alien country," Seven said, "when you don't know the rules and don't like the looks of the place. Just take my hand and be quiet."

He sounded much more confident than he felt. The area was drenched with personality characteristics that he found most distasteful. Fear was draped invisibly but definitely over everything; like a heavy suffocating vine that choked out all other growth. And anger crawled in and out of all the tiny crevices that suddenly opened up around their feet, spreading like miniature earthquakes. Seven didn't like the feel of it at all. But as yet, the various elements were diversified. By steering Lydia and himself carefully, he managed to follow the few clear spots still open.

At the same time, Oversoul Seven felt the fear and anger collecting itself; it belonged to some*one* or some*thing*.

Lydia hadn't made a wisecrack in what seemed a century. She was beginning to shiver. Instantly she hallucinated a big brown handbag with a revolver inside. The bag swung from shoulder straps that fit over her trench coat.

The automatic hallucination of objects was something Seven had tried to teach her without success until now. But she was so frightened that she never noticed her success.

A presence was slowly gathering about them. The fear and anger were literally taking shape. Seven felt a thickness grow before he saw it; a gigantic swirling black-centered demonlike form. Despite himself, he stepped backward. The demon—or whatever it was—*was* definitely there, rising out of the shadow walls. Yet, on the other hand, there was something not-there about it too. Lydia opened her handbag and reached for her revolver.

As she did so, the thing began to speak—or at least words came from somewhere, though Seven knew that the creature's tongue could have no power of its own. And as it spoke, like a giant evil porcupine it sent out darts of terror that stuck into—well, psychological skin—while foul odors slithered like snakes from it, coiling everywhere. Lydia dropped her handbag. The ground beneath it turned into quicksand, swallowing the handbag, revolver and all.

"Well, do something," Lydia stammered.

Seven closed his eyes. He opened them again. Nothing had changed. "We're on our way to visit the gods," he said politely.

A gigantic chuckle began somewhere nearby. And built up. And grew until the sounds drowned out Oversoul Seven's thoughts as well as his hard-earned composure. Giant teeth appeared in the sky, too close to the ground for comfort. They clanked up and down with each god-forsaken gasp of laughter; and the open mouth showed a gullet-path that led into distances too far even for Seven's imagination.

Lydia was sobbing.

Seven was frightened enough; and confused. He whispered to Lydia, "I thought you didn't believe in demons?"

"I don't really know if I believe in gods or not but I believe in demons all right," Lydia muttered, staring at the huge teeth which now were fading, while the original monster-shape came closer.

"There aren't any demons," Seven said urgently. "You've got to believe me."

"Then what's that?" Lydia cried angrily.

"Kneel down and adore me, or be annihilated," demanded the voice issuing from the creature but also seeming to come from the ground beneath their feet, and from the sky as well.

Oversoul Seven finally got his mental footing. "Okay," he said agreeably, borrowing Lydia's expression on purpose.

Lydia grabbed Seven's arm, shouting, "Oh, how *could* you? You'll be bowing to evil!"

"Will you let me handle this?" Seven almost yelled.

"Bow down, with your belly on the ground," insisted the monster, hissing now.

"Never!" Lydia screamed, trembling. She advanced, saying the Lord's Prayer, which she suddenly remembered.

"'Our Father—'"

"Lydia, that's useless," Seven said. But Lydia was beyond listening.

"Bow down and adore me," the monster raged.

"'Who art in Heaven—'" Lydia prayed.

It was going to be a metaphysical shouting match, Seven thought—somewhat angry himself now. "You don't really believe in God the Father," he reminded Lydia, as gently and considerately as he could under the circumstances. "But you *do* believe in demons."

"'Hallowed be Thy name,'" Lydia said, between clenched teeth. She was just yards from the creature, who was now very rapidly approaching, constantly changing shapes.

"Adore me," it commanded, "or be annihilated."

"Annihilated!" Lydia cried, so frightened that she almost forgot to pray.

Seven didn't dare wait any longer. He let his own beliefs predominate until they flooded the entire environment. The monster disappeared just as the huge mouth, momentarily materializing, opened. Seven snatched Lydia away; she was still yelling the Lord's Prayer.

"You're lucky you believe in *me,*" Seven said, disgusted. "That was all your fault back there, and it took me a while to realize what was going on. But would you let me handle it? No. Not until you were scared to death."

"How *did* we get out of there?" Lydia asked.

"I got us out."

"You!" Lydia cried. "You were a coward. Some behavior for an oversoul! You were ready to do anything the demon told you to."

Seven sighed. "It's pretty difficult to explain all this to

you, when we're still in the middle of the action. Look around. What do you see?"

Lydia looked—and looked. On earth, the landscape stayed whatever way it was. Here, it seemed you couldn't be sure of anything. First she thought that she saw a row of trees, prickly shapes in space; and once she was positive she smelled pine needles. But the next instant, the same shapes wiggled and thickened in some odd fashion until they suggested steeples and a medieval street. Although *something* always seemed to be out there, whatever it was kept changing.

"It reminds me of Impressionist painting," Lydia said. "It looks like someone painted wiggly trees with brush strokes that just suggested trees. But when you really look, they aren't trees at all." She didn't like the effect much either. Her literal mind wanted one environment or the other, and she said as much.

Oversoul Seven grinned. He'd changed himself into his version of an artist, a rather antiquated version in Lydia's eyes. For he was wearing a brown robe and beard to match, and gesturing with a paintbrush straight out of the fourteenth century. "Your mind is painting the pictures or forming the environment," he said. "I'm purposely letting your mind predominate right now. Earlier you formed the demon because as far as your beliefs are concerned, gods and demons are connected. Look for one, and you automatically find the other. Worse, your belief in God the Father was far weaker than your certainty about demons. So your prayers were only an exercise in futility; and in a way, they only reinforced your belief in evil. You *really* believe that evil is stronger than good."

"Well, there certainly seems to be more of it on earth," Lydia said tartly. "I don't see how you can sidestep the entire issue. At least I rose to the challenges of the encounter."

"You won't really believe any gods exist unless you meet

some demons along the way, is that it?" Seven asked. "Because if it is, you might get more than you bargained for. And I'd just as soon not watch."

"Watch? You mean you wouldn't help?" It was hard for Lydia to concentrate. The environment turned from a shadowy boulevard to a shadowy back street in some town in Ohio where she remembered living at one time or another. It was as if space kept advancing and retreating, always carrying different images; or like staring into a shop window where the reflections almost came alive and were as real as objects. The gods, she thought, were probably just reflections too. . . .

"Stop staring," Seven cried. "You're getting the edges of your reality blurred, and we aren't ready for that yet."

"For what?" she asked distractedly. She wished that he'd be quiet, because suddenly the images were becoming much clearer, and she could almost hear voices.

"Lydia," Seven shouted, "don't let your mind drift so." But it was too late.

She *wasn't* ready yet, Seven thought miserably. For that matter, he didn't know if he was either. But there was nothing for him to do but follow her—and her beliefs.

The reflections shimmered, thickened into sparkling kaleidoscopes of cubes and circles, piled one on top of the other, all dissected by a strange glinting light against a dark purple sky. Then, in an instant, the whole thing jelled, set, settled into a solidity so perfect that the new castles and palaces carried an air of ancient elegance, a sturdy jeweled splendor that surely was old when the earth was new.

"Why, it's the land of the gods, just as I once imagined it!" Lydia was so excited that she could hardly speak.

Oversoul Seven, still carrying his paintbrush, sighed. He knew, or he thought he knew, where all this would lead them. But he couldn't just step in and direct Lydia—the search would have to follow *her* own desires and beliefs.

Her desires didn't worry him, Seven thought; but her beliefs were another matter. The air was so clear and sparkling, though, that even Seven found himself exhilarated.

"And it's the most fantastic summer day you could ever imagine," Lydia exclaimed.

That's just it, Seven wanted to say, but he didn't.

As Lydia's mood soared, her dungarees and trench coat were replaced by a silver suit of armor like one Joan of Arc had worn in a picture Lydia had seen as a child in her previous life. And here she was, Lydia, brave and young; splendid in her determination, out to find the gods—and more. She'd found them. Or almost.

Seven almost moaned, picking up her images: she'd been eighteen when she'd seen the Joan of Arc illustration and had imagined the present scene.

Which was quite real, of course.

"Well," she said. "We *did* get rid of the demon one way or another, didn't we? He must have guarded the land of the gods."

Seven gave up for the moment. "Right," he said dourly.

The scene was quickly taking on all the dimensions of an actuality. Mountains appeared in the distance, roads and paths arching over them. Trees materialized, growing to full size in the flash of an eye. Lakes almost spilled over with soft water. Lydia said, "Oh, it's all so unbelievable that I have to sit here for a minute and catch my breath."

"You do? You wear *me* out," Seven muttered, but he was proud of her; the environment *was* splendid.

While it lasted, he thought. His robe was hot. He changed it to a silken one, though he was sure that few artists in any century wore silken gowns. Still, there could always be a first, he thought, and with some admiration he stared at Lydia. No one could say that she wasn't independent! There she was, slender, brave, and true, he thought, grinning. Her innocence and intensity were more than he could bear. He wanted to see how far those qualities could take her.

More; a part of him roused up in response so that all of his own beginnings began to merge, surge, ascend. He added his exuberance to hers, as it came tumbling into his experience from all the times and places that he'd known; and the scene took on that incredible clarity that defied any one reality; transcended them all and yet was brilliantly itself, and no other.

The summer-scented path led up to a gigantic building that overlooked the top of the hill. They began to climb.

Chapter Six

Josef's Difficulties

At first the path was easy enough. Then Seven noticed that it gradually became slippery, and the clear air seemed colder. Suddenly, in fact, the wind was so chilly that Oversoul Seven changed his artist's robe to a woolen one and added a scarf.

"Aren't you cold, Lydia?" he called, but there was no answer. Squinting, Seven realized that a fine snow was blowing before his eyes, and for a moment he couldn't see anything at all. "Lydia?"

He called again, when he thought he saw her ahead in the distance. But where had the snow come from? In the next instant, with a sinking heart, he knew. For the figure ahead wasn't Lydia. It was one of his other personalities— Josef, Lydia's father-to-be. Seven had been so involved with Lydia's experiences that he'd almost forgotten Josef entirely. Well, not really. That was an exaggeration, he told himself quickly, guiltily. Yet he was rather impatient at being called away from Lydia, and it didn't help when Seven remembered his last encounter with Josef, who had angrily told Seven to mind his own business and leave him alone.

Seven had to claim these rather uncharitable thoughts about Josef as his own; but as he told Cyprus later, that was before he realized Josef's plight. For almost instantly he sensed the desolation of Josef's spirit; even before he saw Josef's body half frozen, huddled up on the mountain, and the vodka bottle which had rolled halfway down the first slippery hill. It would be difficult to find a more dismal scene. In a flash, Oversoul Seven took it all in. The events involved with Josef's life collected, swirled, flew into Seven's immediate experience—colliding, appearing, and disappearing, until finally they fell into their proper time-space relationships—and Seven could focus clearly in the present, according to Josef's experience.

In the farmhouse hardly visible down the seventeenth-century hills, for example, Josef's wife, Bianka, was approaching labor. Through Josef's dimmed mental vision, Seven saw the scene: Josef had rushed through the house in a frenzy of agony and concern that he was unable to voice. The four fireplaces were all blazing so that the house would be warm for the coming birth, but (because Josef hadn't cleaned out the flues properly) it was overheated, filled with fireplace smoke and the steam from water boiling in the iron pots. Josef kept yelling that the steam would ruin his canvases—sitting there unused for months actually, gathering dust, because he hadn't been able to paint decently for what seemed like ages; but the smell of his turpentine rags had mixed in with the smoke and steam and made him ill. The women were all yelling—Bianka most of all, screaming in bed, so bloated he thought she'd burst; and his mother-in-law chased him out into the barn.

The sudden icy air made him dizzy. He glared back at

the house with loathing and love (all twisted together), grabbed his vodka bottle from where he'd hidden it underneath the hay, and jammed his skis on his feet.

The first slopes had been easy. He sang to lift his spirits and pretended that he was twenty and unmarried—a roaming, frolicsome artist—instead of twenty-six and domesticated. He skied fast and drank faster, not noticing (or pretending not to notice) that darkness was falling; and trying to forget Bianka's staring eyes; determined to run from the pleading screams that terrified him for reasons he couldn't explain. If that was birth, well, damn the gods, if there were any! No wonder Christ wasn't a father! The thought scared him; it was sacrilegious. No mention of Christ having a penis—"Oh God," he moaned, bleary and horrified. Now where had *that* thought come from?

Thinking frightened him to begin with. To forget his thoughts, he tried to plan a painting in his mind. Just then he fell down, twisted his leg, lost one ski, and realized that most of the feeling in both legs had vanished at about the same time. How far from home was he? His clothes were warm enough for working outside for an hour or so, but he'd been out for longer than that, he thought. Or had he? His time sense was all jumbled. How long ago was it that he'd been thrown out of his own house so unceremoniously?

Well, they'd be sorry. His emotions overspilled. He sat up, leaning against a tree, staring down the mountainside. The icy twilight was already descending. Bleak barren hills were snow-crusted, and the air was sharp. He knew that he had no time to waste; he had to get going, claim his other ski and start back, going faster than he'd come. He had to restore his circulation. Yet perversely he sat there, grumbling to himself.

Birth had no right to be so beastly, he thought. He couldn't bear to think what Bianka must be going through. How could their jolly lovemaking lead to such . . . terror? Dear God! And what use was it to pray? What did God know about terror? He himself had no use for Christendom, nor did it have any use for him. Which was all right. But now he wanted some kind of comfort; some reassurance . . . that birth wouldn't be as awful for Bianka as he (and everybody else) thought it would be.

If there *was* a God, if there were *gods*—but they were all children's tales, he thought. A lot of good Bianka's Christ was now. He imagined, just as he lost consciousness, that some ancient Nordic gods shared the hills with him: They would wake him up, welcome him with gigantic feasts and resplendent sword fights, boisterous male laughter, offering him slabs of charred sweet meat—pigs stolen from his neighbors; gods that were eternal and male and didn't need fleshy soft women's bodies; gods that had no need to give bloody birth; ancient Viking gods, banqueting through the long winter night.

"Don't you ever think of anything besides food?" Oversoul Seven said rather peevishly: Josef had definitely broadened girth-wise since he'd last looked at him closely.

Josef opened his mental eyes. His physical ones were nearly frosted shut.

Seven took the shape of an old wise man. "You've very nearly done it this time," he said.

"Oh, it's you," Josef moaned, then said pathetically, "You've got to get me out of this. I'm half frozen. I'll never make it home."

"I hope you thoroughly realize the serious predicament you've got yourself into," Seven said sternly, looking ancient as the hills, wise and dependable—and somewhat angry.

"This isn't any time for a sermon," Josef said mentally. "I don't even know if I'm really seeing you or not, but whenever I *do* see you, then I'm either dreaming or delirious—"

"You're always delirious," Seven answered. "Here." He hallucinated a bottle of brandy. Josef sat up in his spirit

47

body—unknowingly in this case—and drank, sputtering as he did so, while Seven made a quick mental trip to Josef's house to see what was going on there now. A steam bath. The boiling water steamed up the windows and froze into a glittering glaze in which the candlelight danced. The chimney smoke made a low dark ceiling so that the members of the family went scuttling beneath it; bent over, coughing and spluttering. Bianka was in the master bedroom on the second floor. She looked like a terrified big blonde-haired doll. Her hair, braided for the birth, was wet with perspiration and steam; her light blue eyes vacant one moment, and scared to death the next. Her mother, Mrs. Hosentauf, kept yelling "It's almost time" to three female cousins who kept moaning for no good reason that Seven could discover.

A huge half-finished painting stood on a heavy wooden easel by the hall window, and the rags hanging there stank of the turpentine that Josef cleaned his brushes in, daily, so that Bianka would think he'd been busy painting. All the other rags and pieces of cloth were piled in the bedroom, preparatory to the birth. Seven, invisible, kicked these aside and went over to Bianka.

He'd seen more births than he could remember, and he knew at once that Bianka's pains right now were caused by fear and foreboding. She *was* close, though, he saw, with some very definite feelings of disquietude, and he'd have to accelerate time considerably for Lydia; because when the baby was due—well, Lydia had to be there. Yet he tried to forget his concern about the future birth, so he could concentrate on Bianka's present.

She never saw him. Shaking his head, half vexed with her and Josef and Lydia as well, Seven said mentally, "Bianka, you aren't due yet. Your pains are caused by fear. Breathe deeply. Let yourself go. There now, there's nothing to it. That's right." He sent ripples of energy to her belly, watched them travel to her uterus and down her thighs. Bianka began to doze. Seven patted her stomach good-naturedly and when she began to quiet down, he went downstairs.

The men, Elgren Hosentauf and his brothers, were in the barns along with sawdust and hay, animal breath and manure, and—Seven saw—vodka. The four men were huddled together, squatting and laughing, in one of the cows' stalls; warm and cozy, with pitchforks ready in case one of the women came to fetch them, in which case they would say they'd been working all the time.

"Josef's near frozen and needs your help. He took his favorite ski trail up the mountain." Seven said these words to Elgren, Josef's father-in-law, and at the same time he implanted in Elgren's mind the most pathetic picture of Josef's predicament. Elgren suddenly swore; his fat stomach rumbled; he leaped to his feet. "I just had the awful thought that Josef's taken off somewhere," he squawked. "Where is he, my dumb son-in-law?"

Seeing the commotion safely started, watching the men check for Josef unsuccessfully and then indignantly saddle the horses for rescue, leaving the warmth of the barns for the winter night, Seven returned to Josef. Or rather, he returned the part of him that he'd sent to the house for his mission. To Josef, Seven had been with him all the while.

Seven, however, was worried. Josef believed that he was nearly freezing to death (which he nearly was), and Seven had to let Josef's beliefs predominate. "I'm dying," Josef moaned. "No feeling at all in my legs. I'll never see my firstborn, my son who will grow up to be a fine gentleman."

Seven was more upset than he wanted to admit. Suppose the rescue party didn't arrive in time? There *was* one thing he could do, beliefs or no, he thought. "Close your mental eyes," he said to Josef. "And you're going to have a daughter. That is, you are if everything works out the way it's supposed to."

"I *am* delirious," Josef cried. "I decided I wanted a son, in any case."

"You and Bianka decided on a girl. And we're not going to argue about it out here in the snow," Seven cried. "You're drunk, besides."

"I don't want a boy or a girl," Josef sighed, filled with self-pity. "I want to be single."

"Close your mental eyes and keep quiet," Seven ordered.

"Not on your life," Josef protested. "I still don't know if I'm awake or dreaming."

Seven said calmly, "Look. You always get upset when you come across something you don't understand. So kindly close your eyes for your own benefit."

Josef's mental eyes were terrified. "I don't know if I'm more afraid of freezing to death, or of your help," he moaned.

"You haven't time to wonder about it," Seven said, and in a flash he transported Josef—physical body, mental body, and all—some three miles further down the hill, to a good clear spot where Elgren and his men with their horses and sleigh would find him quicker and easier. Josef was screaming. "I'm dead, for God's sake. I'm flying through the air, carried away by demons." And at the same time, almost slyly, he kept poking his mental body in the ribs, seeing that he was, after all, quite alive.

His dream or mental body had separated from his physical one, though, and suddenly Josef stared, literally beside himself, to see his rumpled, nearly blue, stiff, sodden, and drunken form; eyelids stuck shut, with frost climbing between the thick dark eyebrows; proud brown moustache looking like the ancient white quills of some senile porcupine. He was struck by a sudden forlorn longing for his body, with which he'd made love to Bianka and planted his seed—his bristly, usually vigorous thighs, splendid arms, paint-stained fingers. And he vowed that if he ever got out of this, he'd never complain again; he'd paint masterpieces and be a good husband and father and householder beside.

Oversoul Seven got embarrassed whenever Josef really allowed himself to *feel* his emotions, as opposed to playing with them as he usually did. What would happen if Josef actually allowed himself to—well, honestly experience his feelings, instead of playing the mad artist or buffoon? Easy sentimentality was one thing—and Josef moaned often, loudly, quarrelsomely, bombastically. But these present feelings went deeper. Josef's sudden compassion for his body, in contrast to his usual self-pity, led Seven to say, gently, "Your body will be all right. If you believe me, it *will* be found in time. It won't be damaged to any important degree."

Josef was still staring at it, but the easily manufactured self-pity came back. "It'll freeze, poor thing," he sobbed.

"It just might," Seven cried, exasperated. "Now, listen, I have to get your thoughts off your body somehow. Just forget it, will you?"

"Forget it?" Josef screamed, nearly out of his wits by now.

Nothing, Seven saw, would take Josef's attention away from his body while he could still see it; and it wasn't in any shape for him to get back into.

"Dear gods above," Josef cried dramatically.

And Oversoul Seven thought: What a brilliant idea! It just might work—"Look over there," he told Josef. Josef turned, and with his attention momentarily off his body, Seven was able to whisk him away from it. Josef felt a sudden dizziness; the snow grew dazzling bright all around him, despite the darkness of the moment before. The ledge above him trembled and shifted in some indescribable fashion as he stared at it—and before him stretched a summery path. The air was so warm and lovely in contrast to the earlier iciness that Josef cried out with delight and relief. So did Seven, because Josef's concentration on warmth would help keep his physical body from freezing. That is, it would as long as Seven could keep Josef occupied.

"Where are we?" Josef demanded. "How did we get here?" He spoke so quickly that he nearly stuttered because

51

he looked down at his mental body (thinking it was his physical one) to see fine sun-bronzed limbs, small beads of perspiration running between the merry thigh hairs, as his legs flashed in and out of a brown walking robe. "And look. There's someone else," he shouted.

It was Lydia, still looking like Joan of Arc, only somewhat wearier than before. She gasped when she saw Josef. "What are *you* doing here?"

"I don't even know where here is," Josef said agreeably. "And I don't know you, either." Then, perplexed: "Or do I?"

Lydia looked at Seven, incredulously. "He doesn't remember who I am?" she asked Seven.

"No, and I'd rather you didn't remind him right now," Seven replied quickly. "I have some excellent and important reasons—"

"What are they?" Lydia interrupted. "I really do believe in honesty above all. And as a soul, I don't know if you have the right to hide important information from Josef."

Lydia made a fascinating picture, and Josef was staring at her with open admiration. He was in excellent spirits now, completely involved in this new adventure, his miseries and danger forgotten. (And Seven wanted to keep it that way for a while.) But Lydia indignantly put down the sword that went with her outfit and said, "I really think you owe Josef an explanation."

"That's the spirit!" Josef cried. "You tell him. He always intimidates me. I just see him when I'm drunk or dreaming, and right now I'm not sure of anything."

Lydia frowned. "I know one thing," she said. "I'm sick of looking like Joan of Arc, and I'm tired of changing images all the time. I'd like to stick to one image and one environment. Why can't we camp here for the night and explore the land of the gods tomorrow? If it *is* the land of the gods." She was tired, and peevish, and Seven sighed. The environment about them darkened. The sun was sinking; purple shadows filled a nearby meadow of flowers. And just then, above on the hillside, the lights splashed on in all the palaces and shone from the balconies. Josef stared: He'd never seen so many lights in his life.

Lydia laughed out loud, "The streetlights of the gods." She sobered instantly. "The gods don't really live on any mountain, or anywhere else, for that matter. I know that. I must have picked up the whole idea from mythology." She was her twenty-year-old self now, nervously smoking a cigarette; and critical. She eyed Josef: "You're real enough. I've met you before, even though you've forgotten. And Oversoul Seven is real, even though I used to think he wasn't."

"Now look here. Of course I'm real," Josef shouted. "And I almost seem to remember you. But what are we doing here? I must be dreaming. Are you?"

"We're on a pilgrimage to find the gods—if there really are any," Lydia announced dramatically, half sarcastically, staring at Oversoul Seven, yet unable to keep a certain wavering hope from her voice. "Anyhow, you seem to have joined us," she added. "And that's all I can tell you."

Josef scowled. "I'm not religious, and I think that the priests are mostly rascals, but there's only one God. Talking about gods is blasphemy," he said, honestly outraged, forgetting his own earlier thoughts on the matter. He stared accusingly at Seven. "I knew it," he moaned dejectedly. "Why can't I have an ordinary soul like anyone else, one that I can count on, instead of some renegade kind that sets out on pagan pilgrimages?"

But as soon as he spoke, Josef stopped, considering. Everything that he'd ever heard about pagan gods rushed into his mind. Orgies! He remembered the Norse deities again and almost smelled the meat roasting on spits, thick grease sizzling. (Damn, he was hungry.) The sensual richness overwhelmed him and spread out its tantalizing aura so that Lydia cried, "Something really smells great!"

"Roast pig," Josef shouted. "A feast of such gigantic proportions—"

"He's delirious," Elgren Hosentauf muttered. "Roast pig indeed." He and his two brothers knelt by Josef's body and tried to bundle it up onto the sleigh. It was well below zero. The men felt nearly frozen themselves.

"Wake up, Josef. You have to move around. Wake up!" Elgren shouted in Josef's ear. He and his brothers grabbed Josef's arms and started jerking them up and down; then his legs. Elgren opened the stiff mouth and sloppily poured some brandy down Josef's throat; Josef gagged, sputtered, coughed—and opened his physical eyes. Instead of the summer night he saw the snow and a closeup of Elgren's anxious face, large pores with blackheads, some half hidden at the edges of the red woolen scarf. But most of all, Josef saw Elgren's furious yct frightened cold-swollen eyes. "Oh, God," Elgren was yelling, caught between calling Joscf a blockhead and crying with gratitude as Josef's bleary eyes opened.

"He's come to," Elgren shouted. "Give me a hand." They all loaded Josef on the sleigh, while Elgren sat beside him, constantly moving his arms and legs, forcing him to move— much against his own inclination. "Let me sleep," Josef kept muttering. "Just let me sleep."

"Severe frostbite at the very least," Elgren muttered. "The damned fool, running off like that with his wife about to bear—" At the same time, he and the others found that their moods were lifting. They had needed relief from the house and barns. The excitement of the rescue and its success would make them heroes on their return. Still, Elgren was anxious. He urged the horses on: Josef had been out in the cold far too long. He frowned, cursed under his breath, and kept rubbing Josef's hands, while sipping brandy to keep himself warm. Now and then he forced some more down Josef's throat.

The brandy, Josef thought, was excellent. "Where did

you get this?" He held up a heavy mug and grinned. "It's fit for the gods," he said, while Oversoul Seven looked on anxiously. Josef shrugged. "I thought I felt a cold draught of air, and this really warms me up. But how could I have felt a chill? The air is warm as summer."

"Just your imagination," Seven said.

"I almost heard voices, too," Josef said. Some brandy trickled down his fine brown moustache. He wiped it off with his hand. "Do you hear voices?" he asked.

"It's just the breeze," Seven said quickly. He didn't want Josef to return to his body again until it was thawed out, yet even he could hear Hosentauf's raucous shouts, the horses' gallop—horseshoes now and then breaking through the crusted snow—one horse's forehoof sore. Seven caught himself just in time and closed out the images before he landed all three of them back there with the Hosentauf sleigh.

Lydia, now in blouse and slacks, sat down dejectedly. "I was so excited at first, seeing these mountains. I thought of Mount Olympus. But most likely there's really nothing real up there. Yet why is that scene so tantalizing?"

She stared: The warm bright lights splashed down the summer night hills. "Those *are* Olympian hills," she said moodily. "My God, the universe is vast." She felt as if she were going to cry.

"Don't worry about it," Josef replied. "All of this has to be a dream to begin with." The soft wind enveloped him. He felt full of vigor, and he eyed Lydia with more than just a touch of appreciation. "Let's go sit down beneath those trees," he said, his moustache quivering with his sudden gleeful duplicity.

Lydia understood his intent at once. She almost yelled, "You can't act like that! I'm going to be born as your daughter," but Oversoul Seven mentally stopped her. He didn't want Josef reminded of Bianka or his body until the physical situation was stabilized. Like Josef, the Hosentaufs often exaggerated the most simple events of their lives, and Seven knew that despite her moans and groans at the farmhouse, Bianka wasn't really in labor—yet. Checking, Seven mentally monitored Josef's half-frozen body as it sat slumped in the sleigh, and frowned. Josef could just possibly lose a leg.

For a moment Oversoul Seven felt really disconsolate: He had more trouble than he needed; and what he *really* needed was a good brisk wind behind the sleigh and horses. The horses themselves were tiring. What he really needed was—Seven broke off. Suddenly the Denmark scene became brilliantly clear. A strong wind came sweeping down behind the sleigh, pushing it so fast that Elgren Hosentauf yelled, "Where the devil did that wind come from?"

And in a near kind of distance, Oversoul Seven heard Cyprus say to him, "That's the help you needed. And don't forget your practice teaching dream class."

"I *had* forgotten it," Seven cried mentally. "I—" but Cyprus's presence had vanished.

Josef was saying, "I know what I'd like to do," and leering at Lydia.

"Can't you do something with him?" she asked Seven impatiently. Her black hair gently tangled in the wind. She swept the loose locks back uneasily, wondering if she felt any desire for Josef. There was warm moisture around his brown eyes and broad forehead; his glance was certainly inviting, but she couldn't forget that she would be his daughter; maybe, anyway. But more than that, she kept relating to him from a viewpoint of a whole lifetime of different ages. If she stayed at twenty, then Josef was an interesting older man, gallant and almost sophisticated. But then mentally she sprang to thirty-five and from *there,* he seemed amusingly inept and bumbling.

She was quite lost in these thoughts, perplexed and near harried, while Josef sat down on a ledge, crossed his legs, and gave her what he considered his deadliest, most suggestive leer.

Mentally, Oversoul Seven heard an invisible Cyprus say, "Look at the mountain." Her presence vanished again before he could comment, and Seven stared at the mountain as directed.

It hadn't changed. Or did he now notice vague figures at one of the distant castle windows?

"Good Zeus, woman, make up your mind," Josef thundered at Lydia.

Chapter Seven

Some Assembled Gods

Looking down from the mountain, Zeus said,

"They're at it again. Their energy and persistence is really incredible."

Christ answered, "Verily so."

"Yet they keep changing the rules," Zeus complained. He leaned back on his velvet couch, surveying the worlds and times that flickered outside of the castle-sized picture windows, drank his wine, and idly fingered the divine spider plant on the bronzed table by the divan.

Christ just smiled. Then he said, "I don't know what *you're* complaining about."

"Oh, the Crucifixion?" Zeus said. "I'll grant you that was no fun."

"Yet the whole concept was," Christ said nostalgically. "There were great moments, moments when I thought I almost got through to them. Jerusalem wasn't Olympus—

but the saga was there, the excitement and educational contrasts."

The two of them sat quietly for a moment (that lasted for centuries), each lost in his own thoughts, watching the nights and dawns flicker off and on across the earth and all of the earths below and around; for outside of the god-place, times and spaces blew gently past the windows, and the paths in the stately gardens outside connected worlds.

Such a place doesn't exist in usual terms, of course, but in—well, extraordinary terms, in palaces of the psyche; in an inner world that is as separated and personified as you and I and as all of the readers of this book. So in that sense, Zeus and Christ and Mohammed and all of the gods do all sit conversing. And in that sense, Oversoul Seven goes out seeking the gods.

Castle or not, however, nothing could conceal the fact that this was an old gods' home. Zeus kept dozing. Christ now and then had nightmares about the Crucifixion. And in one of the courtyards, Mohammed flashed his fiery sword, but none of the attendants even pretended to get out of the way anymore, or played scared, so that Mohammed just kept flailing away at the infidels, cutting the bodies in half or into a zillion pieces which were all in the next moment magically repaired. It was enough, dear Allah, to take the joy out of killing. Mohammed sighed, and Allah, mechanically clapping on the sidelines, was bored.

No one there, Zeus thought, had anything really left but memories.

"But what memories!" Christ answered aloud. "Still; pathetic. They're still fighting about me on Earth, even now. And waiting for the Second Coming. That'll be the blessed day. I'd *really* have to be crazy to go back there."

Zeus lifted his still black, thicker-than-forest eyebrows and said with a thunderous-enough laugh, "Come on, now. You love it. They still think of you, and it's the only thing that keeps you going. Admit it."

A flash of the old zest illuminated Christ's eyes so that electron worlds within his pupils veered dangerously; and on forgotten islands in time, small volcanoes erupted. "I *should* go back and teach them all a lesson. Hypocrites and liars! Deliberately twisting a god's words. Hypocrites and liars!" Christ banged his golden cane on the massive floorboards, sending sharp splinters of light everywhere, and Zeus said soothingly, "Forget it. It's all passed now. And don't go into a tantrum. You'll make it rain in—where is it? Ohio? Last time you carried on, they had a flood."

"That's nothing compared to what you did in Greece, and the entire Mediterranean, for that matter," Christ said, recovering. But then he shook his great head, untended graying curls cascading to the shoulders of his slightly stained sky-blue robe. "Still, it's sad," he said. "This whole place is just filled with old gods. Half of them have forgotten who they are. And no one comes to visit except those whiny petitioners. Bad enough, they call me by my first name."

"You always did get depressed easily," Zeus said. "We'll rouse again. You wait and see. And if one of us does, we all do, of course."

Into the splendidly appointed solarium came a dark, bent-over, tottering but massive figure of a goddess; gray hair kinky and wiry with leaping electricity; eyes a fury of autumnal ecstasy; ponderous yet so compelling in her mood of dejection that the whole room momentarily darkened. Christ and Zeus eyed each other with a worried air. Zeus coughed apologetically as he always did when Hera, his wife, came out of her private quarters: She was quite insane. She thought she wasn't a god at all. She even believed she was human on bad days (which lasted for centuries, of course).

"She doesn't have a believer left, poor thing," Zeus said.

Hera sat down in the thronelike rocking chair with silver gliders; her face darker than the deepest twilight. She stared out the multidimensional windows for a while, then said finally, "It's you two who are mad. We aren't gods and goddesses. We never *were*. We were all deluded. I'm the only sane one here. You're obsessed: Christ, with his Crucifixion; you, dear husband, with your claims of power; Mohammed with his magic sword, and all the rest. And Christ keeps seeing the head of John the Baptist on a platter, carried by one of the dancing girls. Divine delusions! Obsessions! Sad enough that you've deluded yourselves, but world upon worlds! I can't bear to think about it. If it wasn't that I had Pegasus for company, I *would* lose what mind I have left."

And when she said his name, Pegasus appeared, his huge wings decorously folded over his sleek horse's back. He'd been galloping to keep in shape for the best part of the century, and now he sauntered over to Hera, smiling with his fine horse teeth. "Still talking about the same old thing? You all need exercise. You know, that's your trouble; you need a good workout." He strutted slightly but nicely and added, "I don't mean to brag either, but being a god and an animal both does seem to give me certain advantages."

Absentmindedly Hera stroked Pegasus's hide, while Zeus turned speculative eyes toward Christ. "Suppose Hera's right? he said. "I mean, suppose her insanity carries a certain understanding of issues . . . ?"

"Of course she's right and utterly wrong at the same time," Christ replied.

Zeus frowned his famous frown. "Now you sound like Buddha," he said irritably. "He can't give a proper yes or no answer either. He's never even made up his mind if he likes existence to begin with."

Pegasus's divine animal nature got the best of him. Gently he disentangled his mane from Hera's stroking fingers and said heartily, "Forgive me. This closed-in atmosphere really gets on my nerves. And I don't give a hoot if people remember *me* or not, though it's nice when someone does. I can always go out and gallop beneath the stars and nibble the grasses. And I'm only sorry you can't do the same."

"He probably doesn't gallop at all, but uses his wings the minute he's out of sight," Christ muttered sourly.

Pegasus heard the remark, but ignored it. In his more sardonic moments he thought that it was his animal nature rather than his divine one that was his salvation, for it was the creature part of him that delighted in details, yet basked in a kind of generalized diffused good spirits that could also be quite gargantuan. Now, outside for example, he could appreciate the tiny trembling of the earth beneath his hooves, sense the dirt sliding beneath the surface—small earthslides that slightly shifted the tunnels in which the cool worms slid—and enjoy the summer moon that ever so slightly lightened the roots of the grasses, its rays traveling downward, staining the sliding underground worms with the slightest tint of silver.

Yet he could, when he wanted, use his wings to soar into the skies; and mentally to send his spirit into realms that were extraordinary even in divine terms. Now he nibbled the grass thoughtfully: There was something in the air—a hint of a change—a foreign scent. He perked up his ears. Extraordinary! There were visitors on the ledges below!

The other gods frequently got lonely. On several occasions they'd gone on pilgrimages to find some followers, but each time, unfortunate circumstances cut short their journeys. Again, being the god of inspiration gave him another edge, Pegasus mused, because his own thoughts were as lively as any company, mortal or divine. In fact, he often thanked his thoughts for their vivid and companionable nature. But now there would be a banquet perhaps, some cheer; excellent conversation and surcease from the eternal boredom of the other gods. No, boredom wasn't the right word, Pegasus thought. The gods were never really *bored*. It was just that they didn't feel wanted anymore.

They'd been put out to pasture, so to speak. They really didn't have any duties to perform.

He didn't either, in the old accepted manner. But he had his robust animal nature, and someone or other was always asking for inspiration, even if they didn't know where it came from. Actually, Pegasus mused as he trotted along, he was called upon in one way or another a good deal of the time, but people often forgot his animal characteristics, or worse, his playful ones. "Ah, well." Pegasus neighed, and headed toward the visitors.

Oversoul Seven heard the hoofbeats first, and cupped his ear. While Pegasus was still in the distance, he neighed a welcome so as not to startle anyone. He reveled in the sound himself, for it was the quintessence of each and any and all horses neighing in greeting and triumph. He stomped up and down, the magnificent muscles luxuriating in each motion. He neighed again, aware of his fine form beneath the Olympian sky, while the full moon shone brightly on all the peaks and ledges.

"What on earth was *that?*" Lydia gasped.

"Why, it sounded like a gigantic horse, or a hundred horses," Josef said, growing uneasy.

Pegasus came slowly and majestically out of the shadows. His godlike, animal-like natures merged so perfectly that even Oversoul Seven just stood there for a moment, staring. Barnyards of earth's past and present and future joined in Pegasus's form, so that before Seven's and Lydia's and Josef's eyes rose images of barns and meadows and wars and battlegrounds: There were horses bravely carrying men, forgetting their own terrors as swords flashed and cannons roared; horses hitched to plows tilling the earth; the odors of manure and grass and grain all intermingled. All of this was sensed in one way or another by Seven, Lydia, and Josef, until the animal part of Pegasus alone was godlike in proportions. But besides this, yet rising from it, Pegasus's divine attributes became natural and physical—

nature knowing itself as a horse, glorifying in power and speed and filled to the brim with creaturehood.

Lydia, who had never been a horsewoman, was terrified at first. Josef, who loved horses, was awed, and almost appalled by his own reactions. He identified with Pegasus's sense of power, imagined the beast galloping down dark hills, and he shuddered, almost dizzy with elation. Oversoul Seven wasn't just elated: He was steadied and restored. His earth nature had seemed to grow new roots in the few moments since the arrival of Pegasus. Seven smiled: Suddenly he understood Lydia's need for a place of her own in the universe, and he felt himself as the earthroot soul out of which all of his personalities emerged. At the same time, he experienced a rush of almost unendurable sorrow. It vanished almost at once, but lasted long enough for him to sense the sharp, private earth realities in which each human individual lived—

Seven was so fascinated by Pegasus, though, that he'd taken his attention away from Josef, who had just noticed Pegasus's wings and was muttering, shaken, "I never saw a horse with wings before." And for a moment, Josef's consciousness was in two places at once. Elgren Hosentauf said anxiously, "Hear that? Talking about a horse with wings! He's really delirious." They were unsaddling in the barnyard where the horse manure steamed in the cold air, and with great shouts and bustling they managed to get Josef inside, to the kitchen.

His mother-in-law yelled, "Quick, sit him here." She opened the oven, thrust Josef's legs onto the open door so that his feet were inside, took out the bricks she'd heated, covered them with rags, and placed them between Josef's body and the chair arms. The fire inside the stove was raging. She threw in more kindling.

All this time Josef kept opening and closing his eyes and muttering about the horse with wings. For a few moments, he didn't feel anything. Then the burning, tingling, itching sensation started beneath his woolen stockings, a sodden wet smelly odor rose, someone grabbed his feet and removed the stockings which had been nearly frozen to his feet before, and Josef snapped to.

He looked down to see his feet, distant purple swollen hulks that seemed to belong to someone else. His mother-in-law was trying to force hot cocoa down his throat. One of the cats, having sneaked in from the barns, jumped on his lap and was indignantly chased by a serving girl. "You damned nincompoop," Elgren began. "Trying a fool trick like that at a time like this." Josef moaned, closed his eyes again, and pretended to be unconscious so as to avoid the coming lecture.

Chapter Eight

Lydia Meets Christ
Under Very
Unfortunate Circumstances

As Josef disappeared, Lydia cried, "I never *did* remind him that I'm supposed to be born as his daughter. The least he could do is remember that."

"He's just absentminded," Oversoul Seven muttered. He was trying to discover how Josef was making out at home and listen to Lydia at the same time.

"You seem to be having difficulties," Pegasus said politely. "May I be of help?"

Lydia frowned. "You're only part of a myth come to life," she said sternly. "I remember . . . Pegasus, the god of inspiration—"

"Yes, I helped you often, even though I didn't use this form," Pegasus answered. "You're lucky that I'm one of the gods you believed in, even if your ideas about me were a little confused."

"You're not going to claim credit for all the poetry I wrote in my last life, I hope," Lydia said tartly.

"Are *you?*" Pegasus asked, smiling.

Lydia started to say, "Well, of course. Who else?" when she remembered having often felt that her poetry was hers and not hers at the same time.

"You wrote it," Pegasus said, a bit smugly, "but I carried you out to the rarefied air where the poetry exists."

"All I really wanted to do *then* was write poetry," Lydia said, a bit crossly. "And all I want to do now is find the gods, if there are any—"

"Well, you've found one," Pegasus said, tapping one forefoot modestly enough in the grass.

Lydia tried not to sound disappointed. "I *have* known inspiration in one way or another, as you pointed out," she said. "And without meaning to hurt your feelings, I just didn't expect a god to be a horse. Divine or not, a horse is a horse, even one who speaks as well as you do. Your elocution is excellent," Lydia added, suddenly remembering that she'd also taught English once.

Oversoul Seven had been standing by, letting Lydia carry on, but now he interrupted nervously. "I suggest you end this conversation, Lydia," he said, "or you might regret it. Inspiration *can* be very tricky."

"Well, I'm certain I'd recognize a real god if I met one," Lydia was saying to Pegasus. "But even a horse with wings is a horse. I mean, wings don't necessarily mean divinity."

From nowhere, Seven heard Cyprus's voice: "You'd better remove some of Lydia's misconceptions quickly. They could lead to unnecessary complications."

"You must be kidding," Seven cried, mentally. "She's blindingly stubborn, and you know we have to do this *her* way—"

"But with guidance. And don't forget your practice teaching dream class!"

Seven didn't even have time to answer. He felt time

wrinkle before it actually started to, and he knew that Lydia had gone too far.

He turned to her. She was saying, "I prayed for help during my darkest moments on earth, and no god answered."

"No, no, Lydia," Seven cried. "Change the subject. Fast!"

But she was staring defiantly at Pegasus. "In my darkest moments," she repeated. "And no one answered."

"Are you sure?" Pegasus asked; and the transition was so fast that even Oversoul Seven was startled. He heard time crinkle and Lydia's pilgrimage suddenly turned into a nightmare. He saw at once (in blessed hindsight, Cyprus said later) exactly what happened: Lydia had returned to one of her last life's worst, darkest moments.

Nearing death, she sat in a wheelchair in the solarium of the nursing home in which her grown children had placed her. She frowned, looking out the wide windows down to the hills below. She was strapped into the chair; drugged, but she felt drunk, bleary, so dizzy inside that she could have been guzzling liquor at some wild party for days. Yet, she knew, she'd been nowhere. She hadn't left the old people's home: That much was clear. It was also clear that, wheelchair or no, she'd been somewhere, involved in some kind of mind-traveling that she couldn't understand.

"Time for our pills, sweetie," said the nurse, Mrs. Only.

"I'd like to sweetie her," Lydia thought, in a rage. The rage itself was vitally strong, though its energy didn't budge her arms or legs, which once would have reacted.

"Open our mouth now," Mrs. Only said, with a kind of threatening sweetness.

"Like hell I will," Lydia said to herself, but in utter surprise she felt her jaws drop open, slackly; felt the pill go sliding down that soft but somehow distant tunnel that didn't seem to have anything to do with *her* at all—though again, she knew that once it had.

She stared: The twilight was laid out before the windows. Down the hill, the lights of a gas station glinted. At least, she thought, it always *had* been a gas station and normal enough. But now—she looked with sardonic curiosity— the flying red horse on the neon sign was lifting a foreleg, gently stepping out onto the first shining shelf of air. And he was taking off, wings stirring the early night clouds in ripples; *neighing*. How was it that no one else seemed to hear? She grinned, at least mentally, because she couldn't tell if her lips actually moved at all. But there were farms nearby. She imagined the flying horse neighing to all those farm horses below; liberating them, giving them wings too, so that hundreds of horses just flew off in the middle of fields while startled farmers watched aghast.

Seeing all of this mentally, she shook her head. The pills, she supposed; they were making her crazy. For a minute she strained at *her* bonds, just when the magic horse flew off the gas station sign—but by the time the whole thing was over, she just sank back, struck by desolation. Dimly her predicament came through to her. Not only was she tied up, legally shut up so that there was no justice to resort to, but the world itself was all changing. Nothing was permanent anymore; either it was the result of the goddamned drugs they gave her, or they knew this happened and they didn't want the old people to tell the young ones. The secret was that the world really changed all the while, and that when you dropped out of it, you saw the truth.

"Oh, Lydia, that's it but not it at the same time," Seven exclaimed. "You don't have to re-experience the nursing home." But Lydia didn't hear him, because when she was alive she didn't believe she had a soul, and so Seven just waited for an opportunity to free her whatever way he could.

Maybe when you died, things cleared up again, she thought, but she doubted it. Her ideas rolled down the hill of her mind so quickly that she could only catch a few of them. The rest disappeared. Where did they go?

"Dinnie-din time," said Mrs. Only, coming close with a dinner tray.

Lydia tried to rearrange herself more comfortably.

"Be careful. Don't dump all the hot food now," Mrs. Only said in a terrible voice.

Lydia looked down to see the plate on her lap, the heat of the food rearousing her thighs. Mrs. Only unstrapped her for eating but Lydia didn't want any of their goddamned food. It took all of her will power—she collected herself, for parts of her seemed off in their own unknown places— but she focused precisely and brilliantly, gripped the insides of her own muscles, directed them as deliberately as she ever had, and sent the tray—plate, silverware, cream pitcher, and all—flying.

Then, satisfied, she sat back and tried to say, crisply, "That's what I think of your damned drugged food," but her lips and mouth seemed to turn into cotton, making soft white fluffy sounds that said nothing. "Dear God," cried Lydia inside her mind.

Mrs. Only was picking up the food when Lydia noticed something else, a change in her fellow patients. They'd been beside her all the while in their chairs, but she ignored them. They always ignored each other when the nurses were around, pretending to be dumber than they were. So she'd also ignored their background whining. But now their voices no longer whispered, but suddenly turned full and real and vital. And damn near thunderous; damn near louder than any thunder she'd ever heard.

"True resurrections are the kind we just observed," Christ said. His eyes glowed dimly.

"Who on earth are you?" Lydia gasped, noticing that she was speaking normally for a change.

"Jesus Christ," Christ said cordially.

"And Zeus, at your service," said Zeus.

How was it that she could speak properly, Lydia wondered, ignoring her companions as new patients. "Everybody thinks they're gods here," she said finally, admiring the tone of her own irony. How *was* it that suddenly she could think clearly too?

"Of course," Zeus answered. "We all are."

"You all *think* you are," Hera said, entering the room and sitting down, spreading her gigantic velvet skirt over the gold divan. "They're . . . divinely touched," Hera said to Lydia. "Quite mad, though, I admit, in a charming fashion. Without their obsessions, who would they be, after all? Or are they really senile gods?"

Lydia didn't dare say anything.

"And you don't have to look so dreadful, do you?" Hera asked. "Do change yourself into someone more pleasant. Even if Christ and Zeus aren't really gods, they *do* think that they are, and I try to treat them accordingly."

Lydia looked down at herself to see the spilled food crusting on her nightgown.

"Here, dear," Hera said, handing Lydia a silver mirror.

Lydia looked, shocked, to see her old face—a bony, wrinkled, yet satisfying face, but one filled with bitterness, anger, and dismay. Even in her bewilderment Lydia realized that *here,* dissatisfaction was somehow out of place. "What do you expect me to do?" she asked. "This is how I look. This is me."

"It's just *one* you, dearie," Hera said, with just the gentlest touch of displeasure. "Come now, change for dinner."

"Fish from Galilee," Christ said.

"The finest geese from Rome, a banquet fit for the gods," Zeus said.

"Do change," Hera coaxed, and Lydia stared, for in the mirror she saw her own face, seven years old and pouting. Instantly she remembered the moment: First grade. She'd thrown a temper tantrum and the teacher forced her to look into a mirror at her own angry face until she herself was forced to laugh. Now those earnest, self-righteous, furious young eyes glared out at her; so freshly, innocently outraged that Lydia wanted to cry. The child's face was so . . . cosmically funny, so comic in ways that she felt but couldn't understand, that Lydia suddenly grinned at the child's mirror face.

"That's so much better," Hera (and the first-grade teacher) said.

And—Lydia gasped again—because the child she had been, saw *her:* the old woman, grinning, and it was *that* face all wrinkled yet sunny that the child saw and liked; the face that had forced her to laugh and forget her tantrum.

The mirror's surface wrinkled. The child's face vanished. Lydia was seeing a dignified, funny, perfectly old smiling face that was her own.

"There, that wasn't hard, was it?" Hera (and the first-grade teacher) said. "You can change the wheelchair too," Hera suggested gently as she rearranged her own gown and added a summer wrap.

Lydia was so confused that she didn't know what she was doing. She stared down to see that she was no longer tied to the chair, but that was because they'd untied her for dinner. Wasn't it?

"Do help her, Christ," Hera said.

Christ leaned forward graciously. "Do you understand who I am?" he asked.

Lydia squinted at him uneasily. Was he the old man next to her in the nursing home, a senile old coot like herself? Or was he an old Christ, such as she'd never seen in pictures or read about in the Bible? In any case, she decided, he was nice; so why hurt his feelings? "You're Christ," she said, sighing.

"Verily," Christ answered. "And I say to you that you are you, whether you're young or old or male or female at any given time. You don't have to be old and sick right now. Certainly not *here*. Or there, either. So turn into the image that you like best."

"And then maybe we can get on to dinner," Zeus muttered. But Lydia didn't hear him. She was staring at Christ. He sounded so absurdly *sure*. His gray-white curls quivered with conviction as he nodded his head. His brown eyes didn't blink. They were wide open with that innocent look the very senile get. He wanted her to change her image so badly; she hated to break his heart.

"Daughter," he said.

And she suddenly was a daughter in fact! That is, she was young, glowing, incredulous.

"That was beautifully done, Christ," Hera said.

"Yes, I still have the old touch," Christ answered. He rubbed his wrinkled hands together with obvious satisfaction.

"Well, let's get on with dinner, then," Zeus shouted. He clapped his hands and a table appeared, loaded with delicacies. "Now that everyone's settled, what did you come here for?" he asked, reaching out not too gracefully toward a leg of mutton.

Lydia looked up to answer and she paused in bewilderment. Suddenly his eyes were young and hearty—and very, very familiar. They belonged to Oversoul Seven and just as Lydia realized *that*, that scene vanished and everything came back to her. "Whatever happened?" she cried. "Oh, that was terrible. I relived one of the darkest moments—"

"And you asked for help and got it," Seven replied. "Something you'd conveniently forgotten. I had a bad enough time myself, waiting until I could get through to you. Now I'm exhausted. Besides that, I have an appointment that I'm not looking forward to at all: a dream class with a student who is particularly difficult." He wanted to say, "Just like you," but he didn't. For one thing, Lydia's mistakes were at least exciting, and for another, he was too wise to start an argument. Instead he said, "I've been so involved in your difficulties that I completely forgot someone else who needs me badly. Well, I *almost* forgot," he amended, in case Cyprus was listening.

Seven had whisked Lydia out into one of the endless corridors that connected the various areas of the Gods' Rest Home. "Can I trust you to just wait here until I get back?" he asked. "Anyhow, you need to be alone awhile to digest your experiences."

Lydia was so glad to be healthy and strong again that she just nodded. There were some more things Seven wanted to say to her, but as he began to speak, the environment began to change; or rather, he was moving out of it. "Lydia, don't forget that—" he began, but Lydia didn't hear him, of course.

Chapter Nine

Oversoul Seven's Student, Will, Wants to Drop Life Class

"What did you say?" asked Seven's student, Will, because Seven's words to Lydia were actually spoken in the dream classroom to which Seven was unceremoniously swept.

"Sorry I'm late. I was talking to someone else," Seven muttered, catching his breath. "Now, let's run through the world's problems one more time." He tried not to look at the hallucinatory school clock that hung on the equally unreal but definite walls of the dream classroom. Practice teaching wasn't his cup of tea, but he'd resolved not to be a clock-watcher either. When he thought the words "cup of tea," pleased with his use of earth vernacular, a cup of tea *did* instantly appear on a china saucer next to the copy of the textbook, *The Physical Universe As Idea Construction*.

"That cup of tea shouldn't be there," shouted Will at once. "It isn't a primary construction." He was a husky young man, smiling (or so it seemed to Seven) with unnecessary satisfaction.

"I was testing you," Seven said quickly. "You're quite right: The tea was the result of a stray thought that I deliberately allowed prominence. Just to show you . . . how inappropriate earth conditions can *seem* to appear for no reason."

"Bullshit," exclaimed the young man. "If you'll forgive me, you just made a mistake and now you're trying to cover it up!"

"There *are* no mistakes," Seven said, more sternly than necessary. "If you remembered that, you wouldn't still be in this class, and you wouldn't need me as a private tutor."

"I wish *you'd* remember that, Seven!" The voice, heard only by Seven, belonged to Cyprus, who was monitoring Seven's performance with Will. She was invisible, while Seven had adopted the image of a young man just out of graduate school. Seven said mentally to Cyprus, "Remember that this is my first practice teaching of a dream class, will you? 'Practical Living: The Formation of Private and World Conditions'—well, that's a pretty big subject from *any* point of view."

Cyprus didn't answer.

"Again, there are no mistakes," Seven said to Will. Absentmindedly, he took a sip of the tea and grinned, despite himself. "Actually the tea is delicious," he said. "So this is an example of how a *seemingly* trivial mistake can result in a positive experience if you don't police your thoughts too rigidly."

Cyprus groaned, symbolically speaking. "That's called self-justification, whether or not what you said was true," she exclaimed.

Will didn't hear her, of course. He was standing up, leaning rather indolently against his desk. He smiled in a superior fashion (or so it seemed to Seven) and said, "Now you're justifying yourself again. I think I could teach this class myself if I didn't dislike the subject matter so much."

Silence.

"What an impeccable young man!" Cyprus said, but she smiled compassionately at Seven.

Seven sighed. "Will," he said, "you've taken the course three times before, I hear. You can't even pass it, much less teach it. So sit down."

Will shrugged angrily and sat down. Seven felt sorry for him then, so he sent over the rest of the tea. The cup sailed smoothly through the air, landing by Will's right hand. Seven projected a slice of lemon on the china saucer as an accompaniment and said, "Don't feel too badly. The construction of physical reality *is* an advanced course by many standards."

"If I don't pass this time, I'm going to bow out," Will grumbled. "I told you that before."

"You need permission to drop a course once you've signed up, and I hate paperwork, so forget it," Seven replied, quickly.

"Then give me a passing grade and get rid of me," Will yelled. As he reacted to Will's anger, Oversoul Seven automatically changed his image. What Will needed was a father figure, Seven thought, and in a flash he turned into one—an old man wearing a mantle, sandals, and brown robe.

"Ultimately your teacher doesn't grade you: You grade yourself," Seven (as the old man) said. "Come now; you're very creative and filled with energy. Don't be so impatient with yourself."

Will calmed down some, but he stood up, frowning. "This kind of thing always happens in these classes," he said. "The teacher keeps changing into you, or vice versa. I like you better, though, I'll say that. He's too near my age to know much more than I do."

"So *that's* it," Seven said.

"Well, at least you're old enough to have learned something," Will replied. Then, suspiciously, "Am I awake or dreaming? I'm never sure of that, either, when I'm here."

77

"Both," Seven answered. "You should know that by now."

"Know? I don't *know* anything," Will blurted. "And besides, I think that Physical Reality is a lousy course."

"Then why did you take it to begin with?" Seven asked. He almost turned back into the young graduate teacher, but caught himself just in time.

"To prove I could do it, that's why," Will yelled.

In consternation, Seven forgot himself and called out to Cyprus, "Did you hear that?" Then, to Will, he said as calmly as he could, "That's your trouble right there. You don't have to prove yourself to anyone; including yourself!"

Before Will could answer, Cyprus materialized, and for once Will just stood there silently, staring; for with Cyprus's image an indefinable sense of power and assurance came to him. Suddenly he *knew* that he was somehow secure despite all of his difficulties; yet he couldn't tell for the life of him *who* stood before him.

For one thing, Cyprus reminded him of his mother and his sister, not as they were, necessarily (for they often annoyed him), but as he wished they might be. At the same time, Cyprus seemed to be someone else—the woman (not girl) that he often dreamed of meeting and falling in love with. All of these images were merged in the woman he saw before him, so that it was impossible to separate them. And, for reasons he didn't understand, Will felt more and more assured.

"You're the feminine principle? Or the female muse? Or"—he snapped his dream fingers—"Mother Goddess? I *do* have considerable education on earth," he said, when she didn't answer. "I'm not as stupid as I sometimes seem."

Amazing, thought Seven as he watched, for now Will looked nonchalant and even half insolent. He strolled over to Cyprus. "You *are* damnably attractive, whoever you are," he said. And the closer to her he came, the more powerful and assured he felt.

Yet suddenly he stopped and felt that he should go no further. At the same time, an image opened in his mind so

78

that he *saw* himself—foolishly strutting, petty somehow—approaching what?

The image of the woman blurred, but grew larger at the same time, and he could feel some peak of intensity moving within it. "You *are* the female principle!" he cried, unable to stop himself, even while some part of him knew instantly that he was wrong. But even as he yelled out, he'd approached too closely. He was suddenly in the midst of an incredible calm that gripped him—that is, he could feel the calm's edges holding his mind, or trying to. He told himself frantically that dreams often went from the ludicrous to the horrible, while at the same time he wondered what was so awful about accepting this . . . terrible calm assurance? Why was he frightened of it? Because it was his own, beyond male or female connections, the vast security in which he had his being. But it was too gigantic, he thought despairingly, and when he said that, or rather yelled it out loud, it was all over. He was sitting up in bed, in a cold sweat.

A strange calm filled the room, and he stared about suspiciously. Was there an odd white-grayish mist against the usual night darkness? Or was that the effect of fog and the open window? Nervously, he reached for a joint.

"He half glimpsed us," Cyprus said. "Whenever he lets himself feel the dimensions between fact and fiction, then he's able to sense other realities."

"You were too hard on him," Seven said moodily. "He couldn't identify with his own vitality, really. He'd treat it like an enemy."

"Or call it the female principle," Cyprus said, smiling.

Still more moodily, Seven said, "I don't like practice dream teaching much, either."

"Is there anyone here?" Will asked. He was half awake, staring into the darkness, and speaking mentally.

"Nobody. Go to sleep," Seven answered.

"That's good because I just had a *scare*. A near nightmare," Will said, thinking that he was holding a mental dialogue with himself. He stood up, naked, and walked to the window.

"He's beautiful," Seven said to Cyprus. "Look at that healthy body; that pose—"

Will *was* posing and aware of his world-weary expression, dark brows lowered thoughtfully, as he savored his young-man-alone-in-the-world stance. What an unusual experience he'd just had! Obviously he was brilliant and psychic to have had such events happen at all, even if they *were* dreams. Yet he even felt that his pose was a pose or as if *any* emotion he felt would be bound to be vaguely . . . manufactured. Or perhaps he was actually far more assured and confident than even he knew? Anyhow, he thought, he did feel better than he had before he went to bed. He decided to grin philosophically, and he did.

"Will he remember anything important?" Seven asked.

"Not too many details, but I hope that he'll begin to sense his own vitality more. It will take a while for him to correlate what he's learned, though, because it can't be vocalized."

"*Did* he learn anything?" Seven asked dejectedly. "Sometimes I wonder—"

"Did *you* learn anything? That's more to the point," Cyprus answered. "I helped you out with Will this time, but from now on, you're on your own with him. Remember, you chose this experience yourself too, even though there are some things that you have to forget on purpose for a while. So tell yourself that you'll know how to help Will— and you *will!*"

She and Seven had both turned into points of light. Seeing them, Will thought that they were reflections from the neon sign of the all-night supermarket across the way. The lights flashed back and forth from his fingertips, as he drummed them up and down on the windowsill.

Chapter Ten

Jeffery's Notes and Questions Without Answers

I haven't had time to write here, because I've been so busy with "The Further Education of Oversoul Seven," and except for my academic work, my life now almost seems organized about the book. In my sleep sometimes part of a chapter will suddenly awaken me, so I've taken to keeping a notebook by the bedside. Otherwise the "writing" takes me about three hours a night. I sit down; the words and sense of exhilaration come, some part of me gets carried away by what is being written, and all sense of time vanishes.

Of course, I've told no one what I'm doing. The fact is that I don't know what odd venture this is that I've embarked upon. I'm certainly not writing "Education" in usual terms. I have no idea what is going to happen next to the characters. For that matter, I have no idea where the words themselves are coming from. The concepts involved are hardly to be taken seriously, but as fantasy I suppose they're acceptable enough. In any case, this certainly involves me in the oddest behavior, and so I've decided to study everything that happens as closely as possible.

My sanity does not seem threatened as I first suspected. Nothing else in my life has altered (so far, Jeffy-boy, I remind myself). Well, to be more honest, nothing in my *exterior* situation has changed. I do have the impression that my dreams are different than they used to be, more numerous perhaps, and colorful. I haven't remembered any dreams, however, though as mentioned I have awakened with portions of this manuscript suddenly just here, as if freshly minted.

I try to look at the script objectively and then work backward, trying to figure out what kind of person would ordinarily write this kind of book; and I'm as far from being that kind of person as anyone I know. Or is the unconscious that playful and creative? That is, could the manuscript be the result of my own unconscious productivity? I can't really accept such a thesis, since I'm not at all convinced that the unconscious operates in such a manner. I've always thought of it as containing the suppressed, primitive, unsavory aspects of the self that, quite rightly, we've been conditioned to repress. The conditioning process: Everything must return to that basis. And somewhere, in that framework, there must be an answer to my current experience. Yet—nothing in my own background seems to present an adequate explanation.

I am trying a small experiment. A few days before the manuscript "began," I'd started taking vitamin C. Surely I see no connections. Nevertheless, today I began accelerating the dose of vitamin C to ascertain if there is any resulting alteration in my production of the book. Perhaps in a way that we don't understand, some vitamins cause an overstimulation of certain hormones that further trigger the creative abilities. I don't for the moment believe this, but I refuse to discount such a theory either.

One thing in particular bothers me: Why does the material come all prepared, without any conscious work on my part at all? And why do I have the feeling that "someone" is giving it to me? Well, I finally admitted it: More and more I become aware that there is a personified source behind the manuscript. Is such a feeling only the conscious mind's astonishment with the products of the unconscious processes? This is the most likely explanation, of course. Yet, granting that the unconscious has such abilities—and I'm not at all certain that it does—then why are they showing in my life now, suddenly, and never before?

I'm not doubting the unconscious origin of creativity, but I'm almost certain that conditioning directs its activity. Each act must have its reason, but the reason may simply be the reaction to learned sequences of nerve patterns. So my acts must, it seems to me, be the result of *some* kind of conditioned response.

I don't like it. We had a cat when I was a boy. He came without being called, when he heard the noise of the can opener. He was conditioned: He knew that the sound of the can opener, when it wasn't family mealtime, meant food for him—because we never fed him when we ate. Then, what "conditions" me to sit down and "get" that book each evening after a full day teaching? What element out of my past is wielding the can opener? And what kinds of learning processes are taking place?

Ridiculous rubbish—the last paragraph. Yet, granting the validity of conditioning and the learning aspects of behavior, there is no other alternative except that the answers to my experience lie in those directions.

Thus far I've ignored the contents of the manuscript, being by nature more fascinated by processes than by art; so the process of the book's production fascinates me, while the contents can best be judged by storytellers. Yet a few disquieting thoughts have come to me involving the book's scenes or characters and, try as I will to dismiss them, they keep returning to my mind. For the record, I'll try to put these unfortunate musings in some kind of order.

For one thing, the book's description of the rest home of the gods instantly reminds me of Ram-Ram and his Queen Alice at the mental institution. Even the "gods" are reminiscent of the inmates who seemed to regard me with such annoying condescension when I visited Ram-Ram. I don't even know why such a correspondence comes to mind, or why it makes me more uneasy than I'm willing to admit.

The descriptions of the gods in the book thus far don't bother me at all, of course. How can one get upset over the actions or conditions of mythic characters? I refuse to define my own position on the "gods" or "God," for that matter, in any religious terms at all. That is, the word "atheist" presupposes the existence of a God, if only in the minds of others. I myself believe in a chance universe and in Darwinian principles; and in that framework, the idea of a God (or gods) cannot enter, though some evolutionists try to eat their cake and have it too by inserting a Divinity who set the universe and evolution into motion. In any case, for all of those reasons, the descriptions of the gods do not offend me; only the curious correspondence between their environment and Ram-Ram's quite real institution.

But, just lately, a new issue caught my attention, or riveted it, to be more accurate. So here I will record my uneasy feelings about the chapter just previous to these notes. The first time Will, the young man, was introduced in the classroom dream sequence, I felt a most unwelcome sense of identification with him. For one thing, I wrote the introductory passages or, rather, took them down just after tutoring a particularly difficult student. As I started my nightly writing stint, a small shock went through me to find that Oversoul Seven was also tutoring a student. I shrugged and went on taking down the words that came—as the manuscript has, to date—as fast as I can type.

It was a muggy evening. The window was open, letting in a late February heavy air. Below my windows, a few groups of students or professors and their wives went by; their footsteps coming up to me with a curious intensity, undoubtedly carried, I thought, by the humidity. Someone went to the garbage cans and opened one. The lid as it was slammed down on the ground sounded so loud to me that I might have been standing beside it. It seemed as if the contents of my own mind were clattering.

If I remember properly, I got goose pimples. At the same time, however, I was typing the dream class sequence and my identification with the character, Will, grew quite insidiously. I was never aware of any . . . transition of consciousness, for example, yet by the middle of that chapter, in my mind at least, I was almost speaking Will's lines. I was speaking for him or he was speaking for me; it's impossible for me to express this clearly.

Nothing in the manuscript said so, but I was somehow certain that Will's threat to bow out of the course was actually a threat of suicide. Yet the main character, Oversoul Seven, hardly seemed concerned, so why should I be?

Another connection hit me when Will saw Cyprus as the feminine principle—for when he did, *I* saw my ex-wife, Sarah, in my mind's eye, almost as clearly as I've ever seen her, physically. It came to me that I'd refused Sarah a child—as I mentioned earlier, she's pregnant now by another man—because I saw no reason to bring another vulnerable human being into such a chaotic existence. And if I'm right about Will, then he sees no reason to continue his *own* life. Perhaps I am making too much of all of this, and I do note with some humor that Will was at least rational in his dismissal of life as meaningful, feeling no idiotic compulsion to search for any gods or divine varieties.

For that matter, now that I think more deeply, there *is* a rational reason, if only a small one, for my sense of identification with Will. For he does remind me somewhat of myself in my own undergraduate days, even though any

85

young student probably has certain characteristics that a grown adult might find reminiscent. My body is rather stocky, not unattractive, but it has none of the grace that seems to be assigned to Will's, and I was never that nonchalant or charming or contemptuous. I was too aware of my pompousness, for one thing, even though I couldn't do anything about it then. Or now. But I feel almost threatened in any case by that identification. I didn't like my own participation, emotionally, in the chapter. And I admit that I'm rather abashed at the small coincidence that set me off on this tangent: My full name is Jeffery *William* Blodgett.

I have the sneaking suspicion that the book is playing a trick on me; that "someone" knew I would be discomforted by such a similarity of names. Furthermore, I suspect that the "someone" may be watching for my reactions.

So except for these notes, I refused to react. I took down the entire chapter as if nothing bothered me at all; as if I had not participated in the scenes; as if the sounds from below the window didn't sound unreasonably loud and intense; as if I wasn't suddenly struck by the frightening feeling that my own living room was as hallucinatory in nature as Oversoul Seven's classroom. And of course my thoughts were accompanied the entire time by the sound of my typing fingers, which, as if thinking by themselves, pounded out the words with amazing rapidity. It takes me far longer, for example, to type up these notes of mine, and I'm uncomfortably aware of the stiffness of my own prose.

I do wish Will hadn't been introduced into the manuscript, because surely this means that he'll return in other chapters. Now there is no doubt that the book will continue. In the beginning I told myself that each chapter would be the last and I'd be left with an odd but brief psychological adventure and no more. At least I'm not fooling myself any longer in that regard. Now as I write these lines, I decide to close these notes for tonight, with some dismay, for I find myself in the peculiar position of worrying about a fictional character and wondering whether or not he might commit suicide.

No sooner did I write the last sentence when I "knew" that another chapter of "Education" was waiting. But how did I know? How *do* I know? I try to take a moment to examine my feelings, but already in my mind's eye I see myself tearing this page of notes out of the typewriter and inserting a new sheet of paper to begin the next installment.

I can, of course, decide to resist. I know that resistance is possible. So what is it that—

Chapter Eleven

Oversoul Seven Journeys to the Undersides of the Universe

Seven went wandering through the universe. He
wanted to get away from everything he knew, and
since he knew more all the time, he had to go further to
get away. To do this, he just let himself go unmoored in
any given reality, unrelated to any ideas of himself. As
always, some odd inner motion began to take hold, support
him, and carry him along. When this started to happen he
always worried a bit, nothing like he used to, and then
the journey really began. He felt like a seed in the wind,
blowing through universes but never landing.

Somewhere along the way he knew that his thoughts
would start changing too, and he tried to catch this happening. First, it was like thinking backwards, and very
confusing. Just when he seemed to get the knack of this,
his thoughts turned around again, and it was like thinking
sidewards. He was used to the fact that there was really no

up or down to space. But now the up and down quality of his thoughts was gone too, and his sense of subjective direction. That is, thoughts just came—backwards, sidewards, from inside and outside—and none of them were particularly his or anyone else's.

He tried to navigate in all this, because it seemed that there should be one thought of his own to use as a kind of measuring stick. But he'd already let himself go, or begun the process; and at this point he didn't know how to reverse what he'd started. The thoughts came all at once, not one before the other, and then suddenly Seven got scared—or the part of him that still held on got scared—because the thoughts began to mix with each other.

One thought said, "This is the beginning," for example. The thought nearest to that one said, "This is the end," and the two sentences came simultaneously. Then the letters in one sentence mixed into those of the other one, and some part of Seven's mind went in and out, trying to keep track. But at the same time, all the other thoughts he heard started doing the same thing. And parts of Seven kept leaving him to follow those too, as they went jumbling and turning into completely different patterns.

This wasn't Seven's idea of getting away from it at all, and something else happened that had never happened before. The sentences that he heard now came in different languages, so that "This is the beginning" came in every language at once, and so did all the other sentences. He saw the letters mentally also. Before he got used to this— and the sentences switching to all of their language versions—the letters themselves grew bleary and began to shift and break away from each other, turning into waves and particles of light. Now and then one would explode, and the light from that fragment would turn all of the other particles into waves. But in the next moment they'd be particles again, like mosaics, glimmering in the universe, with darkness all around.

Seven blinked: The darkness wasn't at all stationary, but kept slivering off and falling into all of this particle and wave activity, until some of the letters were made of a glowing, brilliant darkness.

"There was light and there was darkness," Seven thought, or thought that he thought. How could there be light-darkness or darkness that was light? That would mean— But before he could finish, the light fragments and the dark-shining fragments changed places or turned into each other. Seven screamed with dismay and shouted with utter amazement all at once. Because suddenly he was on the other side of . . . what? His mind (or what was left of it), he thought (or tried to think), was different.

He'd been traveling far faster than the speed of light in usual terms, but now he discovered that once this happened, there was a sense of complete stillness that existed inside the incredible motion. He calmed down. He was lolling.

When everything went so fast that you could hardly follow, there was a new quiet plateau within or above the speed—if that was the word. Because now all the letters and sentences that he'd heard before just went lolling about too, like clouds, only they were broad waves now, shining, separated, flowing past each other without a care in the world.

Now who thought that last sentence, Seven wondered, and what world did it come from? He didn't recognize it as his own, or as anyone else's, for that matter. He was simply intrigued, watching all of the gentle motion, which he discovered had a slight sound, like the breaking of light into music or the notes that music comes from—and he suddenly felt himself doing just that.

Some tiny part of himself rode piggyback on the rest of him, which was definitely breaking up or falling apart. Not that he had a physical form, because he didn't, but his being had an intangible form and this was gently falling off in bits and pieces, tumbling out into long waves that now and then bunched together in particles, and all of this kept extending outward into—well, whatever was there. In so doing, Seven's consciousness flowed through the lot; rising and falling in the waves, bouncing and gently snapping back—all very enjoyable.

The waves and particles that were his kept flowing through others that weren't, though he didn't know who or what they belonged to. Only a strangeness flowed through him when this happened. It was "sometime later" before he realized that each time this happened, a bit of his consciousness mixed into those waves too, and a bit of the other streams most certainly flowed into him. How many others was he, then? Or how many others were him?

How on earth could you tell?

How on *what?*

Was that thought his?

Whose?

He'd gone to the other side of the universe, or to the other side of the inside of the universe, whatever that meant and whoever or whatever he was.

Was. This was the strangest thought he'd ever had. Nothing, he knew, *was.* Everything *is.* But where was he in this everythingness? And how did somewhere come from nowhere, drifting as he was, spread out into all those waves and particles, each spreading both light and sound? The sound disappeared but was always present. And Seven realized then that he'd quite disappeared. He doubted even Cyprus could find him. He was . . . dispersed.

He was hopscotching all over; or space was everywhere turning into what he was; or he was turning everywhere into what space was, and couldn't tell the difference.

What would happen if—

He shouted, "I am Oversoul Seven," and meant it?

And he did.

At once, or rather before at once, all the waves and particles stopped, wherever they were, for some had vanished beyond the dimensions of his knowledge or attention, fallen over horizons of being that he couldn't fathom. Yet the stopping was so fast and involved such motion that, like a rubber band snapping, particles and waves all moved one into the other, contracted, imploded, shrank, moved faster than light into a different kind of light—and threw Seven back to the side of the universe he'd left earlier.

"To say I was multidimensionally dizzy is an understatement," he said to Cyprus later, and as soon as he said the words he was struck with the meaning of "understatement." He had gone *under* statement; beneath it. He had unstated himself, at least briefly, and he said proudly to Cyprus, "I must have restated myself rather well, too, because here I am."

"Are you?" Cyprus asked gently.

Seven shook his head, figuratively speaking, and said, "I've just been through enough without you trying to confuse me further."

"All right," Cyprus replied. "I'll take pity on you and help you out. If instead of saying, 'Here I am,' you say, 'I am here,' and if you realize that *here* is a noun synonymous with *I*, then you've really learned something."

Seven knew that he'd really learned something vital in his other-side-of-the-universe adventure. He knew that he knew, but he didn't know how to make the knowledge available. Still, he tried. He said, "You're trying to tell me that where I am is always here. No, that isn't it. You're trying to tell me that here is where I am, no matter where that is." His voice trailed off. "No matter *what* it is?"

"No," Cyprus said. "You're making it hopelessly complicated." She paused, waiting. Seven felt as if she was drawing the knowledge out of him; as if she reached down into some invisible closet of wisdom he didn't even know he possessed, and was pulling this seed of knowledge upward. He felt very odd, as if he should go (down?) there and help her. So he did.

Everything that he had felt and sensed in his other-side-of-the-universe experience was happening all over again, only the waves and particles that spread out into unknowable horizons were . . . forming *his* consciousness, and his thoughts were growing out and up and emerging as his words to Cyprus.

"I am here," Seven shouted triumphantly. "Here always happens for me where I am. Or, here and I are one."

"So if Will decides to commit suicide, he takes his here with him," Cyprus said gently. "He turns into a new here, that then knows itself."

"And if Lydia doesn't decide to be reborn as Tweety? Or if she changes her mind?" Seven asked, and added, "Not that she *would*, of course."

"That's enough questions for now," Cyprus said. "For that matter, I'd see just what Lydia was up to if I were you. And Josef. And—"

"I'm going," Seven cried.

Chapter Twelve

A Mother-to-Be Gets a Midnight Surprise

Dejectedly, Lydia wandered through the giant halls of the Gods' Rest Home, her footsteps echoing against the marble floors. She trailed her fingers along the mosaic walls as she passed, frowning vaguely at the gargoyles, busts, and statues of gods and goddesses that lined the hallway. She'd never been so lonely in her life, she thought; well, at least not in the last life, which was the only one she remembered clearly, and probably not in any of the others that she hadn't remembered yet.

Worse, she couldn't seem to make up her mind about anything—her age or sex or clothes. Now that she'd learned a few of Oversoul Seven's tricks, they weren't half the fun she'd expected. She changed into a male page, looking like an illustration she'd once seen in a history book; then into a young girl dancer in Turkish veils; then, bored, back to herself. But even as herself, she had all of those ages to contend with, and none of them contented her or seemed to fit: She wasn't a young girl, for example, without an old woman's knowledge, even if she could look that way. And she wasn't an old woman, with youth behind her forever, either. She was obviously both, and the more she thought about it, the more confused she became.

She supposed that she was out of line, trying to figure out the god business, but on the other hand, she knew that once she was reborn, she wouldn't have the time. Or maybe even the inclination. She was getting tired of pilgrimages, though, particularly since Oversoul Seven had left her alone. Suddenly she realized how important his company had become. She'd met no one since he left her, yet she knew that some people or inhabitants of some kind were invisibly about. Their presence was tantalizingly close and attractive. Now and then she almost heard laughter. Once she almost glimpsed faces. Yet she felt some strange psychological opaqueness, too, that separated her from . . . whoever they were.

Musing, Lydia came to a large window, the first she'd noticed in the long passageway. She paused, looking out, if "out" was the proper word, and what she saw struck Lydia through with nostalgia. There, spread out sparkling before her eyes, separated from her only by the windowpane, was a snowy scene reminiscent of a Christmas card. An old-fashioned, dear scene, she thought, showing farmlands and white-topped mountains; a place where people lived one age at a time, and with only one image to contend with; tucked neatly between night and dawn, birth and death.

She pressed her nose against the window, wanting to cry, feeling at the same time like a coward for yearning—as she was now—for a new birth into space and time. Her eyes sprang open. Of course, she thought, that must be Josef and Bianka's farm! Otherwise why would she be so drawn to it?

More, she felt—again nostalgically—that she already knew each tree and shrub in the yard, each horse in the barn, as if in some indescribable past she'd already lived the life she hadn't yet begun. On the other hand, she was filled with expectation and curiosity, and with such a feeling of suspense that she held her breath; and when she let it out, it suddenly turned into frost against the window.

And the air was cold.

Lydia shivered and looked around anxiously. At once she knew that she was in the farmhouse. A young woman lay on a bed piled high with mattresses. It was apparently late at night. A fireplace in the corner had died out and only a few embers leapt up now and then in the darkness. The woman, nevertheless, was perspiring. She was muttering in her sleep, tossing her blonde-braided head swiftly back and forth, so that the ribboned blue night cap trembled.

Lydia tiptoed closer.

Could that be her future mother? The woman lay on her back, her huge stomach pushing up the coverlets. There were woolen rugs on the floor and a few smaller ones at the foot of the bed. A pitcher of water stood on the bedside table. Lydia nervously hallucinated a cigarette for herself, lit up, and poured herself a glass of water. Forgetting herself, she drank the real thing instead of hallucinating her own, but Bianka, still sleeping, never noticed.

"Damn," Lydia muttered. Bianka was lovely, but her own connections were with Josef. She would be her father's rather than her mother's daughter, in that respect. She prowled around the room, eyes narrowed, considering. Bianka's true labor, as opposed to the false one just passed, couldn't be put off forever.

Just then a motion caught Lydia's eye. She leapt back. Bianka's dream image moved easily up from the bed (pregnant and all) but light-footed and graceful.

"Who's there?" asked the dreaming Bianka.

Lydia froze. She had little experience in dealing with

people's dream selves; and besides she was suddenly confused because in relationship to her twentieth-century life, Bianka had been dead for centuries. But the same applied to Josef, and she met him fairly often, she thought. And she was, after all, being born back into the past only from the very limited viewpoint of "the living."

She said softly, "It's Lydia. Well, it's really Tweety. I'm supposed to be born as your daughter."

"No. No. No," Oversoul Seven cried, suddenly appearing. "Look *younger*. You aren't born adult!"

Startled, Lydia turned into a three-year-old pudgy blonde-haired little girl with round face and unswerving earnest eyes.

"Oh," Bianka cried. She bent over, smiling.

But Lydia was suddenly frightened.

"Oh, you'll be my baby!" Bianka exclaimed. "And until now I wasn't really sure that I wanted a baby at all! But just to see you—"

Quickly Lydia turned back into herself. She strode toward Oversoul Seven. "Somehow you engineered this . . . somehow—"

"She had second thoughts too, but she doesn't have them now," Seven said, grinning and pointing at Bianka, who stood staring. She wore her nightgown and carried a hallucinatory candle.

"Well, I *still* have second thoughts," Lydia whispered angrily.

"Oh, I thought I saw my future baby," Bianka cried. Her dream image grew agitated, blurred, was drawn to her body on the bed and, crying, "I saw my baby," Bianka woke up.

"What? What?" muttered Josef from his cot in the hall where his mother-in-law had put him for the night. He struggled awake, hearing Bianka's cries through the door. He frowned, wiped his eyes. The bricks that they'd placed at his feet were cold. There were no windows in the hall, and he hated closed places. Bianka called again. He cursed, not too softly, sat on the edge of the cot and held his head. Besides everything else, he had a hangover. And he missed his own bed. The women had put him out to make room for the cousins, and even his wife seemed to belong to them, or to the house, or to the baby that was supposed to be coming—to anyone, in short, but him.

He got out of bed, put his robe on over his nightgown, and opened Bianka's door. The moonlight made a golden white path from the curtained window, reflecting on the kettles and pails that earlier had held boiling water. They sat on the floor by the cold fireplace now, with the light glittering on them; and the piles of rags and other cloths were neatly stacked and ready on the chair. Josef frowned; he'd decorated the chair himself, painted on the flower designs that Bianka wanted, and there it sat—blue and pink for the baby's room—if the baby ever came. And the chair reminded him of his own painting, and of the time wasted on the rosebuds, and of the hours yet to come when he'd fail in one way or another to do what he kept telling himself he was determined to do—become a good artist.

"Josef?" said Bianka in a small voice. She was on the side of the bed away from the moonlight, so he could hardly see her at all. His head throbbed and his feet hurt, but at the sound of her voice, he blushed deeply in the darkness, in shame at his part in her predicament, in anger—after all, women were supposed to know how to handle such things more easily—and at his own unexpected response to her half-crying voice: He was sexually aroused. He remembered how long it had been since they'd really bedded, and before he could stop himself, he saw her in his mind's eyes as she had been: naked, and if not actually slim, well, not as fat as a pregnant cow. The comparison made him further ashamed of himself. He sat on the side of the bed.

"Here I am," he said glumly.

"I dreamed I saw our baby, only she was about three years old."

"She?" Josef stuttered, half because he always said he wanted a boy, and half because he was cold. Besides, conversation about the baby bothered him. He kept getting the feeling that he actually knew more about the affair than was good for him to know. Snatches of dream encounters with Lydia stirred in his mind.

"She looked like you," Bianka said, "except that she was blonde-haired like me."

"If she looks like me, God help her," Josef said, snorting.

"Maybe it was a true dream. Maybe I really saw her—"

"Old wives' tales. It was just a plain dream," Josef said, more gruffly than he intended, because Bianka's dream actually made him uneasy in a way he couldn't fathom. His brown moustache bristled. He stared around, suspiciously.

"What are you looking for? The stork?" Bianka asked. She giggled suddenly. "You look so funny, so gruff. And scared."

"I'm not scared. Scared of what?" he demanded.

"Of being a father," she said, adding half coquettishly, "You should have thought of that before."

"Before what?" he asked, grinning but still uncomfortable in the big bed where he had to treat her as if she were a virgin instead of a wife. The goose-feather mattress softly followed her body contours. He imagined the two of them yelling and shouting in homey ecstasy. He reached out for her, stopped his hand in midair and, instead, lit the bedside candle. "I'll just be glad when we can do it again," he muttered.

"It? It? Do what?" she asked softly. She was growing drowsy. She wondered if the baby was sleeping inside her now. "It'll all be over soon," she said.

He didn't answer, though he wanted to; because, he brooded, she'd never really be the same again. She'd be nursing the baby for months, for one thing. He blushed, thinking of it, mentally seeing the full bared breasts, bodice-loosened. They'd cavort again, but not, he was sure, as they *had*, like merry damn puppies without a care in the world. His youth, at twenty-six, was gone, and hers at twenty-three. And they were lucky. But Christ, the trouble was that their youth *wasn't* gone. It kept lingering and wouldn't give up. "You'd do it in a minute if you could, wouldn't you?" he asked, feeling better momentarily. After all, he wasn't dead yet!

"I'm a born slut," she said sleepily; smiling because the phrase always cheered him up and made him feel more like an artist with his mistress than like a farmer with his wife. She half roused. It made her feel that way too.

Lydia said nervously, "Let's get out of here. I feel claustrophobic." She and Seven had been silently and invisibly standing there.

Josef managed a fake smile. He said, "Your mother gave me one of the straw cots to sleep on. She treats me like a kitchen hand."

"She does not!"

"Now, snuggling down in those goose feathers with you would be more like it." Josef joked because he thought it was the time for it, but he was growing tired.

"I don't think I can do it," Lydia said.

"Do what?" Seven asked, innocently.

"You know what. Be born again. Why can't people just be born at ten? Just arrive somehow, full-blown?"

"You better get out of here, though," Bianka said. "If my mother catches you in here now, she'll start yelling and you'll yell back. You aren't supposed to be in here until it's all over."

"If it's ever over," Josef exclaimed. "Do you feel the baby now? Is it kicking or anything?"

"I don't now, but I did. Oh God, did I! Now the baby's sleeping, I think."

"Maybe it will just go away," Josef muttered.

"Some father he'll make," Lydia said. "We make all

these agreements when he's in the dream state, but he sure doesn't remember them when he's awake. And not all the time when he's dreaming, either."

Just then dawn streaked across the sky. A gray light filled the room. Sound came from downstairs. A cock crowed. "You'd better get back to the cot," Bianka cried.

Lydia disconsolately looked at Seven, then at the frost-coated window and beyond to the snowy hills. The activity downstairs quickened, and through the window Lydia saw Bianka's brother, Jonathan Hosentauf, go out to the barn, rubbing his gloved hands together, puffing out his cheeks. Smoke was coming from one of the chimneys, and Lydia suddenly realized that now she was looking at the entire scene from above, and that the scene was withdrawing, or she was withdrawing from it.

In the next second she found herself standing back in the long corridor with her face pressed to the gigantic sparkling window, the marble floors beneath her feet and the entire snowy scene so distant a view from the window that she could hardly make it out at all.

She looked around, almost peevishly. For one thing, Oversoul Seven was gone, which made her angry, and for another she felt even more indecisive than she had before. Did she really want to be reborn or not? She didn't know, and yet she wasn't pleased with the present situation either. Just thinking about it made her angrier, and at the same time she suddenly felt vehemently, wildly, independent. She was tired of going off willy-nilly. She wanted a place of her own, a point of familiarity she could always count on and return to, a place where even Oversoul Seven would be expected to knock first before entering.

She wanted—

And breathlessly, joyfully, she saw the transition taking place. She'd imagined a trailer by the ocean; herself, fairly young, there alone, writing poetry (not, as in her last life, marrying and having children, with poetry second-best), but going it alone as—funny, she thought—Josef wished sometimes that he had.

"Oh," she exclaimed, for the trailer grew up around her, Formica-topped table in front of wide windows, a fake geranium partially faded but so homey, notebooks piled on the leather built-in benches. She peered out the window: The trailer was only feet from the water. "Oh, God!" She ran out, twenty and barefooted, so delighted that she thought she was—well, alive, and that the ocean would be visited by tourists at least occasionally, just when she felt like company. And she'd pretend that she had just one space and time to contend with. *And* she wasn't going to budge, she told herself, until she was good and ready.

Chapter Thirteen

Between Ages:
Lydia Meets Tweety and an
Old Love

Lydia sat in her trailer, glowering. The ocean at her doorstep sparkled in sunlight. A few palm trees were visible in the distance; she was drinking coffee and she *smelled* the aroma. She was gloriously, triumphantly young, having chosen to be twenty-three after hours of changing back and forth, studying the subtle differences between each age from twenty to thirty. She was inspired enough; at least she'd been writing poetry. The scene, her own image—everything was perfect, the epitome of everything she'd always wanted. But she wasn't happy.

Who would read her poetry, for one thing? She was lonely. Between worlds. She felt dissatisfied with herself, as if she were still wanting a certain kind of understanding; as if she were really only half aware of the realities about her. Now and then she sensed vast activity, all around her, but beyond her reach or perception.

Yet to be born again seemed to demand more courage than she possessed, she thought, and her pilgrimage to the gods was dependent upon Seven's help (for without him, she seemed to get nowhere in her search), and Seven had disappeared once again. She suspected that he was letting her stew in her own juices.

She had sons and a daughter still living, but it was difficult to understand that now, Lydia thought. They seemed like storybook people. That was because she related better to poetry and to the natural world than she did to her own family; it had always been hard for her to take people seriously.

"You'd better hurry up," a child's voice said.

"What?" Lydia stared out of the trailer window, seeing no one at first. In the next moment a small child was visible at the horizon, yet moving toward Lydia with impossible speed. Before Lydia got over her surprise, wondering how she heard the voice when the child was so far away, she noticed something else. This was a little girl, wearing a snowsuit. The beach dunes glittered. Then the child was in front of her.

"You'd really better hurry," she said reproachfully. She was pudgy, with wide, earnest, light blue eyes and a firm jaw, although her face otherwise was round enough.

"I'd better hurry for what?" Lydia asked.

"You're not the only person in the universe, you know," the little girl answered, again reproachfully.

"What's your name? And what do you want? And for heaven's sake, why are you wearing a snowsuit?"

"I want to go home now," the little girl said soberly. "You'd better come back now too."

Lydia started to reply, but she stopped, considering. The little girl was about six years old, and she looked very familiar and very . . . foreign or exotic or *something* at once.

"Come on," the child said gravely. Yet at the same time

there was also a note of gaiety in her clear, high voice. "You *are* coming, aren't you? I have to go back," she said, "and if you don't come, I don't know what will happen."

"Tweety, Tweety," came still another voice.

"I'm here," the little girl called back, and Lydia stared. *Tweety?* Her own future self? Provided she was reborn, of course! But how could the child be Tweety when she hadn't been born yet? "Just who are you?" she cried angrily. She was almost tempted to shake the little girl's shoulders when another child, a boy, also in snow attire, suddenly appeared in the distance. He was about eight years old, puffing, out of breath.

"It's suppertime. Where have you been? You'll get a licking if you don't hurry." He paused, seeing Lydia, and asked uneasily, "Who is that?"

He stared.

Lydia stared back. It was—Lawrence. It was—

"Don't you dare tell him!" cried Tweety.

As Lydia stepped back in astonishment, she noticed the farmhouse for the first time, and suddenly realized that for the entire interview, the bright sand had been transforming itself gradually, granules turning to packed snow; sunlight darkening until now it was twilight with blue shadows covering the winter landscape. She looked around anxiously for her trailer, for the sun—

The little boy asked again, "Who is the lady?" though, and she forgot everything else, as buried memories from her last life suddenly were reclaimed. She and Lawrence as young people in isolated scenes—she and Lawrence, old and stubborn, defying the establishment. And this little boy was Lawrence. She knew it. What then, Lawrence born again? How could she have forgotten him? And what else had she forgotten? And why?

"The little boy is my cousin," Tweety said gently to Lydia, speaking too meaningfully for a child.

Lydia just kept staring. The boy's eyes as he stared back

were so innocent and guileless and clear, and so ignorant of her, that Lydia wanted to cry. But already the boy had turned, made a snowball in his snow-caked mittens, and run to the farmhouse. The back door opened, a slice of light illuminating the dark barnyard. Tweety said, "I *have* to go. You have to come—" and she, too, ran toward the farm.

Lydia gasped and moved automatically toward the house, drawn by Tweety, but more, toward the memory of Lawrence. How was it that the children had found her to begin with? Why didn't the boy know he was Lawrence and recognize her? Why—

The children had disappeared inside the house, and moving closer to it, Lydia gasped again. How *could* she ever have forgotten her love of Lawrence, she wondered, more desperately than she had before. Because now all at once and in a rush, Lydia's full memory and feeling returned full-blast, richer than anything she could imagine, more important than the meaning of life or finding the gods. The feelings roused—what? Desire for life, whether or not she understood it.

At the same time, she peered through the windows of the house. They were iced over on the outside and steamed over on the inside, so she chipped off some small patches of ice in order to see more clearly. What she saw filled her with the oddest nostalgia. The family was gathered at the table in the dining room, bright in fireplace light and further lit by two fat candles. On the thick wooden table sat a gigantic platter of smoked fish, along with loaves of brown crusty bread to which Josef was helping himself. Elgren Hosentauf sat at the head of the table with his eldest son, Jonathan, while Elgren's wife, Avona, bustled back and forth. The two children slyly eyed each other; they only had soup, no fish, and Bianka, Tweety's mother, grown stout, was saying: "Lars goes home tomorrow. His parents are coming for him, and that's that." Tweety mumbled under her breath, and the boy, Lars, lowered his head.

Lydia was almost crying: Lawrence would be called Lars, then, and be her cousin—that is, if she was born as Tweety. She yearned to tell the small boy, to make him understand. Mentally she cried, "Oh, don't you remember? We were lovers. You died on our trailer trip together."

"I'm a grown-up man really," Lars said, puffing out his chest for Tweety's benefit.

"Children do not speak at dinner," old man Hosentauf thundered.

"I am too grown up," Lars boasted, gesturing wildly, and spilling his soup. Tweety giggled and ducked to avoid the heel of bread thrown by her grandfather. It landed in her mother's soup instead, splashing, and everybody laughed.

"You'll just get him in trouble. And Tweety too," said a terribly familiar voice.

Lydia spun around. There stood Lawrence, exactly as she remembered him—in his late twenties, as he'd been when they first met.

"I couldn't talk to you until you wanted to remember," Lawrence said. He didn't look at her, though, but stared through the window. "Fascinating, isn't it, to see ourselves as we'll be?" he asked.

"Forget *them*. We're us," Lydia cried. "You mean, you remembered me? How I could have forgotten you, I'll never know."

He wore a black opera cape and carried a fresh bouquet of roses that flashed against the snow as the window light fell against the ground.

"Oh, Lawrence—Larry," she exclaimed; and for a moment she felt that they were still having their early affair, and she was still married to—

"Roger. You were married to Roger," Lawrence said.

"But I'm not married now," Lydia cried. "And we're young again."

"Are we? Or are we just between ages?" Lawrence asked, smiling. He handed her the flowers and said, "What will you do with them? Put them in a vase on a living room table? Don't you understand? We're ageless. But to be really *young*, we have to go back in time. We have to be born again."

"We can stay just as we are," she said.

"You'll like it less and less," he answered. "We really don't know enough yet to stay here, without physical lives. There's more, too. You've been living in your own mental world. Even I couldn't get your notice earlier—" But he broke off; embarrassed, worried for her and ill at ease himself. He knew the look in her eyes too well, and she was growing more desirable and lovely by the minute.

"Uh, I have this lovely little hallucinatory trailer by the ocean . . ." she said, shrugging her shoulders, raising those arched black brows with exaggerated, humorous, but quite effective invitation.

"Lydia, for God's sake, listen," he said. "Look in that window! Look at that child, Tweety. She exists in a certain reality, one that may or may not take place. The same applies to Lars. Doesn't that mean anything to you?"

"You were easier to get along with when we were alive," she said, glaring at him. "Besides, I'm being born as Tweety *in the past*, at least from our point of view. So, somehow, Tweety *was* born, no matter what I decide *now*. I've already figured that out."

"You're wrong," Lawrence said anxiously. "All the time is at once. There isn't really any past or future, so—" But her anger had taken her away where his love couldn't reach. She'd vanished, along with the farmhouse and landscape. And Lawrence knew that he had to try and find her again as quickly as he could.

To Lydia, *Lawrence* had vanished. "Larry? Where did you go?" she cried.

Right beside her, he asked the same question of her. But neither one saw or heard the other, and each of them felt disconsolate; Lydia the most, because her memories of Lawrence kept swirling around her, vivid scenes appearing and disappearing. It was inconceivable, she thought for the tenth time, that she'd forgotten him. But he'd obviously returned because of their love, and to help her. Perhaps to warn her. But about what? And again, if she'd forgotten Lawrence, what else had she forgotten? And why?

Then, seemingly for no reason, she remembered the voices and presences she'd sensed about her at various times—the images that almost but not quite materialized, the voices that almost spoke.

She'd often suspected that she was surrounded by an entire different dimension of actuality. For one thing, the sounds were too fast for her to follow, and the images that she felt would change too quickly for her to perceive them. She realized that she had the same sensations now, of straining to hear or see some indefinable activity. She sensed motion of a kind, replete with people—a world that somehow existed right now, beyond her grasp, but a world into which she was trying to materialize. But what kind of a world? And who was there? Would she find Lawrence there too?

And as soon as she thought of Lawrence, the name Roger came to mind. And she thought, Of course: Roger was my husband. But somehow that didn't seem to be the right answer. Yet the name kept ringing in her mind until she could think of nothing else. And all about her, images began to waver and wobble and form.

Chapter Fourteen

Lydia Attends a Séance, Shocks the Sitters, and Keeps a Promise

"It's Roger. Roger. Can you hear me?" Lydia spun around. She heard the voice but saw no one.

"If you can hear us, give us a sign."

The voice, if that's what it was, Lydia thought, came out of nowhere as far as she was concerned. She heard it, but didn't hear it at the same time. That is, the voice seemed composed of a small mountain of sounds in some dim distance, and if she turned her attention in that direction, then she felt the sounds stacked up there, falling down into soundlessness or building up again—she couldn't tell which—when somehow she felt the words.

She'd just been thinking of Roger, her husband, trying to recall their life together, so maybe this was a message of sorts from him, she thought. Yet again, the name and the voice didn't seem to go together.

"It's Roger Junior," Lydia's living son said for the tenth time, following the medium's directions and feeling like a damned fool.

The candlelight flickered on the fringed table covering, touching the gilt-framed picture of Christ on the nearest knickknack-filled shelf, dancing on the edge of his sister Anna's huge diamond ring, and on the little gold bell that sat at the medium's fingertips. Roger's eyes followed the candlelight as it flickered from object to object. He shifted his weight in the straight-backed chair. He was tired of the whole affair and he'd come only because he had promised Anna that he would.

"The vibrations are changing," the medium, Mrs. Always, said. She swayed gently. Her voice changed timbre. Roger looked at the glittering reflections again: They made Christ look cross-eyed, he thought nervously.

"Call her name again," Anna whispered, in a small spooky voice. She remembered playing with a Ouija board once as a child, when the pointer suddenly went speeding across the board, seemingly all by itself. Whether it was all bunk, as Roger said, or not—one never knew. "One never knows," she whispered.

The medium said, "Think. Concentrate. Close your eyes and try to see your mother in your mind's eye."

Roger did. He saw the bony finger, the boyish frame at about seventy, the intense, ironic eyes, the tailored suit she wore when she gave poetry readings. He saw her in the dungarees she used to wear most of the time and he saw her running off with that man—what was his name? Lawrence somebody—when she was past seventy. Christ; he tried to squash the image of the two bony old bodies making love in a trailer alcove. He was still scandalized by the whole affair.

"She's here! Your mother's here. I can always feel it," Mrs. Always said. She meant it. She wasn't lying. Her thoughts unwound like pink girlish ribbons, garnishes of

111

sentimentality twirling on them everywhere: She believed wholeheartedly and with grim determination in Mother Love as the strongest force on earth, or anywhere else for that matter; and now she was convinced that she felt that force materializing. She listened inwardly. She sweated; an indignity gladly accepted for the sake of such a worthy task. And finally she saw a mental image. She whispered, "I see her. Your mother. In a lovely blue gown. She's standing to the left, over there. She says, 'Give my dear son my love. Roger, I'm with you still.'"

Mrs. Always's misty, half-closed eyes lit on Roger's face so that he tried to freeze his expression into an acceptable one for the occasion.

"Your mother says that your father is here, too," Mrs. Always said. "And so you see, true love is reunited."

"She and father never got along," Roger muttered. He wanted to ask, "What about that old reprobate she took off with at an age when she should have known better? Is he there too?"

But his sister, Anna, said in a small girlish voice, "Mama? Is it really you?"

Roger blushed uncomfortably. His sister was past fifty, for God's sake, and she hadn't called Lydia "Mama" since she was a girl.

"Is it *really* you?" Anna asked. She knew it wasn't, she told herself; but suddenly she felt very forlorn and childlike—overweight and dyed red hair to the contrary—and the room seemed depressing and sad in contrast to the medium's face, which was filled with a saintly innocence that she certainly wasn't faking. Was she?

"Your mother says that she and your father are both happy," Mrs. Always said. "Your mother is standing by me now. A man is with her. He's medium-sized with white hair and blue eyes. Is that your father?"

"No. He died quite young," Roger said meanly.

"Oh, well, maybe he's your mother's father. Even mediums can't always be sure. He died of a severe illness."

Christ, most people do, Roger thought. He was ready to get up and leave.

"He worked in—leather. Yes, that's it," Mrs. Always said. Roger and Anna both gasped. Anna grabbed her lace handkerchief and buried her face in it; it was drenched with perfume, and the scent made Roger sneeze violently.

"Oh, dear! Do be still," Mrs. Always cried. "You'll ruin the vibrations."

Roger was white-faced and almost sick to his stomach. "Tell us more about the man," he said, looking meaningfully at Anna, who was horrified: It would be doubly scandalous, she thought, for her dead mother's elderly lover to turn up at a séance. But he *did* work in leather. She remembered perfectly that he'd upholstered the trailer love nest when he and Lydia ran off.

"Oh, it couldn't be *him*," Anna whispered.

Mrs. Always knew that she'd really hit upon something, but she didn't know what it was. The word "leather" had just come to her out of nowhere. Neither of the sitters looked very happy about the connection, though. The man was glowering and the stout woman looked scared to death. "I sense a great love, a love that lasts beyond the grave," she said shrewdly, hopefully.

"Oh," cried Anna.

"Anything else?" Roger asked. He was beginning to collect himself again.

"A long journey," Mrs. Always said. She was growing tired. She was never sure where her impressions came from: Some were conscious guesses, but some . . . definitely had a different source.

Roger grumphed. Was that a lucky guess or did it really refer to the cross-country journey with the old man and woman, half out of their blessed minds, on their last wicked binge?

"She's leaving. Everything is getting dim," Mrs. Always said. "Good-bye, dear lady, your two children ask that you remember them," she said to the ceiling.

Children, Lydia thought; that was it. Out of curiosity she'd followed the voices that seemed to act like steps down inverted corridors with endless mirrors, until she emerged into this room. With surprise she saw that she was indeed on earth, obviously after her own death, but the rest of the proceedings at first were incomprehensible.

Two of the people looked very familiar, and from the dialogue she'd overheard, these must be her children, Anna and Roger. But they were older than she remembered. Next to them, invisibly, she was a jaunty twenty-five or maybe even thirty-five, and she was wondering whether or not to be born again as a baby. Lydia stared and tried to bring herself into the environment more clearly.

"There's something over there," Anna cried. "I swear it."

"Don't move," Mrs. Always whispered. In fact, the medium nearly sprang out of her chair, for in a flash she saw Lydia quite clearly in one of the few legitimate psychic experiences of her lifetime.

So séances worked, Lydia thought, catching on. When she was alive, she wouldn't have been caught dead at one! Mrs. Always was pointing at her, her face contorted. Roger was shouting something, and Anna was crying in her handkerchief. The relationships were so complex that Lydia wanted to laugh and cry at once. Yet she related from her own present. It was almost impossible for her to find the part of her that meant so much to these two middle-aged people. They'd never really been close. Had they forgotten?

"Over there, I see something over there," Anna shouted to Roger.

Mrs. Always cried out, "You've left the physical plane. You're dead. Rest in peace, dear soul."

"I know I'm dead," Lydia shouted, but no one heard her.

"There isn't anything there. Or anyone. It's all your imagination," Roger said. "I don't hear or see anything."

"That figures," Lydia muttered, thoroughly disgusted.

"Oh, Mama," Anna cried; and this time when Lydia

heard Anna's voice, the room shimmered. The walls and tables and people turned into flying fragments of stained-glasslike jigsaw images that rearranged themselves until a new picture was formed. Now Anna was five and Roger was twelve and they were in the living room, playing, on some heretofore-forgotten spring evening. The white curtains were blowing in the wind. A dog howled outside, and the sweet damp night odor rushed through the open window.

"Where do the dead go, Mama?" Anna asked.

And Lydia saw herself, the young mother with her children at her feet, and she felt stabs of tenderness. "The dead go everywhere, honey," Lydia the young mother said.

But Roger stood up suddenly, his earnest face filled with rage; with the deep inexplicable passion of a child. He shouted, "You're just saying that, but it isn't true. When you're dead, you aren't people anymore. Dead people don't really come back, like sometimes in the movies. It's scary!"

Then it seemed—to Lydia, the young mother—that the night itself waited, that everything waited for her answer to the child, as if the question itself had implications she only felt but didn't understand. She said clearly, lightly, smiling, "I'll come back years from now, when I'm dead, and tell you all about it when I know more. Okay?"

As she said the words, Lydia the young mother shivered and glanced at her son. Did he smile slyly? Did the child send the mother out ahead of time where he would be afraid to go? Awful thoughts, she told herself, as the young mother—as the mother still remembered by the grown children. And now Lydia thought that it was those children lingering in the adults, who still asked the question, and for whom she'd momentarily returned.

Roger said, "Promise?", frightened, biting his lips, feeling his new youth rising in the suburban night.

"Promise," Lydia the young mother said.

"I'll believe it when I see it," answered young Roger, just as the middle-aged Roger said the same thing.

Lydia stared. She was back in the séance room. The

115

medium was passing small glasses of wine to Anna and Roger, and they were excitedly discussing the evening's events. No one sensed her presence this time at all. Broodingly, she took on the old woman image she had died with. She tried hard to tug at her memories. It was like putting someone else's thoughts on, but finally she managed to sort out from all of her other experiences the one Lydia they seemed to be talking about; and from that standpoint she responded to the conversation.

She saw them now as through a mist; Roger and Anna, sipping the wine, gazing into the nervous face of Mrs. Always, who was more shaken than she wanted to admit. "Your mother must have been extraordinary. I've never sensed such a presence. Oh, I'm still nervous. I saw her so clearly." She fanned herself with her hand. "I've seen many, many apparitions—" Her voice trailed off; with a sinking in her stomach, she realized that the others had all been . . . imaginative images, because she wanted to *see* so badly. "I just hope she finds peace," she said quickly.

"She never particularly looked for peace when she was alive," Roger said glumly. "She was unconventional, a rebel until the last. I guess she enjoyed showing us how dull we were by contrast."

"That's not nice to say about her," Anna cried, looking around nervously.

Lydia stared at their faces. She'd loved them enough, she saw. But she'd judged them too harshly. Her poetry, and later, Lawrence, had been her life. And as she thought that, she suddenly saw Josef's face in her mind's eye: As *his* daughter, she'd have to relate emotionally. She imaged herself as a child in the middle of his bustling household.

"Do you think she's still around?" Anna asked, and Lydia said mentally, "Good-bye dear Anna, dear Roger. I kept my promise. Forgive me for liking you better as children. . . . " Why couldn't Anna show some flair? Why couldn't Roger display just a touch of gallantry? Why—

She broke the thoughts off, struck by a new realization. The conversation with the children about life after death had taken place one spring night after she'd met Lawrence. She'd returned home, rather guiltily, after a secret meeting with him. She'd met him downtown, supposedly by chance but actually by prearrangement.

And suddenly she *was* downtown. The séance room was gone. No one saw her. It was 6 P.M. by the town hall clock. It took Lydia a moment to orient herself, and longer to discover whether or not she was really walking down the world's streets.

It was windy; people went by bundled in scarfs and coats; and cold. Lydia shivered, though she didn't feel the crisp air or the wind. Traffic zoomed by. Newspapers and debris blew in the gutters, and watching, she felt very lonely. She saw everything clearly, but she didn't really smell anything, she noticed. And she only heard the traffic sounds dimly, though cars rushed by just feet away.

She didn't feel any particular sense of contact with the ground either, though nostalgically she remembered how the click, click, click of her high heels used to accompany her wherever she went; or the soft pouncing jounce of sneakers, or—

She really felt, well, ghostly, for the first time since her death. Was this Oversoul Seven's way of making her feel uncomfortable, so she'd want to be born again? Though she didn't sense his presence, Lydia wasn't sure just how many of her experiences were the natural results of her own thoughts—or how many were directed by Seven. She sighed petulantly: her search for the gods had certainly been cut short; here she was, earthbound enough.

People were all around her, busy, concentrating completely in their cozy time and place, with appointments to keep, and with the arrangement of events so neat and simple! Despite herself, Lydia grinned; without even noticing it, she'd turned back into a woman in her late thirties. She'd

117

never realized before how little of yourself was available when you were alive. In life you didn't have to worry about balancing youth's energy and innocence with the wisdom or experience of age, because by the time you got old, you'd lost touch with your own youth. Now she could switch back and forth at will—a mixed blessing, she thought, because she passed a store window and saw that she left no reflection there.

Yet, perversely, she refused to focus all of her energy where she was, in which case she would be able to really smell and feel the air, hear the traffic. But that would be a mockery. A mockery of what? Between ages, Lawrence had said. She sighed again. And suddenly she realized that she was being followed. Being followed? She started to laugh, her unseen image flickering back and forth and changing colors with the extent of her mirth. Who could be following her *here*?

She turned to see Lawrence several feet away, pretending to look in a shop window (Dear God, opera cape and all), and as insubstantial to others as she was. Until she saw him, she'd only sensed that she'd been lonely. Now she realized that she felt completely cut off, and no sooner did she see him than at once the entire scene burst into full brilliance so quickly that she leapt back in astonishment. The squeaks and squeals of the traffic, the cutting chill of wind, and all of the scents and sounds of the street came alive, with a vengeance, it seemed, an assaulting vividness. Automatically Lydia hallucinated a hat, coat, and scarf; and Lawrence was beside her, smiling.

"You're a real bitch to track down," he said, looking about twenty-five—as he did when she first knew him, fifteen years younger than she, dark hair mussed in the wind, opera cape blowing.

"Larry, that cape," she said, laughing, and time collapsed or the edges of it met, and the two of them actually *were* alive and meeting secretly; he dressed for his part in a play, on his way to rehearsal, and she—supposedly—at the library.

He kissed her quickly, excitedly. "How do you like my garb? I'm supposed to commit suicide in it. Can't you see my cape fluttering as I leap to my death? Some part. Maybe I should just concentrate on my crafts and leather work, open up a shop, and forget this acting nonsense."

"You look utterly fantastic," she cried. She was dizzy with exuberance, and the two of them stood there, so vital in each other's attention that nothing else mattered. In that moment Lydia had access to everything that had been in that earlier Lydia's mind, so that in blinding rapidity she was almost overwhelmed by emotions and a series of images. First she felt her love for Lawrence as he stood before her; then she saw the evening they'd later spent together— the small restaurant, red and white tablecloth, dinner, the candles and wine; she heard their own excited chatter and felt her own worry about the two children left at home with a sitter. Last of all a rush of guilt assaulted her, because her husband, Roger, who was on a brief business trip, thought she was at home. And with the guilt, the instant burst. She and Lawrence, two insubstantial images, stood facing each other on the busy twilight street with people passing by, not seeing them.

"Oh," Lydia whispered.

Lawrence said, "We were going to go away together after the play closed. You can recall all of it if you want."

"Do *you* remember?" she asked.

He nodded. "I'm here to help you revive your memories, if you want to. You seemed to close them out."

She said slowly, "You never did make it as an actor, and you did end up with a leather shop—"

"There's something else," he said. "The meeting we just re-experienced . . . was the last time we saw each other for about twenty years."

She just stared at him.

"You even considered suicide once," he said, not looking at her.

"Suicide? Why? Not me, not in a million years," she exclaimed. "Tell me. What have I forgotten?"

But Lawrence was gone, and the environment itself was disappearing.

Chapter Fifteen

Oversoul Seven Has His Troubles and Will Tries to Drop Out

"I keep telling you, suicide is not on the agenda," Seven was saying. "I'm just not getting through to you at all, am I?" Seven sighed, not even trying to hide his disappointment. He'd appeared as the compassionate but wise young graduate teacher, and as the compassionate but wise old man as well, but Will was in such a rotten mood that nothing seemed to reach him at all. "I am supposed to be your soul," Seven said, "but we certainly don't seem to have much in common. I wonder if someone made a mistake somewhere?" Almost absentmindedly, Seven lit up a joint (of marijuana, dear reader) and puffed it in just the correct tender fashion.

"What do you think you're doing?" Will asked. "It's all sham. I know that. You're just smoking grass to make me feel at home or bridge the generation gap or something.

And this classroom is all a dream hallucination too. And waking life is the same thing. Even dreaming, I'm not stupid, for God's sake."

Seven, as the old man, lowered his eyes and began to pace the classroom floor—perfect hardwood, sun splashing across the wood in just the right fashion—all gone to waste. He started to feel sorry for himself.

"You're some guru," Will said accusingly. "You can't teach me anything anyhow, because all learning is meaningless. Everything is senseless. I know that I'm asleep in bed, and awake here at the same time. So what? This place is as senseless as earth is. Or life is. I don't belong anywhere. And when your own soul doesn't like you, you may as well give up." Will finished speaking and stood staring at Seven broodingly, dark brows raised loftily; the picture of young, nonchalant, studied, contemptuous disdain. Then he said evenly, "Life is meaningless, and I don't intend to dignify it by staying around."

"You've *got* to stay around," Seven shouted, trying to think of something. "You can't commit suicide anyhow without taking a course in methods. If you have your heart set on suicide, you might as well do it right. Besides," he added, "suicide is a hard act to follow."

This time Will came toward Seven threateningly, fists raised, yelling at the top of his lungs. "I don't want to *follow* it with anything. You still don't understand. I want it to end. I want *me* to end."

"But why?" Seven asked for the hundredth time as he stepped back judiciously. "You have youth, health, money, intelligence—"

"Life doesn't make it, that's all," Will replied, with such unconscious arrogance that Seven just shook his head.

But Seven stood there stubbornly, and suddenly a great energy possessed him: Will, denying life, was so *full* of life, that Seven decided to try again, and to present Will with his (Will's) own strength and validity. Seven summoned Will as Will was and could be, and when Seven stopped changing shapes, Will stood there gasping, for he was staring at—himself. Only this self was so fulfilled and accomplished and loving that on the one hand, Will couldn't take his eyes away—while on the other hand, he could barely stand to look. All the yearning he'd ever felt in his life was fastened on that image. To be that person! If anyone so marvelous could be considered human. And this super-version of Will smiled at him, and though Will heard no words, he knew that this other self grew up from his own roots—that his, Will's, doubts and challenges had somehow led to this superversion, in which he himself existed.

At the same time, though, and paradoxically, it seemed to him, Will felt his resentment grow in proportion to his appreciation. Because this super-Will wasn't just a better Will, which he could understand, but an Olympian self in ways he sensed but couldn't comprehend; a giant-sized self in terms of power and emotional reality. In fact his ideas of the good self didn't fit this Olympian version at all, which was too powerful to be good, he thought uneasily. Yet he knew it wasn't evil either. And if it wasn't good or evil, then he didn't know how to handle it at all, he thought angrily.

"You don't really exist either," he managed to shout. And the superversion of himself vanished.

Oversoul Seven cleared his throat.

Will was too shaken to pretend that he wasn't impressed. And now that the image was gone, he felt its warmth and vitality, perhaps because he wasn't as frightened. For a moment he felt himself responding, and in a split second he was the superversion of himself, regarding his usual self with the craziest kind of love and sympathy. There was nothing conventionally pious or good about the love, which was emotional and personal yet also composed of some gigantic, objective kind of support. And the sympathy had too much humor in it to be saintly, yet was too full of appreciation to be condescending. Will became so engrossed in trying to figure it all out that he never noticed as the classroom walls disappeared and a grinning Oversoul Seven waved to him from the window just before it vanished.

But Seven's smile vanished at the same time, relatively speaking, because Will had raised an issue that bothered him considerably, at least in retrospect. Did he like Will? Or, more to the point, did he dislike him? Certainly he wished Will well, exuberantly and definitely. Only he found him tiresome because he complained so much and because he was so ungracious inside, when he was so graceful and attractive physically.

"You don't particularly like him," Cyprus said, appearing out of nowhere. "So don't try to wiggle out of it. In any case, I want to talk to you."

"Uh, I was going to check on Bianka," Seven said nervously.

"By all means. I'll go with you," Cyprus replied. "Now, about Will—"

"Well, *he* doesn't like *me* very much either, or anyone else for that matter," Seven grumbled. "He doesn't care for anyone but himself, and of course he doesn't really approve of himself either. And he has this grudge against life that I just don't understand. Lydia's self-absorbed at times, but she *cares*. I mean, she really wants to give Tweety a spiritual heritage and some knowledge of 'the gods.' I know that's why she hasn't made her mind up to be born again! She wants the universe to be right for a new life. It *is*, of course; you and I know that. But—"

Now Oversoul Seven and Cyprus were invisible, and without any forms at all, in what would hopefully be Tweety's bedroom, which was Josef's old studio. They were at rest, yet part of their essences just kept drifting lazily through the bedposts, which Josef in a paternal mood had carved with the heads of animals; and through the bureau, which was quite elegant, an heirloom of Bianka's family, made of rosewood; and through anything else that happened to be there.

Seven eyed the thick icicles that weren't even dripping;

it was so cold outside that the window was almost entirely frosted over. "So I can relate to Lydia now," he said dejectedly. "But Will makes me impatient."

Cyprus turned quite still. With a semblance of surprise, she said, "Seven, I was under the impression that Lydia *had* made up her mind to be born again, and that the search for the gods was more in the nature of a last fling before birth."

"That's what I meant to say," Seven muttered, blushing. "I'm sure she *has* decided—"

Cyprus said sternly, "If I understand what you're trying so hard not to tell me, then Lydia at the least is still hesitating rather vigorously. And Will, who *is* ensconced in a very comfortable life indeed, has decided that he dislikes his existence enough to contemplate suicide, and—"

"Don't say another thing," Seven cried. "All right, I'm beside myself with worry. And I'm trying to go along with human concepts about the gods, though this is *very* trying. Besides that, your Jeffery is identifying so with Will that if Will *does* commit suicide—though I'm sure he won't— I don't know what Jeffery will do. And since he isn't even one of my personalities to begin with, I don't understand his part in any of this at all."

Cyprus smiled one of the most satisfied smiles that Seven had ever seen, as she changed back into the woman teacher image with which she often conducted such discussions. "Jeffery won't commit suicide now," she said. "He has the book to finish."

"But when it's done?" Seven shouted. "Now I'm more upset than ever! He's writing this conversation down, for the book. So he knows we're talking about him. I don't see how you got him to write the book in the first place!"

"Oh, Seven, *I* didn't get him to 'write the book,'" Cyprus said. She started laughing, but with such sympathy and gusto that Seven couldn't be angry, though he tried. "Oh, is *that* what you think?" Cyprus cried. "Well, remember that you decided to forget some things that you know, in order to relate to your personalities better."

THE FURTHER EDUCATION OF OVERSOUL SEVEN

"Well, Jeffery *is* writing this book," Seven began, dubiously now.

"And you're right. He won't be happy with this particular section when he's read what he's written," Cyprus added.

"But he *does* know what we're saying about him!" Seven was so acutely embarrassed and exasperated that he threw his hallucinatory fourteen-year-old arms up in the air with dismay. "But Jeffery doesn't even believe we exist," he shouted.

And Cyprus answered, with an almost Olympian laugh, "He's not as sure of that as he once was. In any case, we've been keeping him very busy, and material about Will *does* always upset him, so shortly we'll have to give him some time to do his own notes."

Seven said, almost accusingly, "All of this just might be too much for Jeffery. I don't like his identification with Will at all, as I told you, or with the suicide question."

This time Cyprus said, "Seven, the trouble with you is that you worry too much. You're always afraid that people will make the 'wrong' choices. You're manipulating Will, or trying to, and he resents it. Manipulation won't work at all. Right now Will's purpose in life seems to be to end it."

Glumly, Seven nodded.

"You *do* have the answer; the way to help him," Cyprus said gently. "But the decisions must be his. And Jeffery's must be *his*, of course."

"What about Jeffery when the book is done?" Seven asked.

"Seven, the book will never be *finished*." A certain sound came into Cyprus's voice and suddenly Seven saw a thousand books or more, each page of each book with its own sequels and probably variations, and each written down by a different probable Jeffery. Oversoul Seven winced. "It's the *one* Jeffery we know that I'm speaking about."

"Exactly," Cyprus answered.

Seven started to reply, but the icicle he was staring at

suddenly began to melt, dripping past the windowsill that Seven saw was Will's, not Josef's. "Will must be in trouble," he cried to Cyprus. "Here we've been talking and—" Seven forgot what he was saying. The icicle was almost gone. The sun glittered on its vanishing remains for just a moment, and Will, staring at it, thought that he'd vanish from life as easily as the icicles melted in the sun. He'd take sleeping pills.

Will had a plastic Cheshire cat that he'd found in a second-hand store. Seven liked to sit inside it, when Will was in one of his moods, so that he could look out from a point of relative safety. Inside it now, he had an excellent view of Will, who was rigidly sitting on the side of the rumpled bed, staring hard-eyed out the window at the point where the icicle had just vanished.

"Shit," Will muttered. He'd awakened with a dream memory that infuriated him, and though the memory was already nearly gone, his anger grew. Now all he recalled was the feeling that he'd dreamed about himself, only a self so accomplished that next to that image, he was worthless. Or nearly worthless. Dead, at least his poor empty body would get some attention. Dead; he'd make them question, his friends and so-called friends, his traveling-free parents and prissy professors. How could you have let such a young man die? Will cursed: There he was, full of self-pity again! Well, sleeping pills would take care of that, too.

"You don't even like to swallow aspirin," Seven said mentally.

"No, pills won't do," Will mused, accepting Seven's thought without wondering where it came from. Neither would drugs. If he was going to die, he wanted to make an impact. He smiled brightly, dramatically: If he was going to do it, he'd do it right.

As Will thought *that,* the truly black despondent mood that had been curling around the edges of his mind suddenly overtook him. He didn't even try to fight it, because he thought life was so . . . shitty, that nothing really mattered. At the same time, as this blackness clouded his thoughts, his feelings got faster and clearer in a particular dark fashion. His despair accelerated and had its own dizzy excitement, and pulsated with energy and action. While all this was going on, so as not to frighten himself overmuch, Will thought almost airily that he'd make no decision. To hell with it. He'd leave it all to the fates. Suspense to the last moment. And even as he decided to leave it all open, Will was going out of the room, down the steps to the front of the house where his motorcycle waited in the driveway. Waited—he thought—like a black monster or like a knight's rescuing steed. Which would it be?

He felt wild and free, devil-may-care, yet he was smiling inside himself like death, he thought; and liking the expression, he thought it again.

There was still some, not much, slush in the streets, which glistened wet, almost shining black in the bright sunlight. And the stores were like cutouts of cardboard to be knocked down like soggy playing cards. It was all sham. He was dead anyhow, no matter what he did, he told himself. He didn't feel like other people did. He was unaffected, untouched.

The sound of the cycle came thundering up, disturbing the entire neighborhood, he hoped, rousing any people taking afternoon naps. The furious whirl of Will starting up death's engine. The sound was so loud and he was traveling so fast that he laughed and cried at once, wearing no helmet so that the cold March wind could eat holes in his head. A great image! Why did he feel so damned creative at a time like this? He wished to hell he'd stop commenting on his own goddamned thoughts.

He stopped at a traffic light and decided to ride slower so that the cops wouldn't stop him for breaking some stupid traffic rule. Grinning coldly, he hit the highway out of town and forgot about driving slowly. The speedometer said 80.

There was a bridge, an open mesh affair, very dangerous when wet, and he headed toward it. This wasn't going to be a suicide, but a test. A contest. He'd hit the bridge as fast as he could go. If the cycle crashed and he died—well, his problems were over. If not, then he'd take it as a sign that someone or something wanted him to live, and that he had a place in the universe, even if he hadn't found it yet.

Shit. He was losing the edge of his anger and he wanted to sustain it.

On the back of the motorcycle, an invisible Oversoul Seven groaned as he monitored Will's thoughts and tried to discover exactly how dangerous Will's course was. He kept transmitting Will's favorite memories into Will's stream of thought, but Will kept blocking them out. Instead, stubbornly, he concentrated on the distant bridge. Quickly, Seven got a mental glimpse of it—there it was, about ten miles away, just as slippery as Will hoped, and it arched over a precipice, of course, with a river far below. A curve at the far end. And two houses close to the road. Seven grimaced: The trouble was that he had to allow Will his free will. And a free Will could be a dead Will.

The cycle was approaching 90. It was a light B.S.A. that Will called, euphemistically, a gentleman's machine, and it—"Look out," Seven shouted to Will, who had just missed hitting a car that came speeding around a blind spot in the road. But neither Will nor the other driver wanted to kill anyone else, Seven saw; each wanted to go out in a *private* blaze of glory. Seven threw a sigh of sympathy and understanding to the other driver's oversoul as Will shakily eyed the bridge which now came into view.

Really desperate, Seven scanned the neighborhood and contemplated his new clue: Will didn't want to take anybody with him if he died. Then (did Cyprus send him the inspiration just in time?) Seven remembered Will's love of kittens. How long did it take a motorcycle to stop? What was the safety factor? In a flash, Seven hallucinated a kitten,

129

choosing a tabby which seemed to be Will's favorite. The kitten, with a sore paw, sat mewing in the center of the bridge.

Then it was up to Will, who saw the kitten and cursed. He'd take the damned thing out of its misery with him. To hell with it. The universe didn't give a shit about a kitten. He squinted; the cat had something wrong with it, or it would be running away. All Will could see now was the kitten, getting bigger and bigger as he approached it. Maybe *it* was committing suicide. It could crawl away, couldn't it? What was the matter with the dumb, stupid thing? Even if he swerved, he might hit it. It'd probably stay on the side of the bridge for days because nobody cared. Who'd bury a dead kitten?

Miserably the kitten tried to scramble to its feet. Sensing triumph, Seven made it the most pathetic kitten imaginable, as it mewed, stood, tottered over.

"Oh double and triple shit," Will screamed, screamed, and screamed, as the hottest, wildest pity overcame him and he felt himself slowing down, stopping his own death, because in the whole cruel universe, he wasn't going to add to the misery of it all by killing some dumb, stupid creature. The motorcycle skidded, skidded some more, as Will tried to stop in time, his fury and pity almost blinding him. He'd slow down, but not enough. He swerved, avoided the kitten, and was thrown off the cycle just before it slammed into the side of the bridge.

Everything seemed unrealistically still. Will landed on his hands and knees. He was a mess of scrapes and bruises, but he wasn't hurt badly. And he definitely wasn't dead. Turning around to look for the kitten, he shouted, "You dumb cat. That's one of your nine lives."

And Oversoul Seven, exhausted, sighed, "Look who's talking."

Chapter Sixteen

Jeffy-boy's Uneasiness Grows and Ram-Ram Does a Disappearing Act

When I was finished with what you have read thus far, I stared at the manuscript, appalled beyond description. The characters in the book were discussing me, and quite objectively, with the oddest kind of sympathy for my predicament. This concern added to my anxiety beyond measure. The constant use of third person references to me, "he" this, or "he" that, struck me with a sense of panic. If the analysis of my character hadn't been so astute, perhaps I wouldn't have been so bothered, but several passages that I reread described me with a . . . loving detachment that I found most disconcerting.

All of this represented some important alteration in the pattern of activity thus far; and I recognized this at the time only opaquely, afraid to follow the matter through for fear, I suppose, of where it might lead. But the shock went even deeper than the realization that the relationship between the manuscript and myself was changing. No matter what they were, or how the book was being written, Oversoul Seven and Cyprus were fictional characters. Their criticism, even their awareness of my own existence, somehow upset the very foundations of all my beliefs. I found myself saying, "They have no right to do this, no right at all," before I realized the implications and irony of my own remark.

Intrusion enough—this weird book and its method of delivery—but I had begun to think that it might be good enough to publish, without, of course, giving any hint of the way it was produced. This made me wonder how many other manuscripts had been written in the same manner, with the "authors" smart enough to keep their mouths shut and cut out any passages that might give them away.

But this added development (I took it almost like an insult) was a further intrusion in which unreality dared to comment upon life; where Art refused to stay where it belonged (if this *was* Art of a most peculiar nature), and began a concerted program of entry into normal reality. The characters were becoming real, turning on their creator and daring to examine his abilities and characteristics. I looked at these latest developments in this way for some time, even though I realized that the premise wasn't acceptable to begin with, since to all intents and purposes I wasn't writing the book, but only taking down its dictation. Did that mean that whoever *was* originating it felt quite safe in dissecting my character, as I might feel in, say, examining the characteristics of a laboratory animal?

As far as Will's near disastrous motorcycle ride is concerned, of course I was somewhat anxious and carried along by the suspense, as anyone *is*, even when just reading such adventurous passages in any book. If I was relieved at the end, surely my reaction was no more than natural. In that regard, I am sure that my "identification" with Will was overexaggerated by Cyprus and Seven in those passages where they refer to it. It's highly unlikely that they know me better than I know myself, for example. Though we all have a few suicidal thoughts in our lives, I've been no more given to them than anyone else.

In any case, whenever you read in "Education" any references to myself, you can pretty well imagine my own invisible reactions. For one thing, while writing down the script, I had no way of retorting to any such passages, of explaining my thoughts, or, in short, of speaking back. I was only barely aware of what I was writing to start with and didn't even realize that I *was* being mentioned until I read the material over. It was impossible for me to insert any comments into the script, even later. In the craziest fashion, my reactions didn't or *wouldn't* fit. My own sentences literally could not be inserted into the book itself. It was almost as if two different kinds of order were involved that could co-exist, but not . . . mix. This further added to my anger, of course. If *they* could insert themselves so smugly into my reality and arrange for me to write their book, then why couldn't I at least report my own reactions within the script itself? Since I obviously cannot, however, these notes are really my parallel statements; the *other* side or my side of their book or world, if you prefer; the one in which the laboratory animals keep their own reports.

I *am* worried: Will I end up bragging about how well I performed at a series of clever psychological mazes? And is that actually what I'm being led to do? Yet even laboratory animals are given incentives, so what reward am I being offered? What stimuli am I unconsciously reacting to? The question itself suddenly excited me so that I stopped writing for a moment, filled with anticipation. If I'm running a different kind of maze than laboratory animals, a "multi-dimensional" one, to coin one of "Education" 's terms, then, of course, the psychological rewards are being held out like the carrot before the horse.

And that simple enough statement sounds very much like Ram-Ram's agitated first conversation with me in connection with the experiments he suggested—experiments, incidentally, that were never quite explained to me . . . But in any case, surely I'm being offered a boon of a kind: the opportunity of studying this bizarre experience from the inside, at first hand, in the most isolated laboratory of all, in a way—my own mind. I seem to be both subject and analyst, and thus in a position to study behavioral conditioning from a unique standpoint. For the first time I see some kind of logic that I can understand in all of this. If I'm right, then each further intrusion of the "book world" into mine is actually the insertion of a new stimulus to the laboratory situation. My reactions are being watched, then. Why didn't this occur to me before? Well, any number can play that game.

So: Tomorrow I won't write a line on the infernal manuscript, and *I'll* wait for *their* reactions. Am I being crafty, suitably clever, or in playing the game, have I already lost the fine edges of sanity? Now I question whether or not sanity has fine edges. I do wish I knew some truly knowledgeable colleague, familiar with all fields of psychology, with whom I could discuss what's happening. Actually I'm beyond that point now; I don't really feel that anyone else can help me. At the same time, I'm afraid, sometimes at least, that I'll end up like Ram-Ram or worse. Even the prospect of being considered a mere fool is a terrible one to me, when I've been so used to considering my psychological stance impeccable.

All of this concentrated thought must be wearing me out. I feel unusually tired and can hardly keep my eyes open. My fingers keep lingering over the typewriter keys as if uncertain whether or not to continue—

As I wrote the last sentence, a knock came at the door. I was glad enough of the interruption and called, "Come in," expecting some student perhaps, or associate. Instead to my surprise there was Ram-Ram, standing in the hallway, grinning, with a cigarette in one hand and a drink in the other. I leaped to my feet. "What are you doing out of the sanatorium?" I sputtered, sorry at once for the question.

"Well, you're cured, then. They released you?" I was so relieved to see him that I grasped his arm and pulled him inside, feeling that he was the only person in the world to whom I could talk. Granting he *was* sane, of course.

"I'm as sane *as you are*," he said, as if reading my mind. "And that's a loaded statement."

"Is it?" I answered, thinking, if he only knew how loaded.

"In any case, I felt that you wanted to see me," he said, now ensconced in the wicker chair that literally groaned beneath his weight. "Actually, I'm as sane as the doctors are, which isn't saying much. Or rather, I'm saner, which places me in a peculiar situation—"

He was joking, in excellent spirits, but I said uncomfortably, "Saner than sane? That sounds suspicious."

"Can't tell if I'm sane or not, huh? That puts *you* in a peculiar position, for which I apologize. So since I'm here, in your territory, we'll play it your way. You can assure yourself that I'm sane, using your definition of the word— presuming you know what you mean by it, of course. Now, since my glass is empty, I'd like to suggest that you offer me a drink."

"Sorry. Of course." I made us each one, leaving the liquor bottle out on the table.

"So, I've been given a clean bill of mental health," he said.

"I'm more relieved than I can say," I said, meaning it.

"I know you are," he said, and I had the curious impression that his words were double-edged, or that he knew more than he was letting on. But about what? Or was his attitude simply a hangover of his condition, a sly reminder of psychological duplicity? "How is Queen Alice?" I asked, testing.

"Fine. As well as can be expected," he answered—which told me nothing, of course.

"But you've been writing a report or thesis or book of sorts, haven't you?" he asked.

I stared at him. He looked no different. He didn't act as

if he realized that he was talking about something he had no way of knowing was true.

"What's the matter? Secret, huh? Well, I've heard your typewriter going up here for hours at a time, from my rooms below. Not complaining, you understand. But I took it for granted that you were working on a manuscript of some sort."

The terrible nervousness that had assaulted me the moment he first mentioned a book subsided so quickly that I was giddy. Of course, I thought; he'd been in his apartment downstairs, not at the sanatorium. It would have been odd if he *hadn't* heard the typewriter since you could hear a sneeze in this building two floors away. "Beginning a thesis," I said, probably too quickly. "I suppose it could run into a book."

"Excellent. Excellent. Yes, yes, yes. Our boy is catching up," Ram-Ram said, rubbing his pudgy hands together. I caught the third person reference to myself uneasily, then remembered that this was his habit of speech, not only with me but with others. It was apparent that I'd been overreacting, and with new relief I poured myself another drink, though Ram-Ram was still sipping his.

"Anyhow, I'm delighted that you've been given a clean bill of health," I said. "Do you have to go back for any kind of follow-up?"

"I have to go back to keep track of our Queen Alice," Ram-Ram said, shifting in the chair. This time the wicker creaked more warningly than ever, and Ram-Ram grinned.

"Take the blue chair instead," I said quickly. "I've got to throw the wicker one away anyhow. Go ahead, the blue one is much more comfortable. I'll even stick the wicker out in the hall while I'm thinking about it." And as Ram-Ram moved, taking his drink, pack of cigarettes, and ashtray with him, I stuck the old chair just outside the door, planning to cart it down to the trash heap later.

Ram-Ram crossed his legs and made himself generally

comfortable, this time on the couch. "Yes, I want to keep an eye on Queen Alice," he said. Then, looking at me speculatively, "I see that you don't want to tell me what *you've* been up to, though. Well, that's easily understandable, but right now I'm giving you a demonstration of sorts that you won't understand until I'm gone."

"Now, what does that mean?" I asked.

"You're a good psychologist. You'll figure it out," Ram-Ram answered. "I'm delighted with our little chat, though. Yes, yes, yes, our boy is doing fine." He stood up, rubbing his hands together in a quick, nervous, yet almost smug gesture, and grinned like a Cheshire cat. And disappeared.

I mean, he *disappeared*. I stood there, not believing my eyes: He was gone. Suddenly I felt woozy, spun around or thought that I did, and found myself sitting at my desk, head slumped over on it, resting on my arms. Ram-Ram definitely was not in the room. The only conclusion I could rationally draw was that I'd fallen asleep after he left, and dreamed that he'd disappeared. Then why didn't I remember him leaving? I reached for my drink. It wasn't there! My gaze flew about the room. There were no used glasses on the end tables. There was no bottle of liquor either. I rushed into the kitchen and to my amazement found the bottle in the cupboard with no indication it had been moved.

Nearly beside myself, I walked as calmly as I could back to the living room. The wicker chair sat where it always had. This time I poured myself a real drink and sat down to collect my thoughts. Ram-Ram hadn't been here at all. I hadn't moved the wicker chair into the hall. The entire episode had been a dream then, I decided. As soon as I finished my notes, I must have fallen asleep and my concern about Ram-Ram and my need to talk to someone must have triggered—

My thoughts broke off. The dream explanation just wouldn't do. The entire interview had been too clear. I began to think that despite . . . everything . . . in some way, Ram-Ram *had* been here. Had I moved the chair in the same unknown fashion? Was Ram-Ram actually still in the hospital? I tried not to ask the next question, but could not avoid it. Had Ram-Ram been here in an out-of-body state?

He couldn't have heard the typewriter if he wasn't home. So how did he know about the manuscript? Or, impossible as it seemed, was the affair all my own creation, not a dream, but a complete hallucination? If so, I was in trouble. Again I worried for my own sanity, but I was actually too angry—healthily angry, I thought—to think I was mad. I *had* seen Ram-Ram. Now I refused to doubt my own perception. And I hate practical jokers. So if Ram-Ram had played some kind of psychological or psychic trick on me, I was going to get to the bottom of it.

In other words, I decided to go over to the sanatorium later that very afternoon.

Chapter Seventeen

Ram-Ram the Godologist and Case History 9871: J. Christ

The godologists were tucked away in a small corner of the universe, though once their domain had been extensive. Godology, it seemed, was a dying art, Seven thought. Not really, of course, since no arts die, but in the context of the times he was dealing with, godology wasn't the exciting pursuit it used to be. Seven shook his head with some dismay. The lawns and shrubs were in need of trimming; dust settled over the once ivied towers, and the buildings themselves had shrunken. Once they'd been so large that it took centuries to get from one complex to another, and now the same buildings could be seen in the twinkling of an eye.

The godologists were a peculiar breed anyhow, for their profession demanded that they mix godly and human characteristics, an uneasy blend, a transspecies really, that made them—well, a trifle eccentric. He had to have some psychological profiles on the gods for Lydia's benefit, though, so Seven resolutely hurried on.

The particular godologist Seven wanted to see was one he affectionately called Ram-Ram, because the godologist always seemed to be butting his head up against divinities that he couldn't understand. Names don't mean much to souls, so it was only when Seven actually entered the godologists' domain that it occurred to him that his godologist and Jeffy-boy's psychologist friend had the same name. Some godologists had physical lives going on, and some didn't. Since Seven didn't know Ram-Ram's status in that regard, he forgot the entire matter in the press of more serious issues. He'd promised Lydia that he'd discover what he could about the gods as they existed in terms of the world she was used to. So Seven sent out mental feelers for Ram-Ram as soon as he approached the nearly deserted grounds.

From somewhere inside, Ram-Ram flashed his mental welcome. "My, my, my. Yes, yes. What have we here? Seven! Delighted," and he sent Seven directions. Briskly now Seven went past empty consultation rooms to find Ram-Ram's small cubicle.

"How long has it been?" Ram-Ram asked at once. "How times fly. In any case, we've made some changes here since I saw you last. Not all for the best, of course. But at least I'm onto something vital." Because Seven was of earth-soul stock, Ram-Ram took human form, appearing as a sly old godologist, white kinky hair getting caught in the silver halo that was the sign of his station. He had a pink flawless complexion that was far too youthful for the rest of his image, Seven saw, wondering indeed if the godologist was getting out of touch with his earthly connections. No real human would take Ram-Ram as just another wise old man, and of course the halo was a dead giveaway too. Seven just grinned, though, and said nothing. He didn't want to hurt

Ram-Ram's feelings for one thing, and for another he knew that the godologists, being academics, were very jealous of their rank, and the halo marked Ram-Ram as having ten doctorates of Divinity.

"Uh, they have cut down on your space a bit," Seven said. He wasn't quite sure how to relate to Ram-Ram after all this time, so Seven kept changing shapes until, watching him, Ram-Ram smiled brilliantly and said, "Yes, yes. That one is fine." Seven stabilized: He had his fourteen-year-old image on and it wore a humble brown woolen robe, as befitted a seeker after truth. Seven grinned and Ram-Ram said, "I haven't had a real student in ages, so I hope you don't mind looking like one for a while. It's such a joy just to imagine that godologists have apprentices again."

"I'll look even younger if you want," Seven offered. Then, to make Ram-Ram feel better, Seven went on. "I *am* a student, though, and I'm on a pilgrimage to find the gods, on behalf of my human personalities. I don't pretend to know why this is all so important to them, to one of them anyhow, Lydia. I'm under the impression that human concepts of divinity are so limited that—"

"Exactly. Exactly," Ram-Ram cried excitedly. "Look, I've something very important to show you that proves that very point!"

Ram-Ram rambled through his massive file cabinet as he talked. "I've done some excellent new studies," he said. "But one in particular should be of special interest to you, since so many of your personalities are involved with Christendom. Look at this. Christ's case history. I prepared it myself!" Ram-Ram's enthusiasm was infectious, but Seven shook his head.

"I'm not interested in case histories, but in *living* divine personalities," he said.

"But here you have it all!" Ram-Ram exclaimed. "It's a thorough investigation. Here you find divine motivation individually and specifically apparent. Here you see the birth of a god, hear the first primal scream as godhood tears itself from nonexistence into divine reality, ripped from the womb of eternity—"

"I never heard such nonsense in any of my lives or before or after," Seven said, scandalized. "Gods come into being because they want to."

"Yes, yes, yes," Ram-Ram said impatiently. "That doesn't mean birth is easy. Any birth is hard, and a god's birth is— well, spectacular, and harder than most. The files show this to be true. The statistics make it clear. Interviews with divine personages confirm the facts."

"Haven't you ever examined your own existence?" Seven asked. "I mean, I understood that all godologists were part divine. Albeit minor god connections. But still. What about your own birth? Or births?"

"Examining my own existence wouldn't be scientific," Ram-Ram said severely. "I *do* have a counterpart on earth, a psychologist who's examining existence from a human standpoint. Granted, I don't give him a lot of attention, and I'm not even sure if he acknowledges the existence of the soul, but—"

Seven bristled despite himself, but he said politely, "If you'll excuse me, dividing yourself in half in order to study the whole seems silly to me. I hope I'm not hurting your feelings, but what happened to the art of godology? Now it's a science?"

"It always *was*. Art is too neither-here-nor-there. We want to be more specific. And a scientist's feelings can't be hurt, because he's too objective to have feelings to *be* hurt," Ram-Ram said rather proudly. "Now do you want to see this case history or don't you? It's Jesus of Nazareth: Case History 9871."

"Okay. That would be fine," Seven said, using his snappiest earth vernacular because he saw that, scientist or no, Ram-Ram's feelings *were* hurt. "I would really appreciate it," Seven added heartily.

Ram-Ram's face brightened, but he coughed, cleared his throat, and began to speak in his professorial style.

"The birth data are all here," he said. "Christ was carried in the womb of time and he had to fight his way through centuries, misplacing stars, galaxies, even; warping the universe, falling through black holes, tumbling from one to the other; seeking, seeking, seeking that one time and space, that one earthly womb, that one microscopic slit in the soil of time . . ."

Seven tried not to yawn. He was thinking that overall he liked Jeffy-boy's Ram-Ram better. At least he had a sense of humor. But the godologist went on, quite carried away by his own presentation. He kept interrupting himself, saying, "Yes, yes, yes," or, "Indeed, that's the way it was," then continuing, growing more excited until Seven became quite alarmed. Again, privately, he wondered if Ram-Ram was really mad. More, Seven couldn't get a word in edgewise, and right then and there he resolved never again to "lecture at" Will in his dream classes. Not that he ever really did, of course, but—

Ram-Ram finally stopped to clear his throat, and Seven said, "Where did you get all that, uh, information?"

"From Christ himself," Ram-Ram said. "Under hypnosis, it all came out." He rubbed his hands together triumphantly. "I have it all in the case history."

And Seven said, "Well, would you mind showing me the case history itself? Then you won't have to go to all the bother of describing it."

Ram-Ram turned on the eternal recording machine, saying, "All of these images came directly from Christ's mind, but first, here's an exterior shot of the experiment conditions. Look." He aimed the machine at the eastern wall of the godologists' building, and the wall disappeared for all practical purposes. Instead, the projections from the machine flashed out against the sky—somewhat like a drive-in theater, Seven thought, except that the whole sky was the screen. He wondered how many others were watching.

Christ lay on a golden couch, spread with royal velvet robes, his eyes closed, his long brown-gray ringlets in disarray about his face, his hands folded upon his chest, and a coverlet pulled up where his johnny robe left off. He seemed to be asleep or dreaming. Occasionally one divine toe twitched beneath the coverlet. Beside him sat Ram-Ram, in his professional capacity. "Now, count backward slowly," he was saying, "from one million back to zero."

"That must have taken forever," Seven whispered.

Ram-Ram, rather annoyed, said, "Never mind, we'll dispense with the hypnotic induction and the count." He touched a lever. "I'll skip ahead a bit. Ahah, here we are: Prenatal memories."

Seven leapt back as a gigantic Lucifer appeared in the sky projection. His form took a thousand images at once, while, overall, one huge leering visage remained.

"The original bogeyman," Ram-Ram said, with great satisfaction. "Quite effective, don't you think? You might say that Lucifer was Christ's shadow, and represented all the portions of his personality that he had to deny: the love of power, lust for knowledge, and the sheer automatic vitality, or the masculine aspects in earthly terminology. Christ's gentleness, understanding, and so forth, stressed the feminine—'The meek shall inherit the earth' and all of *that*. Well, Lucifer in a way is the exaggerated other side of that image: the uninhibited—"

"Couldn't you just be quiet for a minute?" Seven interrupted uneasily. He stared at the Lucifer image, and cautiously dematerialized at the same time. He'd never seen such a terrifying figure. Though it didn't speak, it raged. The mouth moved insinuatingly as if it were calling out for blood and vengeance in a thousand unspoken languages.

Ram-Ram said proudly, "That image was projected directly from Christ's mind. In a way, it was born with him."

Seven stepped back even further as the giant-sized Lucifer changed into a shouting Jehovah, threatening the Israelites and demanding sacrifices. A mountain appeared, and out of a dreadful yet splendid cloud glimmered God the Father's hands, perfect yet somehow frightening, delivering the tablets with the Ten Commandments to Moses. But even Moses looked insane, Seven thought unhappily: ecstatic, alive to a frenzy.

"That's prenatal memory also," Ram-Ram said. "Finally, of course, Lucifer and God the Father behave in rather similar ways for all intents and purposes, so that afterwards the case history gets more complicated."

"It's complicated enough for me right now," Seven exclaimed. "And scary. Doesn't any of this bother you at all?"

"You forget, I've seen it all before," Ram-Ram said just a trifle smugly. "But watch, now."

Seven really wanted to leave. He remembered how Lydia felt once as a child during a frightening movie. She was afraid to move for fear that if she turned her back on the screen, the feared images would chase her down the aisle. He really wasn't *that* worried, he told himself, and besides he didn't want Ram-Ram to think he was a coward. So he stayed.

Now the sky-screen showed a thriving city. Donkeys, horses, and people filled the streets. Vendors in stalls surrounded palaces and temples. The tumult was tremendous, as Ram-Ram took a close-up so that Seven could hear the individual voices, when in the next moment, the entire city was destroyed. Seven couldn't tell what had happened—there was fire, brimstone, smoke; there were buildings toppling, stalls squashed, horses and people making agonizing sounds, a donkey with its head just cut off by flying debris . . . Seven stared: The donkey was still braying, or so it seemed. Then the sound was cut off as quickly as the head had been.

"You'd think Lucifer did all that," Ram-Ram said. "But

it was Jehovah. You see? With prenatal memories like that, and a father who wiped out whole populations if they angered him—well, even a divine son would be bound to have problems. To that, add the fact that Christ had a human, not a divine, mother. Jehovah didn't have a divine mate; he was too ill-tempered. No goddess would put up with him. So in a way, Christ was a half-orphan, divinely speaking. He was the son of a father who was basically impotent—hence, the *angel* appeared to Mary—a father who took his frustrations out on earth, and," Ram-Ram added triumphantly, "on his son. Why else did he send Christ to be crucified? And no matter how he pretended, Christ knew that his father hated him. Couldn't face the truth, though, so he projected his father's hateful qualities onto Lucifer."

"I wish you wouldn't interpret the pictures for me," Seven cried, exasperated, because now the twelve disciples appeared with John closest to Christ, his head bowed near Christ's chest, and Ram-Ram said, "The relationship between the twelve men was interesting also, especially Christ's with John—the tenderness that should have gone to women . . ." Ram-Ram lifted his shaggy white brows significantly. His halo wobbled slightly. He straightened it impatiently and started to continue.

"How many others are viewing these slides?" Seven asked, before Ram-Ram could get going again. "All those images are just splashed out against the sky for anyone to see. I should think Christ could get you for invasion of divine privacy, and I wouldn't want to get Jehovah or Lucifer mad either! Lucifer at least has a sense of humor, but I'm sure Jehovah wouldn't understand at all."

"But basically, Jehovah and Lucifer are both projections of Christ's mind," Ram-Ram said.

"Then how come the sky is getting so dark?" Seven whispered.

"Aha! That must be Christ's anxieties emerging and taking form," Ram-Ram said appreciatively.

"But don't you feel even a trifle uneasy?" Seven asked. "The sky is getting darker by the moment."

"No. Like true scientists, we godologists turn our feelings off in order to do our work. We can't afford to become involved in subjectivity." Ram-Ram spoke very kindly, but rather condescendingly.

"Well, you'd better turn your feelings back on if you can," Seven said, "because mine tell me that we're in for some trouble."

The sky had darkened to such a degree that Seven found it almost impossible to remember what daylight looked like. All of the projections disappeared, yet in a strange way they remained, imprinted in the darkness itself; spooky giant-sized negatives made of layered dark on dark, and in the center of all this, Seven sensed a motion he didn't like at all.

"Magnificent depths of psychological activity," Ram-Ram breathed. "Christ's mind is now reacting to the projections set up by itself and—"

"Will you be quiet?" Seven glared at the godologist, who shrugged and continued his musings, only silently. But Seven was fully and genuinely frightened by now. Who knew what divine psychological mechanisms they were tampering with? And once set into motion, who but a god could stop them? And Seven felt that they *were* tampering. Let Christ's mind keep its secrets. Let the gods save their divine privacy. Let—

Seven broke off his thoughts. The darkness was now swooping into itself at an incredible rate, and in the heart of the activity, a small microscopic image was forming. It was tinier than Seven thought anything could be and still be visible; an image of such intensity that its vitality completely invalidated its size, so that now Seven wondered how he'd ever thought that importance and size were connected in any way at all. He stared at the image because there seemed to be nothing else he *could* do, and discovered that it was actually composed of glittering lights that some-how existed on the . . . other side of darkness.

"I'll teach them something about hypnosis," Christ chuckled.

Zeus said uneasily, "I still think you're going too far."

"Nonsense," Christ said. He and Zeus were whiling away the afternoon. They'd watched Ram-Ram's projections, which had appeared outside of the rest home's huge win-dows, flickering in dimensions too vast for mortal eyes to follow.

"Still, it was a damn good show," Zeus thundered.

"I gave that idiot godologist just what he wanted," Christ said. "Verily, I told him just what he wanted to hear. It's not my fault if he has to deal with the consequences."

The tiny image that Ram-Ram and Seven were staring at now made up the entire contents of the universe as far as they were concerned, and each of them interpreted it in his own, frightening way.

Every one of the separate glowing details he saw made sense to Seven, for example, yet none of the details taken together formed anything at all, while in each eternal mo-ment they seemed just about to; and the suspense was almost unbearable.

"What about Oversoul Six?" Zeus asked.

"Seven. It's Oversoul Seven, though if he doesn't watch it, he'll be Oversoul Five," Christ muttered. "Verily, he's been asking for this. It'll do him good, and it will teach him not to go to the godologists expecting to learn anything of merit. It'll certainly give him a better perspective."

Ram-Ram was seeing himself, in a million different pieces, scattered, throbbing, changing relationships. His memories kept getting organized in different ways, like jigsaw images constantly changing shape and forming new pictures. The dark yet bright images held his attention so that it seemed nothing else had ever existed, or ever would.

"Now, *that's* hypnosis," Christ chuckled again.

"Still, that part about Jehovah was good," Zeus said, drinking his wine and at the same time wondering if it were nearly time for supper. He eyed Christ slyly, rubbing his black beard, trembling with a laughter that sent the royal floorboards quaking. "I didn't know you hated your father all that much!"

"It's no joke," Christ said irritably. "Mythology is full of such nonsense, and overloaded with divine murders. Humans always want the gods to handle their problems for them and commit their murders for them as well." He broke off, musing. "That's why Allah did so nicely. He didn't hide the facts."

"Well, never mind," Zeus chided. "Hadn't you better snap those two out of whatever spell you've thrown them into? They're really likely to get lost, you know. Besides, it's time for dinner."

"I should make that godologist count from a million backwards—a million times. Did you ever hear of such idiocy?" Christ tried to sound humorous, but he *was* upset. Invasion of divine privacy was involved; Oversoul Seven was right.

"Bring them back in," Zeus said soothingly.

"They expect me to retaliate," Christ said stubbornly. "I'm only acting out my role."

"Give them a break anyway," Zeus said. "You're supposed to be merciful too. At least take pity on *me;* we'll never eat at this rate."

"I knew you just wanted your dinner," Christ said, laughing because Zeus's good humor *was* godly in its proportions. (Of course, his ire at times could be equally impressive.) But Zeus didn't brood as he did, Christ thought. So he said, "Verily."

Ram-Ram's and Seven's consciousnesses were more or less captured by the multidimensional images that glittered in the doubled-in-upon-itself darkness of the sky. Christ called out good-naturedly, "There they are," reached out a

149

royal hand that magically extended out through galaxies, and brought Seven and Ram-Ram back in.

"Like two poor fish," Zeus said.

This time Christ smiled indulgently. With one stare of his mind he destroyed Ram-Ram's case history 9871; with another, he deposited Ram-Ram on the floor of the godologists' main building; and with another he brought a bewildered Oversoul Seven directly to his golden couch.

Chapter Eighteen

*Seven's Disquieting Interview
with Christ, a Multidimensional
Happening Turns into an
Insane Vision, and Jeffy-boy
Becomes a Character in a Book*

Oversoul Seven found himself in front of Christ's
golden couch, and he was so confused that he kept
changing images faster than even he thought he could, in
an effort to settle on one that might placate the glowering
Christ whose commanding eyes never left Seven's face for
one divine moment. "He didn't even blink," Seven told
Cyprus later. Seven felt an apology on the tip of his newly
formed tongue: He took the shape of the fourteen-year-old,
since he understood that Christ particularly liked children.

"Well, what do you have to say for yourself?" Christ
demanded. Then, as Seven's boy-image stabilized: "Oh,
you're a very young soul," Christ exclaimed in a somewhat
mollified voice. "Well, verily," he added, in a still softer
tone.

"I'm terribly sorry that you were crucified to begin with,"

Seven replied quickly. "I hope you don't hold a grudge against the world, though. I mean, well, I didn't have a thing to do with it at all."

Someone chuckled, and Seven suddenly became aware of Zeus, who appeared at Christ's right side. Zeus was eating from a leg of roasted mutton. Still laughing, he offered some to Christ, who shook his gray curls impatiently and said, "No. This whole affair has taken away my appetite for dinner."

Zeus stared rather compassionately at Seven, who was just beginning to get his breath, and asked in a voice that was somehow sweet and threatening at the same time, "So you have a taste for the gods, huh?"

Seven whispered, "Render unto Caesar the things that are Caesar's and unto God the things that are God's. No, that isn't right. It's render unto God the things that . . . Um, well, surely you recognize the quote. What I mean is that I let the gods go their way, and hopefully they allow me to do the same." Seven paused, then added to Christ, "The quote was yours, wasn't it, uh, Sir? Or perhaps I should say, 'Your Excellency'?"

"Oh, all right. I'll take a bit of that mutton," Christ said quarrelsomely to Zeus. And to Seven, "I don't care how you address me, but that quote isn't mine. I never said that. I don't care if it makes good sense or poor sense, the fact is that I never said those words in that manner."

"I didn't mean to misquote you," Seven said uneasily. "If you say you didn't say it, well, that's enough for me." Actually, Seven was growing more ill at ease every moment. Earlier he'd been frightened, but now Christ's power seemed to be diminishing to a point where Seven was almost embarrassed for him. Christ was nibbling from the mutton, for example: eating without a knife or fork—he and Zeus both taking very full mouthfuls, with Christ having trouble with the tougher portions. As Seven tried to look away politely, Zeus put his chunk of meat down on the coffee table and said thoughtfully, "You know, Christ, you could have said that Give-to-Caesar quote, and forgotten. In a lifetime, a person, even a god, speaks so many words that surely it's possible that your divine tongue enunciated that particular verbal sequence and—"

Christ's eyes blazed dangerously. He spat out a bit of meat into his napkin and said, very emphatically and deliberately, "I did not say those words. And I didn't curse the poor fig tree either. Being misquoted is one of the worst things that can happen to a god's message, and it happens all the time. Then of course, it's repeated endlessly. Endlessly." Christ's voice grew morose. His divine eyes wandered. Seven thought that if this kind of behavior kept up, Christ might even forget that he was there, and he could sneak away.

"Endlessly," Christ repeated, staring at Seven.

It *was* quite possible, Seven thought, that Christ's memory was slipping, but even as Seven thought those words, Christ's head snapped forward. The divine eyes came afire and Christ said, "So you think I'm losing my memory, do you? I remember the beginning of the world." Once more his eyes dimmed. "Those were the days," he muttered.

Seven was ready to weep. If this was Christ, the legends far surpassed the reality. He was almost always disappointed meeting an author in person, but this! He lowered his eyes and looked at the floorboards. They began to shimmer. Somewhere, Seven thought that he heard Zeus and Christ laugh—massive chuckles that disrupted birds in their flights through a million skies—laughs that emitted divine humor, compassionate but largely lost to any but godly ears. Gradually the chuckles changed in character though they continued until Seven thought that they'd sounded for eternity.

Realizing that he'd closed his eyes, he opened them. Then he rubbed them. There were torn magazines on the coffee table where only a moment earlier there had been, instead, a plate of mutton. The golden couch was replaced

153

by several rickety chairs and instead of Christ and Zeus, Jeffy-boy and *his* Ram-Ram sat with the coffee table between them.

Queen Alice, on the other side of the table, said, "Ideas of sanity are so limiting, don't you think? That's why people who think they're sane get in so much trouble when they realize that they're actually bigger than their concepts give them a right to be."

Jeffery said, "This is ridiculous." He ignored Queen Alice and turned to Ram-Ram, who shrugged his shoulders comically at Queen Alice and said, "Jeffy-boy just can't get all this through his head." Then, to Jeffery, "You want to know if I was really in your apartment the other afternoon. I was. Now, does that answer your question?"

"It does and it doesn't," Jeffery replied with some irritation. "Were you there physically?"

"Definitely not," Ram-Ram said; then, with the kindly old psychologist's smile, "I know, I know. You have more questions, but let's take them one at a time."

"You're the one who's in the mental institution," Jeffery shouted. "So don't give me advice."

"Quite right," Ram-Ram said agreeably.

"If there are gods, they'd be considered insane too," Queen Alice said musingly. She tucked her blue and white checkered shirt in under her dungarees, untucked it again, and said triumphantly, "Many of the insane speak for the gods all the time. Three Christs have come and gone from this very institution since I've been here. And they weren't missed either, I'll tell you. They were all fanatics."

Stoically Jeffery waited until Queen Alice finished speaking. Then he said desperately to Ram-Ram, "I thought that I had an entire conversation with you in my apartment. Then you . . . disappeared. Now you tell me that you *were* there, but not physically. In other words, our insane data agree. Facts that simply cannot be facts—"

"They *are* facts, they are, Jeffy-boy," Ram-Ram shouted

excitedly. "But in a different kind of fact system. That's what I'm trying to get across to you." Ram-Ram broke off. A lovely young girl came over from the other side of the room, offering tiny pieces of a candy bar that she'd obviously slivered into numberless bits of chocolate. She curtseyed. Ram-Ram smiled, said, "Thank you, my dear," in a sweet but grand fashion, offered a piece to Queen Alice, and turned back to Jeffery.

"There's another one," Queen Alice whispered, poking Jeffery, who quickly recoiled. Ram-Ram noticed, and chuckled. Jeffery said, exasperated, "Another what?"

"Why, another Christ. The only one left here, and the nicest we've had by far," Queen Alice said, standing; and despite himself, Jeffery noticed that for all of her years, she was as supple as a girl. Her white hair looked almost blonde for a moment in the afternoon sunlight that came through the yellow plastic curtains at the windows by the TV set. For a wild moment, Jeffery almost felt that she was younger than he was.

"Oh, yes, she thinks she's Christ," Queen Alice said gaily. "The psychologists keep trying to tell her that she must be the Blessed Virgin instead, because there *are* certain conventions to follow whether you're crazy or not." She smiled innocently, rubbing her wrinkled chin with a rather grubby finger, and added, "If you're female and think you're god, then they think you're crazier than a male who thinks the same thing, because at least he has his sexes straight. See?"

Jeffery's eyes widened incredulously. He fumbled nervously with the buttons of his properly rumpled sweater and said to Ram-Ram, "Do you understand what she's talking about?"

"Yes, yes, yes. And she's quite right," exclaimed Ram-Ram. "This place has the richest psychological climate in the world, you know. Cynthia, the girl with the chocolate, doesn't necessarily think that Christ was a woman, but that she is a woman and she is Christ. A subtle difference, don't you see? She annoys our psychological colleagues no end, of course, but she won't back down and be the Virgin Mary. Watch. Look now," Ram-Ram pointed, and Jeffery turned to see Cynthia, a girl in her twenties, move among the multitude. At least, from her manner and bearing, that was certainly what she thought she was doing; offering each inmate a sliver of chocolate; smiling with the sweetest generosity, so that Jeffery himself was almost taken in, at least for a moment. "Why, it's incredible. She obviously believes it," he gasped.

Ram-Ram was getting more and more excited. He wet his lips, and as if addressing a class, he said to Jeffery, "Don't you see? Her father brings her the candy bars. She distributes them instead of fishes—"

Queen Alice said comfortably, "She's writing a bible of her own in her spare time. I might help her type it."

"Oh, God," Jeffery cried. "You really are mad, the both of you!"

"What do you expect? This is a mental institution," Ram-Ram said, laughing; then, slyly, "Without madness, there'd be no sanity in the world. Don't you agree, Queen Alice?"

Jeffery didn't hear her answer. He sat with his head in his arms, overcome by the deepest sense of desolation he'd ever known. "And I must share some of that madness," he said soberly. "I thought I saw you *physically* in my apartment, and physically at least you were here. There must be a kind of contagion, so that the brain no longer distinguishes reality. It must perceive bits and pieces that don't agree. Maybe I mixed a memory of a past visit of yours with reality—"

"Now, now, don't take it so hard," Ram-Ram said. He took Jeffery's hand reassuringly before Jeffery wrenched it away. The girl, Cynthia, hearing the commotion, came over and offered Jeffery another sliver of chocolate. "Take it away," he said angrily. Then, looking up, he saw her eyes.

They weren't Christ's eyes—who knew what Christ's eyes looked like? But they were the eyes Christ should have had, in which all contradictions vanished or were resolved, in whose glance he suddenly saw himself, a person of dignity despite all of his own vast misunderstandings. He took the candy and said, "Thank you," with a simplicity and grace he didn't know he possessed.

Queen Alice was sitting down again, studying her hands. Ram-Ram seemed to have fallen asleep in the hard-backed chair, or he was pretending to be dozing, as a hospital patient might when wishing that a visitor would leave. With a slight shock, Jeffery realized that no one was paying him any attention at all. He might as well have been invisible. Queen Alice picked up a magazine. Someone turned up the volume on the TV set: A ballgame came on, and the spectators' shouts filled the room. It was as if he'd already left, Jeffery thought. He coughed, picked up his jacket and turned to leave . . .

As he did, the sound of the spectators at the televised ballgame seemed to rise in volume, and the applause and shouts suddenly roused Oversoul Seven back to himself. Instantly he remembered the giant chuckles of the gods that had propelled him here. But he'd experienced the entire scene through Jeffery. When he discovered this, Oversoul Seven was considerably shaken and confused. Why Jeffery? he wondered. Jeffery wasn't even one of his own personalities.

And then, as he thought of the gods and Jeffery, between one moment and the next, the two environments—the Olympian rest home and Ram-Ram's mental institution— met and merged, attaining such unmanageable dimensions that Seven called out for Cyprus. There was no answer. Instead, the dizzying transformation continued. The gods' rest home with Zeus and Christ and the golden couch was suddenly transposed over the institution's common room. The magazines on the coffee table fluttered madly through the air, landing on Christ's couch. The television set, still showing the ballgame, now sat in the gods' rest home, with Zeus madly adding his shouts to those of the spectators.

Worse, Jeffery, who was just leaving the common room, suddenly—somehow—turned into Will, and stayed. Queen Alice became Zeus's wife, Hera, and Ram-Ram, like some mad director, was himself and the godologist Ram-Ram as well. Seven was reeling, trying to keep it all straight. In the next moment, however, all the surroundings expanded. Zeus and Christ, all of the inmates of the institution and all of the gods in the rest home, merged into one wildly incoherent supergod, but one so ancient, so grandly senile, so sweetly insane that even the grasses trembled at the very thought of his approach.

For now, in the next scene, Seven saw the world ruled by this spectacular entity, and heard the tempting senile god's voice as it drifted eerily through all the secret places of the universe, into forest corners, into the deepest, most inaccessible ocean caves, into the invisible closets of people's minds. And despite himself, Seven was terrified.

He saw frightened pigeons fly to hiding places. He felt the god's breath shake the world to bits in endless autumns; leaves committing exultant suicide. ("Ah hah," Will yelled, dying with each leaf.) And he felt each living thing tremble, trying to preserve its life in the face of such cosmic temper tantrums. This god's insanity whispered crookedly through men's chromosomes, tainting them with flaws beyond number. The senile god shouted his incoherent truth to the multitudes, who in turn killed their neighbors and rode in bitter triumph through endless savage wars. Mad Mohammed flashed his eternal sword; Jehovah in fits of holy tremors sent down his plagues and flood; Jupiter and Thor threw their thunderbolts while Buddha contemplated his divine navel and in the streets his gurus sprinkled holy ash.

Seven screamed, "Stop!"

The insane god, who was at once Jehovah, Buddha, and

all of the others, paused and seemed to notice Oversoul Seven for the first time. The earth that Seven was seeing took on the god's features, so that Seven saw the treetops spinning in the wind as the shaken, tousled curls of Christ's head; the oceans, the depthless pools of his insane delight and the unendurable realization of his plight; for this god knew he was a demon, raging, possessing the earth, tuning it to his own cosmic insane pitch until surely one day— today or tomorrow or in a million years—that pitch would become so agonizing that the god's mind would split; divine neurons spilling out into mortality, the blessed essence contaminated beyond degree, and lost.

This *was* an insane vision. Seven tried to clear his consciousness, to shake it loose from the strands of despair that threatened to send him reeling into extinction. Hopelessly, he suddenly saw Lydia and Will falling through unnumbered days that wound back to the insane god's infancy.

"I won't live in such a world," Will was shouting. His voice splintered the air beneath him, and at the same time his memories poured out of his mind into space.

And Lydia, furiously angry, stood for a moment, shaking her fists at the universe. "I won't be born again in that mad world!" She was going to say more, but the insane god's eye blinked and Lydia twirled, turning smaller and smaller, blown willy-nilly by the thunderous power of that divine blinking eye.

Seven's astonishment at all of this slowed his reactions. What nightmare was this? But he couldn't seem to break its spell, and the psychological implications of this disastrous vision were all too clear. He had to break away for Lydia and Will, and if they were lost . . . But how could they be? Again Seven cried out for Cyprus. This time she responded so abruptly and severely that Seven was snapped back to himself—so quickly that he felt as if a million shocks surged through the most vital portions of his consciousness.

159

"Seven, how *could* you have allowed such a thing to happen?" Cyprus exclaimed, though "exclaimed" isn't quite the word. Seven felt her disapproval, or rather, her sorrow. But before he could respond, he watched as her image appeared simultaneously to Will and Lydia, who seemed to be in the distance below him. Lydia looked incredulous and angry. Will looked defiant and scared to death. Seven watched as Cyprus formed a gentle summertime hill beneath them. Then she talked to them quietly, before returning to Seven.

"What happened?" Seven asked impatiently. "What did I do wrong, and how much will Lydia and Will remember? Was Will on drugs or something?" He was still shaken himself, and he noticed that Cyprus wasn't consoling *him*. Instead she said, "Look for yourself." And she and Seven stood invisibly in Will's "bedroom."

Will lived in a loosely knit commune; that is, young people constantly came and went. Will's cot, with his name painted on it, sat behind a huge rubber plant, and beside this sat the two orange crates that Will used as a desk. The plant and crates marked this corner of the large room as Will's property, and above the bed a poster of Buddha stared blissfully over Will's pillow. Will considered himself quite lucky since his corner possessed a window, half of which he'd covered with a map of the world.

Now he lay curled up at the head of the cot, wondering if he felt strong enough to make it to the communal sink to wash his face, or even further to the refrigerator where his food—oranges—was stacked on the third shelf. There were ten other cots scattered around the room, each one marked in one way or another as private property, but for now, Will was alone.

He'd just awakened from a terrible nightmare, or so he thought, except for the ending where he was sunbathing on a hill; and he supposed that one or a combination of the drugs he'd been taking had caused the particularly frightening sense of insanity he dimly remembered. But now everything looked normal, which meant shitty and dismal, he thought. Reaching under his mattress, he felt around until his trembling fingers found his potpourri of pills, his cache, that he kept hidden there. Without even looking to see what particular pills he'd grabbed, he popped two.

Oversoul Seven said to Cyprus, "He does it all the time."

Will's eyelids fluttered. He began muttering. Cyprus sighed. "What you experienced earlier was a nightmare, all right, composed of Will and Lydia's worst fears about god and the universe. And you should have monitored it for them, not fallen into it yourself."

Will's mutterings grew louder. At the same time, he began to rouse in his dream body. "You stay with him now," Cyprus said. "I'll want to have a good talk with you later."

"What about Lydia?" Seven cried. "I should get back to her, shouldn't I?" But there was no reply, and in any case it was too late; Will stood in his dream body, eyeing Seven.

"Well, I've done it again," Will said sheepishly. *"You're* here, and you're one of my most exasperating trips." Actually, he felt quite satisfied with himself for the moment. He knew he was tripping, but he'd decided Oversoul Seven was some kind of symbol that meant he was safe, or nearly. In fact, for no reason at all, he felt cocky. "If you're a figment of my imagination, I'm pretty good," he said to Seven.

"I'm sorry I can't return the compliment," Seven grumbled.

"How come I feel so great?" Will cried.

Seven answered, "Cyprus gave you additional energy; but then you probably wouldn't remember." He himself felt quite glum indeed, and his mood didn't improve as Will ran up and down the room, shouting, "I'm out of my body, I'm out of my body!"

"You're strung out on drugs too," Seven cried angrily, "and if it wasn't for me, who knows what trouble you might be getting into."

"So what?" Will shouted happily. "I'm out of my body

and you're here, and for once we aren't in a classroom. Is my wish your command, by the way?" Will eyed Seven speculatively and added, "Because on my last trip I had a terrible experience about an insane god or something, and I don't want to do that one again. But if you're like a genie, well, I can go where I want to."

"I'm not like a genie," Seven said.

"Well, anyhow. God was miserable. But let's take a trip to see his mother," Will declared.

"Whose mother?" Seven asked, uneasily.

"Why, Christ's. She'd know all about him, wouldn't she?" Will replied. "After all, who knew him better?" Will started giggling.

"Forget it," Seven said. "And anyway, why Christ's mother?"

"Why not?" Will said airily. "If I'm tripping, well, it's *my* trip, isn't it?" He grinned brilliantly and added, "And somehow, I seem to have you where I want you for a change."

"That's what you think," Seven muttered to himself, but there was no doubt that he had to stay with Will for a while, and he didn't like the new turn of events. How much bleed-through was there, actually, from one personality's experience to another's? Without knowing the details, was Will somehow aware of Lydia's search for the gods, and its so far unhappy results? He must be, Seven thought, staring at Will; otherwise, Lydia and Will wouldn't have been involved in the same awful nightmarish experience.

"Well?" Will demanded, and despite himself, Seven was caught between exasperation and appreciation: There Will stood, arrogant and sassy, and looking like a young god himself; filled right now with fresh determination. But determination to do what? Because in the next moment, Will said, "I'm probably going to commit suicide the first chance I get, so you really shouldn't refuse me any favors or you'll be sorry later. And I want to visit the Virgin Mary. If that's within your province, of course."

Seven sighed. Will's last remark made a certain kind of unfortunate sense. "I can't guarantee what will happen," Seven said nervously. "I wish you'd change your mind."

"Not on your life. Not on your life. Not on your life." Will started chanting the words over and over, and Seven wished wholeheartedly that Cyprus hadn't given him quite so much energy.

"Have it your way," Seven said. Will could have sworn that no transition had occurred, but now he and Seven were travelers.

Chapter Nineteen

The Virgin Mary's Tale and an Ego for Buddha

Seven and Will were dressed like humble pilgrims. The street (if such it was) appeared to belong to ancient Jerusalem. Donkeys brayed. Tradesmen went about their business. Mary's small house was set in a bit from the numerous stalls at which vendors sold their wares. The house was actually the strangest combination of a manger, barn, and small sitting room. Outside, two palm trees stood at either side of the entrance. Incongruously enough, there was a small green lawn, and in the center of it were various small statuettes making up a tabloid of the nativity, with Mary, Joseph, and the baby Jesus. Alongside was a plaster image of Christ as a boy of about twelve, and to the right, a huge cross on which a statue of the adult Christ hung, with blood that looked real enough running from his wounds down into a small pond, which drained into the ground. By each palm tree knelt a statue of an angel carrying a sword.

Will just stared. "This isn't real, you know," he said to Oversoul Seven. "And this street just started from no place. If you walked to either end, it would probably just disappear." He shrugged to show that he wasn't impressed, yet there was something terribly impressive about the mixture of junky artifacts and real, braying donkeys; and the cheap-looking plaster-of-Paris angels had the craziest intensity, as if their grotesqueness gave them a life of their own.

Seven just said, "Now, let me handle this, please. And be polite for a change, if you can." He knocked at the door.

Will said, "I can't believe it; knocking at the door of the Virgin Mary. Even for a dream or a drug trip, it's just too much."

The door opened, seemingly by itself. At first the room seemed dim. Seven and Will took a few hesitant steps inside. Then, however, a series of glows lit up the interior, like spotlights, though not as bright. One showed an empty manger; one, a group of oxen, sleeping; and in the light of the third glow, the Virgin Mary sat crocheting.

She said, pleasantly enough, "Welcome. But if you've come to see my son, he isn't here."

"We know that," Oversoul Seven said politely. "It's you we've come to see."

Mary looked alarmed. "You aren't reporters? I don't give interviews anymore," she exclaimed.

Seven assured her that they weren't journalists of any kind, and with a partially worried air, Mary put her crocheting work aside.

Will kept saying to himself, "This is impossible. It can't be happening." To Seven he whispered, "This whole thing is crazy, and besides, she looks like Whistler's Mother." But even as Will spoke the words, he completely changed his mind.

Mary blinked constantly; anxiously. She looked like a

windup doll, dressed in a long blue gown with a brown robe on top, her too-smooth head partly covered by a black veil. Her face was too chinalike, too chiseled, and her eyes looked too mechanical. But for mechanical-looking eyes, they were astounding. Will felt that they'd been weeping for centuries, and indeed they did begin to weep again.

As she started to cry, gently, Mary reached for a Kleenex and said, "Do forgive me. My son was a good boy always. They crucified him, you know. Just the same, people keep coming here and writing, wanting me to intercede for them. Life has its cruelties. And I can never answer all the mail, so people must think I don't care." With one hand, she indicated a corner of the room where stacks of letters and stone tablets and even sheets and rolls of papyrus, along with telegrams, were all piled together. "Mail even comes by wireless now," she said. "And I had to have the phone removed because for years I was on the phone day and night. And my son is in the old gods' home now, you know. I visit him when I can, but he never forgot the Crucifixion. And he's never been the same since. He never really thought that his father would let him die that way, even if it was to a good purpose. The family has scattered since. But I'm sorry for rattling on like this over my own problems. Would you like a glass of wine?"

Oversoul Seven shook his head. Will stood looking out the glassless window at the commotion outside, noticing that the sounds of the street somehow stopped just outside the window, though they should have been only too clear. It was like watching a silent movie, he thought: He could see the merchants' mouths opening as they spoke; see the carts drawn by the donkeys, but no clatter of wheels or raucous shouts entered that room. Wild, he kept thinking: What a trip. He hoped he'd remember it all.

"Do continue," Seven was saying to Mary. Then to Will he said, "And I wish you'd come over here and sit down." Will managed a partially insolent, partially nonchalant stride to show that all of this was too impossible and ridiculous to take his notice for a moment, but he sat down.

Mary gave Will a humble smile as if agreeing that she was, indeed, beneath anyone's serious consideration. Then she rearranged her robes slightly and, head lowered, she continued. "I tried to be a good woman. Joseph, my husband, was only a lowly carpenter; a virtuous one, it's true. But from the moment he was born, I thought Jesus was special and I wanted to give him a heritage to be proud of; a gift no one else had . . ." She paused, looked worried, and eyed Oversoul Seven with an anxious air.

"Do continue. It's fascinating," Seven said, without looking at Will, because he was doubly sorry that he'd let him come. This interview wasn't likely to convince Will that the universe had any sense, Seven told himself. At the same time, Seven had almost forgotten who Mary was supposed to be, in the reality of this woman before him, with her hesitant manner . . . Seven broke off. Or was her manner suddenly confessional? "Don't say anything you don't want to," he said quickly, but it was too late.

"I never could bring myself to discuss . . . things of the flesh with my son. She paused again. "Do you understand?"

"Absolutely," Oversoul Seven said nervously. "Do you want to change the subject?"

"No, it must be said," Mary replied resolutely.

"Well, say it, then," Seven muttered under his breath.

"I told him, my son, that he came from God . . . without the agency of man. It was only a mother's innocent deceit."

"Oh, I knew it," Will shouted, springing to his feet. He lifted his head dramatically and threw his arms skyward. "Sheer idiocy. Behind every religion, every philosophy. At least the Western ones. Oh, sheer idiocy!"

But Oversoul Seven (still looking like a pilgrim) was at Mary's side; truly upset. "Now, now, do calm down," he pleaded.

"My son believed me," Mary cried in an anguished voice. "He became truly deluded."

Her eyes *did* seem made for weeping. Crying, they attained an odd but truly spectacular cast, as if the tears magnified and yet distorted some truth that seemed irreconcilable with the words she was sobbing. "I knew it was a lie," she said, this time as if condemning herself beyond all hope of salvation. "And yet," she began, and as she spoke, her tears stopped abruptly. She lifted her head proudly, staring at the astonished Oversoul Seven, and moved her arm in a triumphant gesture. She was suddenly so authoritative that Seven leapt back just a step, and Will just stared. Mary's voice now was strong; almost hard. "And yet, the lie was the truth, and I knew that, too. Or the lie became the truth. Or maybe it was the truth all along, and I had to pretend it was a lie. But in some way, I *am* the Mother of God."

As she spoke, the air in the room seemed to shimmer. Seven thought uneasily that something could happen that could disturb worlds or disrupt them prematurely if Mary remembered . . . if Mary remembered what?

But she didn't. She almost seemed to have forgotten what she'd just said, for that matter. Dejection once again settled down upon her doll-like features. "So we shared the same delusion," she said in a sad voice. "It was so bad finally that Jesus attempted suicide. They took the knives and forks and all silverware away from him at the rest home. He's not allowed any sharp objects at all."

Seven felt a twinge of guilt for having thought that Christ and Zeus were gluttonous when he saw them eating without forks: He blushed.

Will stood in the center of the room and said, "Well, that's it, all right. If Christ contemplated suicide, it shows he's not all mad, Madam. Still, it *does* make you think twice, doesn't it? When the gods can't stand existence?" He started to giggle. He couldn't help it. He put his hand over his mouth, and sat down on the floor, holding his stomach.

Seven listened to Will with a feeling of dismay, but something else kept bothering him, and he couldn't properly identify what it was—a fact that annoyed him even more. Mary started to weep again; Will had the grace to be quiet for a moment, and Seven mentally explored the many-leveled nature of this interview with the Virgin. Mary was acting; that idea came to him. Christ and Zeus were acting; but no, that wasn't exactly right, either. There *was* a drama though, in which psychological props were being used, Seven thought, and he had to know what part he was playing, along with Lydia and Will before . . . what? Before the pilgrimage to the gods turned into something else entirely. Or had it already? As soon as Seven thought of Lydia, Mary's cottage vanished, or at least he and Will found themselves outside once more, walking down the street.

"Seven! Seven!"

Hearing his name called, Oversoul Seven stopped with surprise. Who could be looking for him *here?* He eyed the street. No one looked familiar. The street hawkers were putting away their wares for the afternoon. Donkeys were reladen with supplies. Dogs and children skittered here and there. Horses slopped water. Men and women in various everyday garbs suddenly began to hurry away—perhaps to simple suppers. Then amid the confusion Seven noticed one figure, also dressed as a pilgrim, running toward him. It was Lydia.

The moment Seven recognized her, he heard another voice, Cyprus's, mentally say, "You forgot someone, didn't you?" Seven started to answer, but by then Lydia was saying breathlessly, "Cyprus sent me here. I had a dreadful experience. I'm not sure what it really was, but there were insane gods and God knows what! I came to on a hillside. But who is this?"

Will was really beginning to enjoy himself, and Oversoul

Seven's obvious discomfiture. "Who are you?" he asked, bowing with mock deference. "The Virgin Mary's sister, I suppose?"

Lydia started to respond rather tartly, when Will immediately went on, "Or Buddha's daughter? Or perhaps Buddha in a woman's guise? Or—"

"Stop that," Seven cried. "Not another word."

But Will was tasting a sense of power. He made a mental note to find out exactly what pills he'd popped because he'd never had such a brilliant, heady, conscious trip before. "That's it," he shouted, snapping his fingers. "You must be Buddha."

Instantly he broke off. Suddenly there were lotus blossoms everywhere. The stalls and people and donkeys were gone. The street disappeared. The silence after all the commotion was the oddest thing of all. Will had never sensed such silent air. Then he, Lydia, and Seven noticed something even stranger. The space around them formed a gigantic transparent image of Buddha, and they stood inside. The softest grass imaginable was beneath their feet, and the loveliest blue air was above; yet all of that was a part of the Buddha's form. Seven stared: The image was now repeated unendingly, it seemed, in miniature transparent images, kaleidoscopic Buddha-shapes, mixing and merging together, forming the grass and sky as well, a million Jell-O-cubes of Buddha images. And the air itself felt different, like the most softly moving gelatin, of different hues, that all blended together. Will, shocked, stuck his finger out and stirred the air; he could feel it nudge against his fingertip as if it had a life of its own.

"What a trip, oh, what a trip!" Will shouted. His voice sent ripples through the jellylike air, set it moving in a slow frenzy.

Oversoul Seven cried, "Be quiet. Listen."

"I don't hear anything," Lydia said. She pulled her pilgrim's robe about her throat and looked around anxiously.

Then Will leapt back. "I hear something," he exclaimed,

for the air was making the most peculiar settling sound, and before their eyes, Seven, Lydia, and Will saw the air visibly thicken, while still retaining its transparent quality. A giant-sized, slightly solidified Buddha image formed in the air just above them. Its parts moved and flowed together, again, like gelatin made out of space itself.

Seven steadied himself and said politely, "Uh, good afternoon."

Lydia didn't say a thing. Will prostrated himself on the ground and said, "Here I am, Master. I've no ego left. I'm done with desire. I've read all about you, and please consider me your servant."

"Get up on your feet and don't make a fool of yourself," Seven whispered.

Will sent Seven a glance of nearly pure hatred, and then addressed the Buddha. "I tell you, I'm done with desire. I'm finished with wants and lusts."

The Buddha lifted his beautiful gelatinous brows and said to Oversoul Seven, "What is he talking about?"

"Excuse me," Lydia interrupted hesitantly. "Are you an Indian god? If you are, I have some questions."

"I am if it suits your fancy," Buddha said. "Now what is that poor fellow saying?" Buddha raised his flowing arm and indicated Will, who was sitting in a lotus position, and doing a rather poor job of it because his sneakers kept getting tangled in his pilgrim's robe.

"Om, om, om," Will chanted, and Buddha snapped, "Will you shut up?" so loudly that Will sprang to his feet.

"Now what's all this nonsense about giving up desire?" Buddha demanded. He spoke an elegant Indian dialect that Seven, Lydia, and Will all understood at once.

"It's a part of your teaching, Master," Will whispered. "I've read it in all of your sacred books."

"Let those who will, give up desire," Buddha said. "It sounds like a lot of nonsense to me, and if anyone said that I made such pronouncements, then I've been grossly misquoted. Shall the bee give up its honey? The cat, its tail?

171

The apple, its core? The fly, its wings? The scalp, its hair? The cow, its moo? The—"

"Uh, we get your point," Seven said.

But the Buddha went on. "The horse must neigh. It cannot meow. But men, when they quote me, put the cat's meow in the horse's mouth." He turned his blessed eyes in the general direction of his navel and sighed, but Seven noticed that his eyes were quite merry, twinkling like gelatin.

"All of this is a bit disconcerting," Seven said, because by now it was apparent that Buddha's form was sometimes softly gelatinous and visible, and sometimes only indicated, except for the navel which remained, like a grape. For a moment the form stabilized again and Buddha's voice rang out, this time more sweetly than before, so that the sounds themselves seemed to glitter through the image's multitudinous jellyish folds.

He said, "Desire not to desire—an impossible situation! For that matter, all realities and situations *are* basically impossible; that is, they would be if they happened, for the reasons mortals suppose they do. Lydia, for example—"

Without thinking, Lydia knelt down, genuflecting. She crossed herself and said, "Yes, Father," in response to an early Catholic conditioning that she thought she'd forgotten. Recovering, she jumped to her feet, glared at Oversoul Seven as if her mistake was his fault, and tried to hide her embarrassment. "I'm sorry, but I don't mean to kneel before anyone anymore," she said. "And, well, a real god wouldn't need adoration."

Buddha's image chuckled, quaked; and the sweet voice went on. "Lydia, a part of you—your desire—is building up someplace else, which is why you feel so discontented now. You haven't followed your desire to be born again. You keep hampering it and setting conditions. You set yourself apart from your desire, examine it, and demand that the gods take responsibility for your lack of decision."

"Why, I do not," Lydia sputtered. "And what do you expect me to do?"

"Just go where your desire dictates," Buddha began.

Will shouted furiously, "You can't say that! The Buddhists believe in rising above desire. Even I know that."

At this, the Buddha laughed, setting his image shaking and quaking, and he shouted, "Ah ha, but I'm not a Buddhist. I'm *Buddha*. And your desire is your inner direction, and you desire death only because it's the only desire left, the only one you allow."

"I don't believe that at all," Will shouted. "And I don't have an ego anymore. I've rid myself of it. I just want to serve, so I can only suppose that your ridiculous remarks are part of a trial to test me. I want to be selfless. I *am* selfless. I am, goddammit," he yelled. Then he stood, staring, too frightened to move. The gelatinous Buddha shuddered, trembled like a cosmic jell-mountain, and began to melt into a trembling mass of semithick liquid that moved purposefully and directly toward Will. First, the edges melted and small puddles reached Will's sneakered feet. He finally screamed, and leapt backward, as the entire mass flowed like cold lava, faster and faster, in his direction.

"No. No," Will screamed, staring upward at the unsteady melting Jell-O Buddha which now threatened to avalanche down upon him.

At the last minute, Oversoul Seven grabbed Will, and the Buddha-flow stopped; uncertain. Will was shaking and muttering, and Seven said sternly to the Buddha, "You didn't have to go *that* far. We get the message." Then, to Will, he said, "Your 'trip' is over, and I'm sure it's more than you counted on. Wake up inside your physical body. And if it's selflessness you want, you nearly got a taste of it, so I hope you've learned a lesson. Anyhow, you're safe now, so you can wake up relieved."

Will just nodded, too shaken to say a thing. He muttered something about never taking drugs again, and disappeared.

The Buddha shrank at the edges, wrinkled, each part shaking
with such humor that Seven almost forgot to be angry; and
then the Buddha was gone. Seven and Lydia stood there a
moment, still dressed in their pilgrim garb, when once again
the air began to thicken into semi-shapes, and Lydia gasped
as the grounds gradually changed to those of the gardens
outside of the gods' rest home. Only this time, Cyprus was
waiting for them.

"This has gone quite far enough. Seven, I want to talk
to you," she said. She took a form that was nearly regal,
so that Oversoul Seven made no protest, though he'd had
one in mind. Even Lydia remained silent, though Seven
was afraid she might complain about some of the less for-
tunate of their recent adventures.

A blue-green cast covered the garden; a twilight that was
at once sad in nature and oddly neutral in quality in a way
that Seven sensed but couldn't fathom.

Dejectedly, Lydia sat down on one of the benches. With
her head bowed she looked medieval in the pilgrim's gown.
She moved; glanced toward the gods' rest home, its stone
structure looming now like a dark cliff in the distance. "I've
made one decision, anyway," she said. "If anyone is interested."

Cyprus was smiling very gently, and yet her smile had
the same neutral quality as the twilight, Seven noticed.
"What did you decide?" Cyprus asked Lydia.

Lydia stood up, one arm resting on the back of the bench,
the pilgrim cowl half obscuring the curve of her cheeks.
She looked tired, defeated, and triumphant all at once. "I'm
definitely ready to be born again. I'm going through with
it after all," she said, but with a hard tone to her voice that
defied her slumped shoulders. "I want earth life again, with
clear boundaries and a framework that I can understand.
And gods or not; God, my life last time made more sense
than the gods do. So who needs a senile Christ and a Jell-
O Buddha? I want to go to Bianka's room again, and check
with Josef, and see how the birth preparations are going. I

174

just can't handle all of this other—" She broke off and threw her arms out in the air. "Nonsense!" she cried.

Seven blushed. Cyprus, with that strange neutrality, took Lydia's hand in hers, and the two of them vanished. For a moment Seven was alone, though he knew that Cyprus would return for their talk; a talk he'd rather forget, he told himself. It was obvious that he'd gone wrong somewhere in this search for the gods, and yet he knew that he had to let Lydia and Will search in their own ways. He'd merely help out as best he could.

In the odd twilight, Seven disentangled himself mentally from his personalities, from Lydia and Will and Josef, and instantly he felt lighter, freer, and playful. The universe *was* safe, spilling over with exuberance; so where, he wondered, had Lydia's and Will's dissatisfaction come from? Granted, the gods seemed—well, a trifle erratic, but they were likeable enough in their own fashions. So just what did Will and Lydia expect of them? And why should either of them suppose, if they did, that those gods had anything to do with running the universe?

He decided to forget about it while he could. Free of restraints, Seven played in the twilight. He turned into a flower, luxuriating in the touch of gentle air. He forgot himself in the very transparency of his being, while all the time knowing that he knew himself better for his temporary unknowing.

At first, Cyprus was only a distant thought to him. Then she appeared. The two of them turned into points of light, sparkling in the garden.

Seven said, "Before you say anything, I'm terribly disappointed. I thought that the gods would have more sense." Cyprus didn't answer at once. The background sounds grew louder. In the distance Oversoul Seven heard the clash of Mohammed's sword as he fought with the infidels, yelling "Allah" and leaping back and forth. "That's what I mean," Seven cried disconsolately.

"They mean well," Cyprus answered. "Don't be so critical. They're giant psychological projections, man's 'divine children' exaggerating their parents' best and worst qualities."

"You mean they aren't real at all?" Seven cried, astounded. "First I didn't believe they existed, and I guess I was better off. Then I thought that if they'd influenced human thought all that much, the gods *must* exist. Then I decided that they were real and I expected them to be—well, at *least* adult, in human terms. Now you're telling me that they weren't real to begin with."

Oversoul Seven felt tired and confused. He glanced around the garden. Birds of all colors flew through the air. The sky was an extraordinary blue-gray. Flowers grew everywhere in tints beyond description. But none of it contented him.

Cyprus kept changing position, appearing first on a leaf, then on a grass blade, and then on the top of Mohammed's sword, so that Seven cried out, "Cyprus, don't do that!"

Cyprus said, "Oh, Seven, you know better than that," and Seven answered, "I know it. Of course you wouldn't get hurt. But I'm too worried to think straight."

"Do stop brooding," Cyprus responded. "The gods are real enough. They're just different than your personalities expected them to be. In a manner of speaking, the gods are born from man's yearning, from man's loves and hates and fears and hopes. Each person contributes to the creation until you have—well, a conglomerate god, made up of part of each individual."

"Then they *aren't* real," Seven shouted.

"Oh, Seven, you haven't met the *real* gods yet, if that's what you mean. I thought you understood that!" Cyprus stared at Seven with amazed dismay, and to cover his confusion Seven took the fourteen-year-old-boy image. Cyprus automatically compensated, adopting her complementary teacher form. She said, "It never occurred to me that you supposed—"

"Supposed what?" Seven asked dismally. "What did you think I supposed?"

Cyprus said gently, "I took it for granted that you realized that you were perceiving Lydia and Will's *versions* of the gods; mostly Lydia's, as they were reflected through her mind and took on those psychological connotations. The gods as understood by mortals are always conventional personifications. They're like religious psychological statues, only possessing more abilities and characteristics. But all in all, highly limited by any standards of excellence or morality. Animated superstars; perhaps that term expresses it best of all."

But Seven was horrified. "I didn't understand that at all," he said angrily. "And certainly Lydia and Will didn't. I didn't believe that the gods, as mortals understand them, had anything to do with running the universe, but . . . I don't know what I thought," he cried.

There was a small pause. Then Cyprus said gently, "You *did* understand that you create your own reality?"

"But the gods' reality is something else again," Seven exclaimed. "How did such a misunderstanding take place? And if there are real gods behind the gods I've met, then how do you find them? If they're always camouflaged by people's beliefs about them, how can anyone find them? You and I know that the universe is safe, and that All That Is is hidden in us, and in everything else as well. But Lydia doesn't know that. And Will thinks he does, only he has some crazy idea that desire is somehow opposed to being. And I don't like Lydia being born again by default, if that's what's behind her decision. If she *is* born as Tweety, I have to give her something, some clues, to help her in her new life; some idea that frees her from—" Seven broke off, really upset. "I hardly know what to think myself," he said. "And what about Will? He was still talking about suicide."

"Which reminds me," Cyprus said. "It's time to give Jeffery a rest, so he can write his own notes. I imagine he might be just a bit upset himself."

177

Chapter Twenty

Jeffery's Notes and Some Upsetting Realizations

Now I must confess my concern over what is certainly a rather unique predicament, for this manuscript has included events from my own life as a part of its narrative. Imagine my horror as I found myself automatically writing down (but not from my viewpoint) the entire happenings that occurred during my last visit to Ram-Ram. I was, in fact, more than halfway through the description before I realized this odd turn of events, for when I am embarked upon writing the book, it's impossible to tell where my mind is. A psychological absence falls upon me. That is the only way I can describe it. There is no amnesia. I know my fingers are working the typewriter keys, and I am aware of my environment, yet I am lost to myself in a way difficult to describe or decipher. When I finally realized that a portion of my own life was appearing as part of this unwelcome book, I was appalled, but my fingers typed on, and some part of me remained strangely neutral and unconcerned. A maddening situation.

My new isolation doesn't help either. Almost everyone has left campus for spring vacation. I stayed, because I expect a letter any time from Sarah: Her baby must be due this week or next, and ex-wife or not, I still bear her good will. In any case, I was alone here the afternoon after my visit to Ram-Ram, when I suddenly found myself reliving the experience through this manuscript itself.

Even the air had a deserted cast. There were no cars in the parking lot beyond the courtyard. The absence of noise was almost annoying; no footsteps to the garbage cans; nothing to distract me, so that as I wrote the words, it seemed as if the written dialogue had its own sound and thundered distantly in my mind. That would have alarmed me in any case, but unfortunately, this was only the beginning.

The sounds grew louder, and as if they were real, they echoed through the nearly empty building. Everything in this place is metal or concrete, it seems, and sounds are always intensified. But these had to be imagined sounds! The chattering of Queen Alice and Ram-Ram's damn chuckles, and even the shouts of the audience at the televised ballgame—all of these rose, and echoed through the entire building. Yet they couldn't have, of course, since the sounds belonged at the mental institution I had visited the day before. So I told myself.

As the sounds grew louder, however, another more bizarre intensification took place, one I'm quite embarrassed to describe. Certainly the entire affair will cast doubts upon my own sanity if and when this manuscript is ever read.

But, just as described in the previous chapter of the book itself, the air seemed to thicken into pseudo-shapes until, as I typed, the scenes were before my eyes that I had actually witnessed the day before at the institution! That is, as the scenes were described, I saw them. The entire common room, with all of the patients, was somehow transposed here, over the contents of my normal living room, so that in a manner of speaking, the book came alive. Nor did the effect end when the description of the affair was done, or with my own exit from the scene. Instead, the insane-god nightmare, or whatever it was, also came alive for me. The feelings of desolation were quite shattering; and I was also involved in the Virgin Mary fiasco and the Buddha scene as well.

When Will was told to waken in his physical body, the dictation ended for the day. I left the typewriter with a sense of great relief, and closed my eyes. But I swear that when I closed them, I looked out of Will's eyes for just a moment and saw the communal room that had been described earlier in the book. I cried out in true alarm, and at once everything returned to normal.

But I had seen enough, apparently through Will's eyes, to trigger a most regrettable response on my part. I saw the poster of Buddha hanging above Will's bed; and following his gaze, a kitchen sink stacked with dirty dishes; a plastic geranium crudded with grease plopped in a coffee cup. That was all, but it was enough. I knew that Will started retching, even though when I cried out, I stood in my own living room.

The scene disappeared, but Will's mood, his memory of the insane-god sequence, or his unaccustomed revulsion at the poster of the Buddha, added up to an emotional turmoil that struck me with full force. I told myself time and time again that Will was simply a character in a book, yet I knew that my own response was far stronger than the kind of identification given to fictional heroes or antiheroes. Memories that I'd purposely suppressed for years rushed almost revengefully into my mind, and with them came all of the attitudes about life that I'd had at the time the events occurred—the time of my own undergraduate studies.

Certainly I didn't live as Will does, or does in this damnable book, but I wished then that I had. How romantic communal living seemed, until, at least, I imagined the intimacy from which there would be no escape. But I recalled with dismay my own brief but intense intellectual journey into Buddhism and various Eastern religions, an episode that until today I had almost completely forgotten. Worse, my own attitudes toward life at that time now returned to assail me, until I realized that I had never forsaken them but only hidden them from conscious awareness.

I barely consider life worth living. How long have I really felt this way?

I would not give my seed back to the earth because I did not agree with the conditions of life.

More, I realize now that I see the universe and everything in it as the accidental chemical creation of mindless elements, with life itself springing from the semen of some insane cosmic Frankenstein—chemicals gone mad, forming a world without reason, and certainly devoid of purpose. So to that degree, Will's insane god and mine were the same, though his was an offshoot of religion, and mine of science.

Those feelings of desolation came crushingly close, reviving long-forgotten, only half-remembered thoughts of suicide: suicide as a rational man's only method of maintaining honor in a world without rules, in which each species survives only by being craftier than another. These realizations, so long buried, were bad enough. With them came the shame of a condemnation I could not escape, for I saw that in my investigations of rats and in my experiments with them, I took out my revenge against the world by literally mutilating the brains of rodents; out of sheer rage. And with this understanding, I fell down on the couch, covered my face with my hands, and wept.

A fine way for a professor of psychology to act! So I tried to examine my own feelings in order to clear my mind. Nothing worked. And nothing could erase my sense of outrage that Ram-Ram and myself were turning into characters in a book—a book written by my fingers, but not by my mind. And I wondered: How could *that* be an accident? I still couldn't see any purpose in the entire affair, yet the wild series of crazy events seem to hint of some strange order that exists completely outside the usual kind of purpose or design.

Why did I care if Will committed suicide? Or, for that matter, if Lydia decided to be born again or not? Yet I suddenly realized that I cared, deeply, and that my anxiety about both issues had been growing steadily, even though I'd resolutely tried to banish such thoughts whenever they came unbidden into my mind. So I asked myself another question: Did Lydia in some way remind me of Sarah? Did I, in my own grotesque imagination, suppose that the birth of Sarah's child was somehow dependent upon Lydia's decision to be reborn? The utter nonsense of such musings strikes me with the deepest scorn, yet I cannot escape realizing that I have, indeed, made such impossible identifications and associations.

Moreover, I don't trust Lydia's decision to be reborn as given in the last chapter. She could change her mind overnight. I'm led to think that there can be no logic at all to these imaginative dissertations of mine, for I also imagine that Sarah and Bianka are *both* waiting for childbirth while (oh, dear Lord) the stubborn Lydia still dallies. At the same time, an irrational-enough hope seizes me, as if Lydia's pilgrimage might yet lead to the discovery of life's purposes; and this despite the fact that I do not admit the existence of the soul (Oversoul Seven to the contrary). And from these skeins of irrationality, how can I possibly have any hopes?

Beside this, though, a general exhaustion overtakes me. I sit here waiting for more dictation. For the first time, almost weak with suspense, I know that the book must be finished, and that I must learn the outcome. And new fears assail me. Suppose whoever or whatever is giving me this manuscript suddenly decides to withhold it?

Chapter Twenty-one

Stage Fright and Preparations for Birth

Oversoul Seven grinned at Cyprus and said, "I hope it isn't as difficult to get Lydia through her birth as it was to get her through her last death. She wouldn't believe that she was dead for the longest time, in her terms, of course. Suppose she doesn't believe in her new birth as Tweety either?"

Seven materialized as the fourteen-year-old male to complement Cyprus's image as a young woman teacher. The two of them stood in a replica of the room in which Lydia would be born, and Seven looked around with a worried air. "These rehearsals always confuse me," he said. "I think I've got it all right. There's the cradle and bureau, complete with linen in the drawers. Everything is perfect seventeenth century. And I've explained Lydia's role to her time and time again. I think she has it down pat: how to orient physically inside the baby, how to organize her perceptions."

Seven had started counting the points he'd mentioned on his fingers, but Cyprus said, "Stop that, Seven. When you worry about details like that, you always make me nervous."

"Details," Seven said, indignantly. "Easy for you to talk! You just instruct, and I'm out in the field, so to speak. Uh, oh—" He broke off, staring at the cradle. He'd materialized it all right. There it stood, made of lovely earth oak wood, but he'd forgotten to make it solid in space, so that even though the shape was right, it stuck up like a piece of flat board.

"It's a good thing that this is just a class situation," Cyprus said, "or you'd be in trouble. No real baby would fit into *that* cradle. Talk about details!"

"Well, I'm glad this isn't an examination because I lose points on details in every examination I take," Seven said. "There, the cradle's right now." He grinned and added, "My marvelous inventiveness makes up for a lot."

Cyprus tried not to smile, and she said with just a gentle touch of severity, "Well, remember, you have to make sure that *everything* is in readiness for Lydia's birth as Tweety. I presume the new parents are all prepared, and that they have all of the necessary background information?"

"Right. Absolutely," Seven said, briskly. "I've talked to Josef over and over in his dream state. He understands why he and Lydia chose to be father and daughter; or rather, why he and Tweety have."

"And Bianka?"

"Bianka understands that she and Lydia will have, uh, certain creative conflicts, in order to help each other resolve challenges they want to work out. But they'll love each other just the same. And—"

Seven broke off again—and groaned. Josef suddenly appeared, wearing a toga. He strode angrily across the room and stood in front of Oversoul Seven. "Here you are in one of my dreams again," he said almost threateningly. "Or I'm in one of yours. I can never tell the difference. I'm in terrible trouble, and you've got to help me."

Cyprus dematerialized diplomatically.

Seven said, "Josef, you do this all the time, come and bother me when you're not supposed to. What is it now?"

Josef began to stride nervously back and forth, scratching his dream head and glowering at Seven. "I never know when I'll have one of these crazy dreams, and I never know what to do in them," he said. "But I knew I'd find you somehow. Now my wife is going to have a baby at any moment. How will I get my painting done? She's made my studio over into a nursery, just to rub it in." He glowered at Seven again. His brown moustache quivered. "I wasn't cut out to be a father," he wailed. "I wasn't even cut out to be a husband." He sat down on the bed, and Seven grinned: The bed creaked just like a real one; not bad for a hallucination, he thought. But Josef put his head in his hands and looked about ready to cry.

"Come on," Seven said, "we've been through all this ten times. You said that you wanted to be a father, so you could understand corporeal creativity as well as creativity through art . . . so you could help form a new life and study living art."

"Well, I take it all back," Josef moaned. "A painter has enough problems; he has no right to father babies. Paintings don't cry and smell and take a woman's attention."

"Why, you're jealous of Tweety already," Seven exclaimed, almost scandalized.

"Bianka's giving her my old studio," Josef shouted, "I didn't know she was going to do that."

"Tweety's going to be your greatest model," Seven said. "She might even coax you into being a really good artist."

"I'd rather use the cat for a model," Josef said, thundering now. "And this is all your fault."

"We oversouls get blamed for everything," said Seven,

shrugging his fourteen-year-old shoulders. "You told me that you wanted to be a father. You and Lydia met in the dream state and settled on each other as parent and child. Bianka went along for her own reasons, but it was all your idea."

Josef looked up, craftily. "Someone told me once that if a woman was shown a black cat, she'd lose her baby," he said.

"It isn't true. It's superstitious nonsense," Seven said quickly and emphatically.

"How do *you* know so much?" Josef asked. "I keep forgetting who you are."

"I'm your *soul*," Seven cried, exasperated. "And that's some job, let me tell you." Seven sighed and turned into the image of an old man, because it was always easier for him to handle Josef that way.

"Oh, it's the old man I see in my dreams. Thank God," Josef said with obvious relief. "Did you hear what I was saying?"

"I did," Seven said, kindly and wisely. He had a white beard, white hair, and the saintliest blue eyes imaginable.

Josef started all over again. "My wife's going to have a baby. Just earlier today, I felt wonderful thinking about it. But now I'm filled with doubts. Besides that, I'm scared and feel like a coward. I should be feeling paternal, and acting like a tower of strength or something like that."

"You can feel any way you want to," Seven said.

"I can?" Josef said, with surprise.

"It's quite natural to be upset and have mixed feelings. Here, I have someone who might make you feel better," Seven said, and mentally he called for Lydia. She materialized in an instant—very cleverly, Seven thought, as a lovely young woman several years younger than Josef.

"Oh, it's you," she said. "You're getting cold feet, are you? Never mind. So am I! How odd it really is. Imagine me being a baby? And calling you Daddy? Or Dadda? Or what shall I call you?"

"Oh, God," Josef said, sputtering and laughing all at once. "I remember the whole thing now."

"This is how I'll look when I'm grown up. Won't I make a great model for you?"

"Model?" Josef said, making a grab for her and grinning.

"Let's not let things get out of hand," Seven said. "Josef, do you feel better now?"

Josef kept grinning and nodding.

"Well, you both have to get out of here then," Seven said. "You're sure it's all settled?"

Josef and Lydia shook hands almost formally. "I feel much better," Josef said. Then he exclaimed "Oh," and disappeared.

"What happened?" Lydia asked.

"He must have awakened, or something startled his body," Seven answered. "But technically, you shouldn't be here either. I'm rehearsing the, uh, inner mechanics involved in the birth. I *did* want you to reassure Josef, though. Now have *you* any more questions?"

"No. Right now I feel fine. How I'll feel when I actually take up residence in a baby's body may be something else again, though." She grinned jauntily and said with a laugh, "It can't be any more confusing than being old and senile, and I got through that all right. But when do I actually become Tweety?"

Seven turned back into his fourteen-year-old image. "I told you, it's your choice, really," he said. "You can become Tweety at the physical birth or just before, or just after. Babies have a body consciousness, and the self or spirit comes in when it wants to, so to speak, of course. But the body consciousness gets lonely if you wait too long; it needs support. But really, you'll just know the proper time."

Lydia smiled and took the form of the old woman she'd been before her death. She had a visor cap set askew on cropped white hair; she wore a pair of slacks, a shirt, and held a cigarette in her hand. "Funny, such a comfortable image in a way," she said. "It sort of heightens the contrast,

187

when I think of being a child again. On the other hand, it makes me feel older than Josef, who's going to be my father. I hope I can handle him all right."

"That's no way for a daughter to talk," Seven said. He started to laugh, but suddenly Lydia turned serious.

She said soberly, "Remember, though, you promised to do something special for me, or for Tweety; to give us some kind of knowledge to compensate for all the distortions we've discovered about the gods. And it must be something a child can understand."

"I promised, and I'll do it," Seven said. "And it *will* give you some inner guidelines to begin your new life."

"And you won't forget me, I mean, *me, Lydia?*" she asked.

"Never. And besides, it doesn't work that way. Good-bye for now, dear Lydia," he said, and Lydia disappeared.

Oversoul Seven waited somewhat nervously for Cyprus to materialize.

"I see you have your work cut out for you," she said, reappearing.

"Have I? I'll say I have," Seven said, grinning all over his fourteen-year-old face. "Aren't they something, though, my personalities? Aren't they unique? I *do* hope they manage everything all right."

Chapter Twenty-two

A Birth

Bianka was definitely in the final stages of labor this time; scared and sweaty; and worse, she still wasn't sure if she wanted the baby who even now was kicking for release. Josef came in now and then, terrified, his hefty weight balanced as carefully as he could so no squeaking floorboards would announce his presence, in which case Bianka's mother would scream and chase him from the room. He could hardly see, anyhow, for the steam from the boiling water that fogged the windows and cleared his sinuses at the same time. He felt frantic. If he'd known that childbirth was so . . . agonizing, would he have left Bianka alone? He squinted his brown eyes with dismay. No, nothing would have kept him away from that lusty body of hers. And in his mind's eye, he saw the two of them in puppylike embrace, filled with an ecstasy that left him confused and triumphant at once.

"Get out," Mrs. Hosentauf screamed. "At least when you're drunk you aren't under foot."

"Josef," cried Bianka, "I'm almost ready."

"Out! Out!" yelled Mrs. Hosentauf.

"AArrr," yelled Josef back, but he lumbered out of the room with one anguished look at Bianka. She'd be small again after the birth, he thought, with a sense of elation he felt guilty about at once; and she'd be his again. And while all of this was going on, Lydia invisibly prowled about the room.

Bianka moaned and closed her eyes, and as she did so, some part of Lydia responded, fluttered, searched for freedom; sought for a beginning in which she could grow into being from a different angle. Suddenly something inside Lydia's personal reality turned as clear as cellophane. She could see through herself—through her subjective surface to her core—and as she did, she felt an exquisite acquiescence and exhilaration, and at the same time, a thrust of aggressive action so strong that it seemed to propel her into a creativity that was too fast to follow.

Oversoul Seven was there, and Lydia felt her experience merge with his, or his with hers. Yet, conversely, her own independence was never clearer. Even now, she could accept new birth or reject it, and if she refused it, there would be other choices. Yet how dear and solitary that bedroom looked, a tableau tucked in time and an infant about to be born in a house anonymous to history. Yet in that birth, or any birth, she suddenly knew that the unknown universe recreated itself into new knowing.

"Quick, the boiling water," Mrs. Hosentauf shouted.

Bianka was only half conscious. The labor pains felt like worlds cracking in her womb, as if more than a baby wanted out . . . as if, she gasped, as if a god wanted out! She caught the blasphemy, tried to mutter, "Forgive me, Lord," in response to her training, yet some wildly triumphant knowledge shouted that, yes, a god wanted out. The god was part her, part Josef, but mostly it was the earth turning into god, and god turning into earth all at once.

The last rays of sunlight struck at the windowpane, one ray leaping through the steamy room, and Lydia felt herself go out into the universe, disperse triumphantly into numberless knowing particles of consciousness, each shaken, cleansed, glowing, and renewed, and coming back together in a new configuration drawn by the shining door that was Bianka's womb, from which, knowing and unknowing, the infant now emerged.

Lydia felt herself sifted through the experiences of Bianka and Josef; woke up inside their molecules so that each of their most unconscious memories were implanted in the infant. She fell through Bianka and Josef's realities back through *their* parents' lives, and back further in dizzying descent; so that in sequences impossible to follow, she touched upon the consciousness and reality of each being ever born. She fell through the chromosomes of Christ and Mohammed, of Mary and the gods of Olympus as they are known to man, and saw that all of them still live, sifted through man's consciousness—distorted yet recreated with each birth, and with each creative thought or vision, with each impulse. Somehow she had to impart that knowledge to Tweety.

"There are no gods to be found," Seven said, "because they were never lost. They're so hidden in ourselves, so much a part of us and everything else, that they just *are;* everywhere. Yet nowhere."

"Feel your own knowing right now," Cyprus advised gently.

And Lydia, inside the infant, stretched her consciousness and felt earth's great endurance; and all of nature's parts were guests to the birth so that she was aware of endless dusks and dawns, numberless seasons, and felt the sweet couch of existence that supported her with such immense safety that it hinted of a love beyond any condemnation—

as the universe in each infant, and in herself, opened its eyes again; *again,* yet for the first time.

The infant slept.

Lydia roused; frightened a bit now by the sense of unity. She wiggled around inside her own consciousness and her own individuality snapped back like a rubber band. She was frightened again: Where had she gone when she'd forgotten herself?

Chapter Twenty-three

After-Birth Complications in Which Lydia Wakes Up in a Probable Life

Inside the baby, Lydia scowled, figuratively speaking. It seemed almost unbelievable that she couldn't talk. So this was what rebirth or any kind of birth was! It certainly wasn't very dignified, and it presented all sorts of difficulties that she'd (conveniently?) forgotten when she decided to be born again.

Again? Or was she being born in many times and places all at once, as Oversoul Seven maintained?

"Of course you are, dear Lydia," Oversoul Seven said.

Lydia saw him mentally. Her eyes, or rather, Tweety's weren't focusing properly, but in any case, Seven and Cyprus weren't visible to Bianka or Josef.

"Seven is here to help you handle the situation intelligently," Cyprus said, "and I'm here to see how well *he* does. But really, Lydia, there's no need to be nervous. None at all."

"We really should call Lydia 'Tweety' now, shouldn't we?" Seven asked. "Or is she still Lydia, learning to be Tweety?"

The baby set up such a howl that Bianka cried, "Josef, listen to her. What shall we do? Her face is all red."

"Arrarh," Josef thundered. "Do something. I'm afraid to touch her."

"Don't yell. You'll frighten her," Bianka cried.

"Josef hasn't changed. I can see that," Oversoul Seven said. "But you took his character into consideration when you decided to be his daughter, of course."

"I suppose it's too late to pull out now?" Lydia asked dryly.

Cyprus smiled. "You sound so much like Seven when you talk like that, but that's to be expected. He's your soul, after all."

The baby quieted. Bianka and Josef tiptoed into the next room. "Thank heaven," Lydia said. She slipped out of Tweety's body and joined Seven and Cyprus by the cradle. Lydia appeared as a young woman of about twenty. She strode vigorously about the room, puffing on a hallucinatory cigarette.

"They don't have cigarettes like that in the seventeenth century, by the way," Cyprus said. She appeared as another young woman for Lydia's benefit. Seven couldn't decide what form to take, so he tried several until Cyprus asked him to settle down.

"I can't help being nervous," he said. "I'm supposed to help Lydia, but how can I when she insists on pacing the room like that?"

"You'd pace the room too, if you were being born again, and into the seventeenth century after you died in the twentieth," Lydia retorted.

"But I *am*," Seven answered. "That's one of the main issues of all this. Only you're the . . . part of me that's closer to the experience." Seven looked hopefully to Cyprus, who said, "You're doing fine; explain it to her yourself."

"That sounds like I'm not myself, just a part of you," Lydia said, puffing on the cigarette.

Tweety started to cry again.

"Oh, hell," Lydia muttered.

"That's no attitude," Seven started to say, but all of a sudden he couldn't get his footing, and with good reason. He was trying to stand up in three different rooms at once. So, seeing his predicament, he dematerialized and regained his balance. Then he realized what was wrong. He was seeing too many times at once, because in one room Lydia was dying in the twentieth century: He recognized at once the surroundings in the old peoples' rest home where she died, but it took a minute for him to put the picture into the correct sequence. In the second room, transposed over the first one, Lydia was being born as Tweety in the seventeenth century, and that was where she belonged in her Now. And in the third room, she was dying again in the life that she was just beginning.

"Seven, stop drifting," Cyprus called from the second room, and sheepishly Seven returned, and stood by Tweety's bedside. He grinned: The baby's head was as fresh as a peach, only two soft open eyes staring up at him, quite like a peach suddenly given sight, he thought; and looking out from itself.

"Will I lose all of my own memories?" Lydia asked anxiously. "I will, won't I?"

"Now don't start worrying about that again," Cyprus answered. "If Seven can remember who *he* is, you certainly can. Attaining to your soulhood is much more taxing in its way; but you don't have to worry about that yet."

Seven frowned. "I wish you'd stop just staring at that baby, Lydia," he said. "You have to identify with her sooner or later. Procrastinating doesn't help matters. You aren't thinking of putting it off at this late date, are you?"

Lydia's eyes flew open. "I never thought of *that*. I didn't

195

realize that I still could change my mind," she exclaimed.

Cyprus said sternly, "Seven! You aren't helping matters one bit. You're just making the whole thing more difficult."

.Seven grimaced, took the form of an earnest young man, and paced the room. "Well, maybe," he said. "But Lydia's one of my personalities after all. She has the right to know that she *can* change her mind, though it's true that such things are frowned upon. You'd have to get a replacement now, Lydia, and someone who's interested in seventeenth-century life. People are very touchy about which centuries they get born into, and the seventeenth century isn't a favorite, in case you're interested. Some wouldn't touch it with a—"

"Seven, that's enough," Cyprus interrupted. "Lydia, try to relax. Just because you're fond of the seventeenth century, Seven doesn't have to be, of course. But he isn't being very diplomatic, either."

The baby stirred. "It's a living organism," Cyprus said gently. "Prepared for you, waiting for your consciousness to make it human. Now it has body consciousness, but no self in your terms. Are you going to give it selfhood or not? Some individuals enter the baby before birth, as you know, and some after. But you *are* dawdling some."

Seven grinned.

Lydia said, almost laughing, "How could I *not*, after that? Of course I will. I just got stage fright, that's all. I know I'm not saying good-bye to myself, but becoming another self while not losing what I am. I'll do my best for Tweety, as Tweety. I'll—"

But the oddest thing was happening, and Lydia opened her eyes to a scene of such suddenly recalled delight that she cried out. There was her bedroom, surely hers, with sun-splashed wallpaper and white ruffled curtains. She was looking down at the bedcovers from the viewpoint of someone sitting up in bed. She was staring at . . . yes, the baby in her arms. She'd just given birth a short while ago; but to whom?

Let me hold this scene, this moment, she thought desperately.

The baby was—oh God, real, still birth-smelly, whatever that meant, and hers, hers, hers! She chanted, dizzy with elation; the warm living curve of her sunshiny arms filled with that new, solid, wiggling flesh. And, how curious, the baby's eyes were so clear, like a tiny animal's, knowing yet unknowing. She'd write a poem about it later, but not now. Only where was Roger? And what was the baby's name? Why couldn't she remember? Suddenly she was scared, and the baby looked almost unfamiliar and strange.

"Roger?" she called. "Rog?"

He came hurrying in, a towel over his arm. "What's wrong?"

And seeing him, so substantial and *there* and solid, for someone so bony and gawky, she started laughing and crying at once. "Oh God, I don't know. I took a nap, as you suggested, and when I woke up, I couldn't remember Rog Junior's name. There, see, I know it now! But my own baby's name! And the room seemed so funny, and I had the feeling of doing all this before."

"Crazy puss," Roger said, bending down to kiss her; but she looked up at him and thought: Now who was *that?* His face was kind, anxious, loving, with funny off-center eyes. But who was it?

"Who is *that?*" Oversoul Seven asked Cyprus.

"You should know," Cyprus answered. "It's Roger, Lydia's husband."

Cyprus and Seven stood invisibly by the bed, and Lydia didn't see them any more than Roger did. Then Lydia began crying.

"Come on," Roger said. "You told me yourself that new mothers can expect all sorts of goofy feelings at first. Forget it. You'll scare the baby. Anyhow, I was going to bring you in a dish of fresh peaches. See what a handy husband I am?"

"Peaches!" Lydia exclaimed. "That's it. I was dreaming about babies and peaches. Or *something*. But God, I must look a wreck. Is my nose all red from crying? Maybe it's the stupid drugs the doctors give you during delivery. No, they wouldn't affect me now, would they?" She paused. "I'm still confused, though. What the devil is the date?"

Roger went "Tut, tut, tut," made a mock bow, and said, "Madame, it's October 18, 1927. Is there anything else you want to know? I'm your personal information service."

Lydia's eyes widened. "Now I remember," she cried. "I was dreaming about the seventeenth century for some reason, and when I woke up, I didn't know where the devil I was." She shivered and added, "Look, the baby's sleeping. God knows what *he's* dreaming about! Put him in the crib, would you? Well, at least I'm flat now and not big as an elephant. I'm going to get up and dress and—"

"Don't drink too much tonight, though, hon. It isn't good for new mothers," Roger said, regretting his words at once.

"Oh, you had to say that, didn't you?" she shouted. "You had to spoil this beautiful afternoon."

"What do you mean, beautiful afternoon? A few minutes ago, you were crying, and I cheered you up," Roger shouted back.

"What's going on?" Seven asked anxiously. "Lydia's in the wrong life. I thought maybe she was just reliving a memory, but she's really into this! She just finished that life. That baby is her son, Roger."

"So I see," Cyprus answered dryly. "Seven, all lives are parallel, you know that. Otherwise Lydia couldn't have gone from the twentieth century to the seventeenth."

"Yes, yes. I know. In theory that works. But in practice, well, Lydia is supposed to be a baby, Tweety, right now. She's not supposed to be *having* a baby in the twentieth century. How do I get her back on the right track?" Seven paused for only a moment, and went on. "Look at her," he said. "Now I remember this particular day! If we don't stop her, she'll live that life all over again, won't she? And that was the day she fell in love with Lawrence, husband or no, and—"

Seven was so upset he dematerialized even to Cyprus, turning into a worried swirl of air that rushed around inside itself. "I've got to stop her," he said, wordlessly, of course. "I'm her soul, after all. And what about Tweety? Cyprus, I'm really upset. Now, help me."

Cyprus sighed and said, "Stop that swirling. You'll make yourself dizzy."

Seven stopped, and turned into a small white worried human face that was invisible to everyone but Cyprus. "Don't you understand what might happen?" he asked. "Lydia has free will, you know."

"Well, of course she has."

"That makes it worse, don't you see? I can't understand why you aren't concerned. If she falls in love with Lawrence today, she'll have to go through the whole thing again. But with free will, suppose she *doesn't* fall in love with him?"

"I don't follow you," Cyprus said, trying not to smile.

"That's exactly what worries me," Seven cried. "You're supposed to be my teacher, but in earth-type orientation I'm beginning to wonder. If Lydia doesn't fall in love with Lawrence, or if she uses her free will to change anything at all in this life, she'll alter everything else. And maybe she won't even be born as Tweety!"

"Seven, look!" Cyprus directed. The whole house opened to Seven's vision; and on the doorstep stood a young man in an opera cape. He carried a bouquet of flowers, and looked so jaunty and pleased with himself, and so conscious of the fine figure he cut, that Cyprus started laughing.

But Oversoul Seven was nearly in a frenzy. "It's Lawrence," he cried. "And he's alone, just like he was the last time this happened. He mustn't go in until I get Lydia out of this and back where she belongs."

"Seven, come back," Cyprus called. But it was too late. Seven changed into a small angry October wind that rushed around the edges of the porch eaves outside, rustled the flowers in Lawrence's hands, and blew his cape out suddenly so that Lawrence shouted, "Whoo! What a wind!"

"Don't go inside," Seven sent the thought directly into Lawrence's mind. "You mustn't go in there." And the wind wrenched the bouquet from Lawrence's hands and sent the flowers flying across the porch, down the steps, and past the geraniums that Lydia had planted by the walk.

"*Damn*nation!" Lawrence shouted, chasing the bouquet.

Seven returned to Lydia's room to find Cyprus smiling a smile in which serenity and amusement were equally mixed. She said, "Do sit down and enjoy Lydia. I'll explain it all to you later. You cause yourself so much trouble. Needlessly."

Lydia was magnificent, Seven had to agree. She was applying makeup from small jars, holding her head so proudly, tilting it to get just the right effect. The dress she wore was very short, with a flounce. Her stockings were sheer and black. Her cropped black hair lay almost flat against her head. She was putting on a pair of triangular silver earrings; and suddenly Seven realized when he'd seen them before.

"Those were the earrings that caught Lawrence's fancy," he shouted. "Lydia, do you know what you're doing? Take those earrings off at once. Come back where you belong. In a few moments you'll see Lawrence in that dumb cape for the first time and fall in love with him. Then I'll never get you out of here. And if you *don't* fall in love with him, I don't know what kind of trouble you'll get us into, because then you'll change everything!"

Roger came into the bedroom. "Ready, hon?" he asked. "I just saw Lawrence coming up the walk. His girl isn't with him, though." He stopped and said, reprovingly, "You're smoking, and you know that's not supposed to be good for—"

"Young mothers; yeah, I know," Lydia said, glowering at him. "You just don't think smoking is feminine, that's all. Well, I'll smoke if I want to."

Seven shouted, "Lydia. Come with me at once."

Cyprus said gently, "Seven, it's no use. Lydia didn't believe she had a soul in that life. And she didn't believe in hearing voices inside her head either. She won't hear a thing you say."

"You just don't understand," Seven exclaimed. "You're too . . . remote. Lydia's my personality, and—" He broke off, groaning, as a grinning, disheveled Lawrence, disarmingly devilish in his infernal cape, stood triumphantly just inside the open front door, his cheeks red from the autumn air. And Lydia stood in the hallway, staring at him; hooked, Seven thought. He turned to Cyprus with dismay.

Lawrence said, "I had the funniest feeling that you didn't want me to come inside. Like something was trying to keep me out."

"Don't be silly. Nothing could be further from the truth." Lydia smiled and came out into the living room while Roger closed the front door. Without knowing why, Roger suddenly felt sad, and watching him, Seven wondered how much Roger knew or remembered. Lydia was obviously ignorant of what was really happening.

And Lawrence was positively gleeful. Roger looked at him and said, uncomfortably, "What happened to your girl?"

"She couldn't make it," Lawrence said cheerfully. "You'll have to share Lydia with me for the evening."

"Why, that's pretty flippant," Lydia said, laughing. She threw herself down on the couch.

"Something else is wrong," Seven said to Cyprus. "I just remembered; Lawrence is supposed to be a good deal younger than Lydia. They fell in love under these circumstances, only she was so much older that the whole idea seemed ridiculous at first. She was at least ten years older, and— "

"And now?" Cyprus asked.

She and Seven were two points of light hovering near the ceiling. Seven looked down and said, "Wait, I'm getting it, I think. Creativity happens constantly, and all existences are open-ended, so somehow Lydia and Lawrence *are* doing it differently this time. They're more or less the same age. But what about Tweety?"

"Let's see for ourselves," Cyprus said. "Watch."

Cyprus and Seven looked down again. The baby, Roger Junior, was crying. Lydia got up and went in to quiet him.

"What a crybaby," she exclaimed; then bending closer, she was struck by the living miracles of his eyes, so clear and brilliant and incredibly dear . . .

Someone was saying, "You see, your memories are alive, and even changeable. You can live them, in all of their dimensions, so there's no need to worry that you'll ever forget your experiences."

For a moment, Lydia didn't know where she was or who was speaking. Then she saw the baby in the cradle and realized that she was standing there too, with Cyprus and Seven.

"*This* baby is Tweety," Seven said, grinning. "And we're back in the seventeenth century."

Lydia stared at the room. It looked as real and solid as the other one had.

"Sit down," Cyprus laughed, "and I'll explain what happened."

"Yes, I wish you would," Seven said a bit tartly.

Lydia nodded. She looked so confused that Oversoul Seven hallucinated a cigarette and lit it for her.

Cyprus said, "Lydia, when you're involved with any birth, then through association you remember other birth experiences sometimes, when you were born, or when you gave birth. Often death experiences are connected in the same way. Except that your memories live, and this time you creatively changed them so that you and Lawrence were the same age. Your father—your *new* father, Josef—can't bear to copy a painting, for example. So when you relived your memories, you changed the circumstances instead of copying them. When you're outside of strict three-dimensional reference, you have considerable freedom with your own experience."

"And *your* experiences form the basis of Tweety's unconscious," Seven said triumphantly.

"I'm glad you understand," Cyprus said.

Seven blushed and said to Lydia, "I forgot too. And when I got confused earlier with the three rooms, then that, plus your confusion, triggered your twentieth-century memories and the whole episode."

"But how many lives can you live at once?" asked Lydia, sounding exasperated.

"You're usually aware of only one at a time," Cyprus answered, smiling. "But before you're really all the way into a life, you're often conscious of—"

Seven interrupted. Looking at Cyprus suspiciously, he said, "I have a feeling that there's more to this than you're letting on. But never mind; Lydia and I can handle whatever comes up. And come on, Lydia. You really have to identify with Tweety now. You just can't go flicking in and out all the time."

Lydia said, "And to think that I used to think that when you were dead, you were just dead and that was the end of it! But this is too much. And I'm wondering: How real was the Lawrence I just met? And what about Roger? And when Lawrence and I meet as cousins, will we remember anything at all? And—"

"See, I told you," Oversoul Seven said. "In your present state of development, you need one life to put yourself into. Otherwise you just get all confused."

"As *you* did, Seven," Cyprus said. "And still do. But

Lydia, by entering fully into Tweety, you journey into the source of creativity. And from this, with your cooperation, the self-consciousness of Tweety will emerge."

Lydia smiled and tried to answer, but suddenly she felt so drawn to the baby that everything else slipped away from her attention.

Chapter Twenty-four

The Birth of Self-Consciousness for Tweety

Cyprus said, "Look at me, Seven. There's something that you must do so that Tweety's new consciousness can be born from Lydia, and yet be unique and hers alone." As Cyprus spoke she began to spin, quicker and quicker, and the motion turned into sound. Oversoul Seven found himself staring at the sound of Cyprus into which, unaccountably, she had vanished. The first sound was a long, deep, drawn-out one and Seven didn't know how to deal with it. Its resonance was so steady and ponderous that it seemed to be the utterance of all physical matter; the heavy voice of mass on mass, or weight on ancient weight. He blinked. How could Cyprus or any part of her sound so . . . *massive?*

He, himself, felt suddenly heavy too, as if he weighed more than worlds, and he began to sink into something (or through something); yet dropping with no sensation of speed or even of motion. How could you fall without feeling motion? he wondered. But the sound had him in its spell. Within it, he was aware of incredibly slow thoughts that took centuries to speak, that were dragged out across the ages, trailing syllables each heavier than the most massive rock imaginable; and of a consciousness so slow, in his terms, that galaxies could rise and fall in one second of its time.

Seven was frightened. By now, Cyprus had disappeared so completely into the sound that he despaired of ever finding her again. And he felt himself congealing within it; its long tones turned his consciousness into something else, so that his own thoughts had the oddest *weight* to them. He was dropping into a deeper mode of feeling than he'd ever known.

"Cyprus, where are you?" he called frantically. Yet even his fright had a slow, heavy sureness about it, and his thoughts sounded drawn-out in his mind, as if they began in some ancient past, finally to emerge in a distant future. The syllables were so slow that by the time Cyprus heard them... if she ever did... he wouldn't need her help, or he'd be beyond all help.

In fact, by the time the first syllable, Cy (of Cyprus), rang through his awareness, he himself had finished the thought that was still being expressed. The sounds in slow motion, deep and ponderous, kept going out from him at an ever slower rate. Again, each vowel was so heavy that Seven felt he could grab onto it for support.

The next sound, wh (from *where*), began and this time Seven could feel its weird mass, so without knowing how he did so, he clung to it. (For dear life, he said later to Cyprus, who laughed.) The sound was falling, and he with it, "whwhwhwhwhwhwhwhwhwhwhere."

"Souls are eternal," Seven thought, so the sound couldn't carry him beyond the time of his being into... And as he thought, the first vowel (of *soul*) started out, stretching, still only beginning to sound when he'd finished the sentence. All the while, the last thought—the cry for Cyprus—was still not yet half formed into sound; and the last syllable, ere (of *where*), went echoing all around him, while the "souls" from the last thought just began to thunder.

Finally Seven couldn't think at all, bombarded by all those belated vowels and syllables. He still clung to the whwh (of *where*) that stretched outward, somehow continually constructing itself without finishing the word. It was a bridge of sound to which he hung, dazed, because now he realized that the sounds really had *mass*. And that mass grew and thickened. Each vowel and syllable, still sounding, fell. Yet a trail of mass built up behind them, and did not disappear. Instead, the sounds formed structures in space, or *of* space.

And the structures were aware.

They had come out of the sound into which Cyprus had disappeared.

For the first time, Seven wondered: Had he disappeared into the sound too? Was he a sound now, and his thoughts variations of what he was? It was all impossible, he thought (or tried to think), when the first syllable of the sentence instantly began its slow, ponderous, undeviating journey. He would have cried, but he didn't know how to—and who knew what sounds *that* would make?

But now, curiously, his own inner thoughts slowed down too, and there was nothing he could do about it. His consciousness sank to some deeper level where thoughts-as-sounds grew out of him like trees from the earth, slowly yet automatically, with great sureness and strength.

A strange triumph seized him, an acquiescent exultation, the feeling of being himself a source; though he didn't understand exactly what this meant. He had sunken as far down as he could. Into what? The heavy long sounds? The resonance? Had he . . . congealed? And his thoughts sprang up slowly out of him, from him, with slow majesty, forming structures that sounded when the words were finished. They were like buildings of sound finally completed, or worlds of matter and form rising from sounds within sounds.

Within him was a slow, sure peace. He wasn't frightened anymore.

> He felt his massive endurance,
> The strength of creativity, sure of
>   itself, unending.
> He rested, while his thoughts kept
>   growing out of him,
> Around him,
> Above and below him.
> The sounds of his thoughts formed
>   into shapes and images.
> In a slow-motion dance, the
>   vowels and syllables
> Congregated, thickened,
>   congealed,
> Until they turned into
> Flowers and trees all around him,
> With him in the center,
> Assured, at peace, creating.
> A bird came to life
> When a vowel joined another,
> Meeting, clicking together
> In seamless commotion.
> And from this came the worlds
> In which his personalities had
> Their living,
> And Seven knew
>   He'd fallen
>   Into the
>   Ground of his being.

"The chord was struck out of which you emerge, said, from another dimension.

The first vowel started out. It would be centuries before the next one reached him, and Cyprus smiled; knowing, wise, aroused and yet unaroused, from the ground of *her* being; from which Seven emerged and was still emerging.

From which Tweety was emerging, in a new Now of being, rising into self-consciousness, yet claiming a consciousness that had always been hers; that now rushed into her knowing.

Tweety opened her eyes and looked about the room.

Chapter Twenty-five

On the Brink with Will and Jeffy-boy

Lydia sat invisibly, legs crossed, watching Tweety navigate in the snow. Tweety and the cat were playing together. The cat, Welheim, daintily ran along the thin-crusted snow until it hit a soft spot and fell in, straight down; then it would begin meowing, scrambling frantically, scaring itself, only to pop up again to start the entire process all over. Tweety watched, squalling delightedly each time the cat disappeared, and each time it re-emerged.

By now Tweety could get along without Lydia monitoring all of her motions, even though she fell down often and didn't really walk properly yet, and Lydia stared across the fields, wondering idly if it was time for supper. She caught herself with a start; it wasn't she, but Tweety, who was hungry and anticipated the mutton chops that Bianka had promised earlier in the day. On the one hand, Lydia thought, it was definitely exciting and fun...delicious...to anticipate the chops with Tweety—she corrected herself, *as* Tweety—and yet, well, it was also just as pleasant to be aware of Tweety's feelings without identifying with them all the way.

As she sat, musing, she smoked, and she was just reaching for another hallucinatory cigarette when a young man appeared, looking rather surprised. She recognized him at once from the Buddha affair, but it was obvious that he considered her a complete stranger. By his clothes and manner, Lydia knew that he was from the twentieth century, and she sprang up with pleasure. "What are *you* doing here?" she asked.

"I'm dreaming and I must be traveling out of my body," Will said a bit smugly. "Anyhow, in answer to your question, I'm life-hunting, though why I'm here particularly is beyond me. Where are we?"

"Seventeenth-century Sweden," Lydia said.

"Great. That figures. I was looking for someplace exotic. What a dreary landscape this is." Will frowned and glanced around rather disdainfully.

"Why, it's lovely here," Lydia protested. "I lived in the twentieth century once, too. That's where you're from. I can tell."

"Wait a minute," Will interrupted. "Then you're dead!"

"No, you're not born yet," Lydia replied with a touch of anger. "Anyhow, you're lucky to be talking to me at all. I'm on a recess, in a way. Actually I'm living my life as that child over there."

Will was appalled. "Why, that's like living backwards," he said. "I mean, you're an adult now, and you'll have to be a child again."

"That's what happens," Lydia said, thoroughly enjoying the company. She related to Will as a contemporary, smiling at him as a young woman at a young man.

He scowled at her. "Smoking is bad for your health," he said.

She started laughing. "I haven't got any health at all," she said, between gasps. "I mean, I haven't got a physical body in usual terms. I just take this form. Tweety has a body, but then, she doesn't smoke. Besides they don't have real cigarettes like these in the seventeenth century anyhow."

"You're absolutely and completely mad," Will shouted.

"Or you are. It's your dream," Lydia replied. "You visited here in your dream, but it isn't a dream to me—" She broke off. Will said something else and she tried to respond, but suddenly from the house the sizzling smell of mutton chops wafted through the air so temptingly that Tweety's senses splashed over. Tweety and Lydia for the moment became indivisible. Tweety forgot the cat and headed clumsily toward the house. Will just stood there. The young woman had completely disappeared.

Will groaned. The dream, or whatever it was, was getting out of hand. He felt very lonely standing there in the strange dreary landscape. He was just beginning to feel really sorry for himself when Lydia reappeared.

"This happens to me more and more," she said uneasily. "I keep forgetting myself and turning into Tweety all the way. See how small this little fenced area is? They put Tweety out here whenever it's not too cold, and to her, it's absolutely vast. While to *me*—"

"I'm going to commit suicide," Will interrupted, but a part of Lydia was suddenly relating to Tweety again, in the kitchen, and she didn't respond.

"I *said*, I'm going to commit suicide," Will repeated.

"Oh, sorry, I wasn't listening," Lydia answered. "I don't think I ever died that way. And you were telling me that smoking was bad for my health. Suicide isn't about to promote good health either, you know."

Silence. "You're terrifically facetious," Will said finally. But his curiosity got the best of him. "How did you die and how many times? Are you putting me on?" he asked suspiciously.

But Lydia more than answered his question. She turned into the image of the old woman she had been before death: white bubbles of hair; thin but somehow jaunty bones dressed in a pair of dungarees and faded shirt. Will stared, horrified at the transformation.

She said, in the old woman's crispy voice, "I looked like this, more or less, when I died the last time. And I was pretty proud of myself in a way. I mean, I considered myself a survivor."

But Will was so startled that he could feel himself starting to wake up in bed; and he didn't want to. He did, though—in a cold sweat. He was somehow terrified. He'd taken quite a few phenobarbitals, and he imagined, *imagined*, he muttered, gritting his teeth, that he'd just fall into a dreamless sleep. But no. Instead he had to have a nightmare in which a beautiful young woman turned into an old hag. Ugh. He tried, unsuccessfully, to remember what else had happened. Then he tried to interpret the whole thing symbolically, and gave up almost at once.

Why, he wondered, would he want to be born again anyhow? And again? And what good would suicide do, if you just woke up in another life? Christ, he grimaced. You could just go on killing yourself in one life, only to be born in another! If you did it fast enough, though, maybe giving yourself ten years to a life, he grinned bitterly—you'd get life, death, life, death, life, death, BAM, BAM, BAM. Shit! He reached beneath his cot and popped some more pills without even checking to see what they were.

Of course, babies wouldn't remember their past lives, at least he hoped not, so for a while, he thought, there'd be some peace—but just the same, you'd have to program yourself ahead of time to commit suicide before you grew up and started the whole thing over. And it wasn't that he was poor or ignorant or sick—he disdained such excuses, he thought proudly—he just didn't like . . . life itself, or the conditions of life.

He lay on the unmade cot, arms behind his head, leering

at himself mentally; thinking that no matter how rotten he felt, he probably looked cool, nonchalant, clever, and sardonic. Because he always did. People always told him so.

"Clever." He hated the word. And people. Because no matter what he *said* to them—and his fluent tongue spoke convincingly—he never really related to them. He didn't know what they were up to. They were as impersonal, as far as he was concerned, as mathematical figures.

His glance went beyond his private corner to the communal kitchen with the greasy fake geranium on the windowsill, to the wooded area outside, and he remembered the cliffs that surrounded the campus and the waterfalls where all the beer parties were held.

And without ever having made any decision, Will dressed languidly, thumbed his nose at the poster Buddha (but making this an elegant, almost classy gesture), to find himself some ten minutes later merrily walking along the slippery edges of the rockbed. Jauntily, whistling, he threw his jacket over his arm and eyed the highest level of the cliffs that he could comfortably reach. No need to wear himself out, even for such an important occasion.

"What important occasion?" he asked himself.

"Who knows?" he answered. His mind felt curiously and beautifully divided, and his body felt so light and transparent that he almost felt invisible, though he knew that he wasn't.

Then, eyes wide and clear, contemptuous and hurt, he looked down.

It wasn't too far.

But far enough.

And he was woozy enough to jump. The drugs had taken the edge off the moment.

All he had to do was

Jump off

the edge

of the moment.

"Shit." Even now he couldn't forget himself, he thought,

or stop watching himself. He almost felt as if he were two selves, neither very likeable, one watching the other, one thinking, "How tragic, yet how handsome and young I look," and the other thinking, "How dumb and cosmically stupid to have such feelings at a time like this." But both of him looked down again.

• • •

This is Jeffery, interrupting dictation of the book. Never have I used so much raw willpower, but as I completed that last sentence, "But both of him looked down again," I knew I *had* to stop writing. To go on could bring disaster. I knew that even as my fingers hovered over the typewriter keys, quite ready for the next sentence. Reason would have to come later; I knew that, too, as I reacted to a sharp, sudden, undeniable sense of personal danger. The next line, or the next, could destroy me.

Sweat ran down my armpits. I took one hand and with it *pulled* the other off the typewriter, feeling as if at any moment my hands would pounce upon the keys with their own will and type out—what? My own death sentence? The pun didn't escape me even as I lit up a cigarette and moved as far away from the accursed typewriter as possible.

I'd been nervous, beginning this section on Will. For one thing, it's the first on the book that I've received in two weeks to the day, for after the chapter on Seven's return to the ground of his being, there was nothing. Did that return, in *our* time, take two weeks? Then beginning this chapter, I found that there was a time lapse in the book also, for Tweety was no longer an infant. She was also becoming more of an individual, so did *my* two-week period somehow correlate with Seven's journey and Tweety's growing self-consciousness? And what about Will? As soon as he appeared in this chapter, I felt alarm signals, until, finally, with that last sentence, I could stand it no longer. I refused to write another line.

Will was only a book character and a poorly developed

one at that. I said this over and over as I stood, growing more and more upset, staring out the window at the balcony, and Oh, God, at the geranium pot on the railing, the same one that fell over during that first dream encounter related in my early notes. Feeling, yes, possessed, I walked slowly out to the balcony (where my first out-of-body experience had occurred). Almost hypnotized, I looked out at the new staggered cement apartment buildings, jutting out indeed like cliffs; and downward at the garbage cans, unfinished lawn, and parking lots.

What on earth was I doing? I knew I was trembling; I felt as if I were tottering at the edge of some chasm between worlds, trying to leap from one to the other.

And I knew that no matter who or what Will was or wasn't, I had to stop him from jumping. I had to reach him somehow. But how did one reach a character in a book? Impossible, I thought. At the same time, I knew that reaching Will was my mission, and if anyone had asked me then what my mission in life was, I would have answered unhesitantly, "To save Will's life."

As this thought came to me, I felt dizzy and off balance. I feared that I'd lost my footing, and would plunge (real body and all) over the railing onto the ground below. But instead, the apartment buildings blurred across the way and almost disappeared in a kind of white glare. Then they turned into the cliffs described in the book as the ones sought out by Will . . . and I saw him, standing on a rocky ledge, looking down.

So I—he—hadn't jumped yet!

Scared to death, horrified, I suddenly realized that I was Will's "other self" mentioned in the last passage of the narrative. I stood beside him—the observer. And he knew it! I mean, he felt an observer-self, though whether or not he realized then that I was real, I don't know.

"Don't jump," I shouted.

"The wheel of life . . . round and round she goes," Will

said, and giggled, an awful sound. Then he threw his arms out dramatically and said in a mournful voice that clearly mocked itself, "This is where Willy-boy gets off, sweet daddy-o."

As he said that, as Will, I felt a dizzy surge of irresponsible power and weird impulses: to let go, to jump, to choose *nothing*, to cheat mortality by courting death. Snapping back to myself, I said urgently, "You've got a future. You're going to be a psychologist. You'll forget all this, the drugs, the emotional bombastics."

Will groaned; there he was, still divided, still arguing with himself. He said, "And the search for excellence in life? What a dumb deluded search that was!"

"Was? You're still alive, aren't you? You can't commit suicide because I'm your future self and I exist," I cried.

Will looked directly where I was standing, not seeing me, surely, yet sensing my presence as his other self and hearing my voice in his head.

"How like me," he said. "Of two minds till the last. It's enough to drive a man to suicide! Still witty, too. God, how I hate myself."

I yelled, "Stop that! If you jump, you'll kill me, too." I shouted, frantic. But I was the real me: He was the storybook character; so how *could* his death possibly affect me? I didn't know, but I knew it could. "You're going to write a really strange book," I cried, on impulse. "I know. I've seen it."

"Who cares?" he said. "And I'm tired of this dumb dialogue with myself anyhow. On the other hand, I might as well talk to myself because I don't have a friend in the world. My parents couldn't care less, either." He shrugged eloquently and moved closer—too close—to the cliff edge.

I sprang forward to stop him, but with his last words I suddenly felt sick to my stomach. Because I had no friends now either. And without further transition, it happened. Will's feelings were no longer just Will's—they were mine, fully, completely. When this odd and terrible transference happened (for that's what it was), I almost fell over the cliff edge myself, with the impact of a despair that suddenly hit me full force.

At the same time, the scene before me took on a clarity beyond description—the gray cliffs interspersed with spring grass and small rocks, the crooked trees newly sprouting. The bottom of the gully beneath me, as if I'd lost all depth perception, now seemed but one mere step downward; hardly dangerous and, moreover, oddly inviting.

The despair and sense of hopelessness I felt was almost sexual in the strangest way, a yearning that sought orgasmic release. On the one hand, I ached to throw myself down through the gap of space I knew did exist despite my illusion of its shallowness. But like a lover, the gully itself changed seductively, seeming closer and closer, so that on the other hand I thought that one small sweet step would end the monstrous psychological pressures that I'd hidden from myself for so long.

And simultaneously, some voice within me whispered that I must be the observer again or Will and I were both lost; but the voice was weak and did not possess the power of my feelings. I listened, but the words seemed to make no sense.

While all this was happening, I was so completely engrossed with my own emotions, so hypnotized and gripped by the temptation to jump, that I almost forgot Will entirely.

"One little step, *shit*," I heard his voice say. The words got my notice. I stared. Will was shaking his head with what seemed to be happy bewilderment. For an instant I thought that he'd lost his reason completely, for the implications of his actions escaped me entirely at first. Giggling again, only this time with a wild, childish, almost animal-like relief, he plopped promptly down on the cliff, took off his shoes and stockings, and with a cackle like a starling's, he heaved his sneakers and socks down to the gully bottom.

I followed them with my eyes. The shoes . . . were they

his or mine? *He* was crying and still giggling with relief, and only when I understood that he was crying with *relief*, did I realize what happened.

His despair, in some way, had been mine all along! When I accepted that almost impossible psychological weight, *he* was free.

Jealously I watched him: the young man's perfect form, set off now by a newly released psyche. *Who* was he? Now I resented him, lolling there on the bank as if he hadn't a care in the world. My own despair was still paramount, only now I was aware of it as *it,* and not quite as lost in its power as I'd been before.

Will turned, stood up, bare feet tentatively testing the path, the twigs and stones impinging on the soles of his bare feet; stinging, bringing tears to his eyes—and a triumphant defiance to his heart. "I almost jumped. Almost." (I caught his thoughts and listened in. He went on:) "I was saved. Something stopped me at the last moment. Something or somebody *cared.* I wouldn't be feeling these stones under my feet if I'd jumped. I wouldn't be thinking. I wouldn't be..." He continued with a chanted list of the things he wouldn't be feeling if he'd jumped; and I found his elation embarrassing.

Then, approaching the path from which he'd come to the cliffs, he paused. Or rather, he was...stopped. I felt his surprise. And, as if he were being magically *pulled,* he returned to where I was invisibly standing, eyeing the spot as if it intrigued him, though he couldn't see me; of that I was sure. Once more he turned toward home and once more he stopped and returned, as if compelled to remain within some mysterious and invisible radius. Almost forgetting my own plight, I watched him perform in the same way several times; ending with his standing irresolutely before me.

Why didn't he leave? My own sense of desolation swaddled me in a mental cloud, almost suffocating all thoughts not pertaining to it. Yet somehow I was as intrigued by

219

Will's actions as he seemed to be, with the spot of ground on which I was invisibly standing. Now he stood staring at it, obviously perplexed. He appeared certain that something or someone was there, and though he didn't see me, he certainly was growing more aware of my presence in some other way.

Again, I thought: "Why didn't he go home? Back to the commune?"

And I thought, "Because he has no future alone."

The realization, I think, came to both of us at once.

His boyhood's life could only be fulfilled in my manhood.

In *my* life!

Was he real?

More real than real?

More real than I had been in years?

If I didn't accept Will as a part of myself, he had no place to go. I looked around. Was the ground I was standing on real? Did the paths go anywhere? Or was there only one that led back to Will's commune?

Will looked, almost desperately, at the path by which he'd come. His face showed fear, and anticipation as well.

"I'm here," I said, wondering if he'd hear me.

"Oh, wow, what I've just been through!" he answered mentally. "And besides that, I tried talking to myself a few minutes ago, and no one answered... like there was no one there. Weird."

"That would have been when I was too frightened myself," I said.

"That makes two of us, but what do we do now? I'm alive, anyhow." He paused. "Aren't I?" he asked. "Suddenly now that I've decided to live, I feel... unreal."

As he spoke, I saw him clearly. He was myself as I'd thought of myself years ago; living in a commune (though actually I never had), but more: so lonely that I could hardly bear to remember. Was I, Will, asking help from a future self? Or was I, the future self, changing the future by going back and altering the past . . . from my present?

So I said, "You'll be me. But I'm learning too. And I'll be different because of you; and because of what just happened."

"You mean, you're real and I'm not? To me, you're just the self I talk to."

"Neither of us is real without the other," I said. "If I denied your reality, I'm sorry. And if I ignored your questions and aspirations, I apologize deeply. But I don't know *how* to accept you, either, even though I desperately want to."

And as I said that, confusion overtook me completely, for suddenly I was *Will,* listening to my words of inner dialogue, and I was myself as myself, speaking the words.

I wasn't sure what was happening as the cliffs shimmered, and Will's image along with them. I know that I had a memory lapse in here somewhere, but the next thing I knew I was standing on my patio again, staring down at the unfinished lawn and at an old pair of men's shoes that someone had thrown beside the garbage cans.

My exhaustion was so complete that I stumbled into the living room and fell almost immediately into a deep sleep. But just before I collapsed, I remembered, as an official part of my own past, when I had stood on a hill, contemplating suicide. I'd completely forgotten the event; blocked it out, of course.

Yet drowsily I wondered: Or had the memory been born just now, and built into the past? And more urgently: Where was Will now? Were either of us still in danger?

Chapter Twenty-six

Ram-Ram Says Good-bye and Tells What He Knows

"I think I get what you mean, but I'm not sure," Oversoul Seven said to Cyprus. The two of them were sitting, invisibly of course, on the chairs on Jeffy-boy's patio. "Will was a past self of Jeffery; *that* sounds simple enough, I guess. But..."

"But what?" Cyprus asked gently. Then she said nonchalantly, "When the lawn is finished, Jeffery will have an excellent view."

"There's something you aren't telling me," Seven said stubbornly. "I'm not fooled at all by your sudden interest in Jeffery's lawn."

"I'm not keeping anything from you," Cyprus said, looking nowhere in particular. "There might be a few things you've kept from *yourself*, though. I'll give you a hint. Jeffery remembered Will, and Lydia is going to have to give *her* memories to Tweety for a while, and—"

"Don't tell me," Seven cried. "I'll think of it myself."

"Good," Cyprus said, smiling. "I just wanted you to know it's all right for you to remember now."

"Sometimes you sound so superior," Seven answered, because no matter how many different ways he cross-referenced his memory—by times, people, events, or probabilities—he couldn't discover anything that he'd really forgotten.

"Oh, Seven, it isn't a matter of superiority," Cyprus began, "it's—"

"Hold on," Seven interrupted.

"On to what? Why?"

"It's just earth vernacular that means 'wait a bit.' Never mind; look there!" Seven cried excitedly, because below them Ram-Ram was ambling up the walk. "You knew he was coming, didn't you?" he asked reproachfully. But Cyprus only smiled.

She said, "Just watch and listen, and maybe you'll remember something important." By now she was laughing so hard that she was afraid she'd hurt Seven's feelings.

But he was too confused to notice. "There are so many unanswered questions," he mumbled. "I still don't know why Jeffery wrote the book for us, or how Lydia is connected to him, or how her full acceptance of Tweety's life has any bearing on Jeffery's future. I'm *still* having my troubles with Lydia, by the way. But why should Jeffery care?"

"Shush. Listen," Cyprus said. She and Oversoul Seven turned into two points of light on the ceiling of Jeffery's living room.

"What's Jeffery going to say when he types this?" Seven asked anxiously. "He'll know we've been listening to his private discussions with Ram-Ram."

"You forget," Cyprus said. "Jeffery thinks we're fictional characters."

Ram-Ram knocked at the door. He had to rap several

times before the sound awakened Jeffery, who was still asleep on the couch. Groggily Jeffery yelled, "Go away."

"It's Ramrod Brail," Ram-Ram called.

"Great. Just who I want to see," Jeffery muttered; but he went to the door anyway and let Ram-Ram in.

"Well, I've been discharged," Ram-Ram exclaimed. He looked very pleased with himself.

"Nice for *you*," Jeffery said irritably. "Is it for real this time?"

"Now, now, now," Ram-Ram said. "I just dropped in to say good-bye. I'm going to take a trip and do some writing. I must say, you don't look very happy to see your partner in crime." He chuckled, and stared passively at the ceiling. "You *do* look pooped, Jeffy-boy, if you don't mind my saying so."

"I mind! And I don't like being called Jeffy-boy," Jeffery said.

"No. Of course you don't. The boy is part of the man, though..."

"Now what do you mean by that?" Jeffery demanded.

Ram-Ram sat down, smiling affably. "Only that you used to be so stuffy. I liked to remind you of the boy buried in there somewhere."

Jeffery stopped, stared, and asked despite himself, "Will? Are you talking about Will?" Even as he spoke, he felt an absence in himself. Where was Will?

"Will?" Ram-Ram asked.

"Nothing," Jeffery answered, with such obvious relief that Ram-Ram pretended not to notice. He stared at the ceiling again. "Of course, scientific journals are out," he said. "You can't prove any of this."

"Ram-Ram sees us," Seven cried.

"Does he?" Cyprus said.

"Prove what?" Jeffery demanded. He sprang up from the couch, displaying more agitation than he'd intended.

"Well...whatever you've been up to," Ram-Ram answered innocently. "I *was* here, out of body, for one thing, though you'd never admit that to any of our colleagues, I don't suppose. My being a mental patient for a while doesn't help you there either. Yes, yes, yes; I do have a good idea of your psychological adventures. You haven't committed yourself to them, at least not all the way."

Jeffery said as calmly as he could, "Just how much do you know about my activities? And *how* do you know whatever you know?" He paused and almost shouted, "Or *think* you know?"

Ram-Ram stood up, turning his back to Jeffery, arms folded behind his back, and walked toward the patio door. He stood, looking out. "I would imagine that you have a manuscript of some sort by now," he said. "But my knowledge of your, ah, bizarre activities isn't as detailed as you might think, or as I'd hoped. Before you called me about your first dream encounter with the two men, I wasn't at all surprised. I'd had a dream of my own about you—"

"I need a drink," Jeffery said abruptly.

"By all means," Ram-Ram replied, beaming as if he were the host, and still talking, he went into the kitchen. Jeffery heard the sounds of ice cubes being clunked into glasses, and Ram-Ram returned with drinks for both of them.

"A toast," he said grandly.

"The dream," Jeffery said.

"Oh, yes, the dream. Now, how would one tell our young man here about such an event? That was my problem, of course. Now you'll understand with no trouble."

"Oh, God," Jeffery yelled. "Will you get on with it?"

Oversoul Seven said to Cyprus, "How jittery Jeffery is! You know, for a moment I almost thought that I remembered something terribly important. But now I have no idea what it was."

"Oh?" Cyprus said, seeming to be quite unconcerned.

Ram-Ram sat down. "I'm not sure of much of this," he said. "But I dreamed of an automatic manuscript that you'd be writing in some way that I've forgotten, and I knew that I'd have a hand in triggering it."

"Go on," Jeffery said. His face was so intent and still that time might have stopped.

Ram-Ram continued. "Years ago, I was very interested in phenomena like out-of-body experiences, hypnosis, and alterations of consciousness in general. I fooled around with them, so to speak. But I was cautious: There was my reputation to consider. Life went on, and I followed the academic line. Then, when I had my dream, I perked up. Just suppose, suppose, there was something to it, I thought. It was several days before your experience, but somehow I awakened from the dream knowing that you had to come to me. So I didn't contact you. But just in case, I took several books out of the library to refresh my own mind on the psychic field in general, and to loan to you *if* by any chance my dream *did* mean anything and you called. As, of course, you did."

"I noticed the library date on the card," Jeffery exclaimed. "I did wonder briefly that the books were taken out before—"

"As you were meant to. So that you'd have some reason to believe me now. Not that anything is proven, but, ah, suggested, at least." Ram-Ram paused and said, "And then, of course, it's not quite over."

"Now what do you mean by that?" Jeffery asked uneasily. At the same time, he wondered if Ram-Ram's remark had anything to do with his own growing anxiety; for Will kept flashing in and out of his consciousness.

Oversoul Seven said to Cyprus, "What I'm supposed to remember has to do with Jeffery's dream...and *this* book...right?"

"Shush," Cyprus said.

"Now, Jeffy-boy, don't you like surprises?" Ram-Ram said, reverting to his humorous, coy air. "But be that as it may, I know this much: Whatever you're involved in isn't quite finished. There's something important you still have to do. Something else: I always sensed an unresolved and unhappy, maybe unloved but turbulent part of you, quite hidden behind your self-conscious professorial psychological attire. Again, that's why I called you Jeffy-boy; teasing you, of course."

Ram-Ram's voice had a hypnotic quality that seemed to fill the room in the growing dusk. Even Oversoul Seven almost nodded. Ram-Ram's small eyes were half closed, yet in their lidded drowsiness there also seemed to be a hidden spring of alertness.

"And more than that," he went on. "I also sensed that in some way you, uh, represented a past unresolved self of mine ... as a young man ... a part that needed help. I wanted to go back into the past and make some changes ... even as, I believe, you've done the same kind of thing in your own case." Smiling softly, Ram-Ram said, "Yes, yes, yes. So it goes."

"I remember!" Oversoul Seven shouted. "How could I have forgotten?"

Just at the same time, Ram-Ram said, "So, to recapitulate, two people came to me in the dream state and somehow set up this entire episode, including the events I know of and those you haven't told me."

"It was me!" Oversoul Seven shouted to Ram-Ram, who didn't hear him, of course.

"And?" Cyprus asked gently.

"And you, too," Seven said, a bit abashed. "But why didn't I remember until now?"

"The *why* is next," Cyprus answered.

Jeffery said, "You're telling me that the two men who I saw here appeared earlier in a dream of *yours?*" The hypnotic effect of Ram-Ram's narrative was broken.

"I've no proof," Ram-Ram answered. "But yes, yes, yes, I'd say so. The descriptions of the men you gave to me matched mine, all right. I'd say that they were the same."

"But what about the mental institution?" Jeffery demanded. "How did that all start? Were you really, uh..."

"It's according to your definition, if you're asking me if I was mad or not..."

"I'll second that question," Seven said to Cyprus. "And I have another. Where's Will? And why do I suddenly feel uneasy about Will and Lydia both?"

"For one thing, Lydia needs you right now," Cyprus said. "There are some things that must be taken care of, and before Jeffy-boy and Ram-Ram finish their conversation. And what happens with Lydia has something to do with Will and Jeffery, too."

"But what?" Seven asked with some dismay. "And there's more for me to remember, too, isn't there?"

"Hurry. Go to Lydia now," Cyprus replied. "Granted, there's really no time, but in your terms there's none to waste."

Chapter Twenty-seven

"The Time Is Now,"
Lydia Says Good-bye and Hello,
and Seven Remembers

The snow bank was blinding: yellow and white sparkles exploding in tiny puffs that Tweety tried to follow with her eyes. The sparkles were on the very top of the snowbank, floating out of the snow beneath like feathers; and with all that swirling, she could hardly see the snowbank beneath, which sat there like a huge white animal. Tweety eyed it suspiciously, to see if it might be dangerous.

Besides this, though, her bottom was wet inside and out. It was sloppy and wiggly on the inside by her underpants where the familiar brown, warm, smelly stuff came out. It squashed when she plopped down on the ground, and she could feel it squishing between her legs. But the wet outside her bottom stuck to the snow, and when she sat in the snow, it was cold and hard. Her face burned with the sunlight and burned—cold, too, and still she sat there, in the snow, where suddenly she'd fallen.

She didn't hurt, but she stung. She started to wonder exactly *where* she stung, and whether or not it was worthwhile to start crying about it, but she kept getting fascinated by the yellow-white, shining snow sparkles that flew out of the snowbank, glittering in the sun. She stared at them, feeling dreamy, but then the cat caught her eye: He was rounding the shedhouse. Then she remembered that she'd just fallen down, and that she wanted to follow the cat.

"Get up, me," she said to herself mentally, because physically she couldn't get the words out right, though they sounded all right inside. Getting the outside like the inside was hard. The cat dashed out into the sunlight again, a blur of activity. Impatient, Tweety tried to get up again, but nothing happened. There was something that the "other her" told her to do at such times. But what?

Then it happened all by itself.

She saw herself get up quite clearly and chase the cat. This picture of herself flashed right out in front of her eyes, and before she realized what had happened, she was up on her feet, following the image of herself. Only then it disappeared, and there was only the cat. For one instant, before it vanished, she was the image of the self she followed . . . and she saw it, herself, in her brown leggings and coat, and bundled up in the hateful orange scarf; running.

But she wasn't running really, just plodding. She couldn't go fast enough yet, and the snow kept rushing up to meet her, and it hurt when it hit her on the bottom. No, she thought, the snow didn't come up at her after all; she kept falling down to meet it. Then she was down again, harder than ever, plopped on her wet bottom, which really stung. She yowled.

Nobody came to get her up; no inside people or outside people. She got scared.

A wind came up and whipped about her. She flailed back at it, but it didn't stop. The sun became brighter so that the snow sparkles glittered all over and she could hardly see.

Tweety shouted angrily at the wind, which now was blowing snow in her face. "Up, me," she said to herself.

"You have to make the picture first," said the "other her" somewhere in her head, and Tweety brightened, not feeling quite so lonesome. She had to make the picture first. That was how it was done. So, she wiggled her forehead and thought about it, and tried, but with no success.

"I guess I'll have to do it for you again," Lydia said, and she projected a mental image of Tweety, so that Tweety could see for herself what her body was supposed to be doing. Tweety saw herself get up and walk into the house, so she got up and followed the image; booted feet against the crisp snow. The sun went beneath some clouds and Tweety stopped, astonished. Where had the brightness gone? Why was the air darker? And colder? And she'd lost a mitten. The snow had changed too. Now it was all dark blue or worse, like upside-down clouds on a thunder day.

She shivered. The dark part of the air felt prickly, as if it had tiny prickers in it from air-bushes she couldn't see. She thrust her pudgy hand out and started giggling; the air stung like the cat's tongue did sometimes when it licked her fingers.

Oh, God, Lydia thought, how incredibly rich Tweety's world was! How much sense data had she explored in the five minutes or so that they'd been in the yard? Bianka never left Tweety out over fifteen minutes at the most, and always watched from the window, a fact Lydia kept in mind, but Tweety usually forgot in the brilliance of present experience. Lydia wanted to cry with nostalgia, and joy too: Feeling it all from Tweety's viewpoint was still shockingly immediate, while she herself had almost forgotten the first explorations of . . . well, life and creaturehood.

A part of Lydia's consciousness stayed with Tweety, and a part dissociated and looked down on Tweety as the child plodded through the snow. Lydia knew the house was only a few feet away, yet through the child's experience, it seemed much more distant. And that seventeenth-century landscape, Lydia thought: It was so dear, so lost in time, yet never lost, of course, because it was somehow or other, a different Now . . . Tweety's Now . . . ever opening up to her senses. What difference, if this was all past from a twentieth-century viewpoint? She had to learn to readjust her thinking, because obviously all time existed at once. No matter how much there might be that she didn't understand; how heroic, how forever meaningful and unique was that one child's wonder in the moment of its Now.

Then why did *she* want to cry?

She knew the answer. She was caught between her own experience and Tweety's. More and more she was drawn to the bright new focus of Tweety's life. Yet if she gave in, she'd lose her own identity and be swept away, at least into momentary oblivion. She'd lose her own freedom, she thought. Yet what did that freedom mean to her, if it locked her out of the incomparable creaturehood focus of one space, one time? So, watching Tweety, and feeling with and through Tweety, Lydia realized that she herself felt homeless, between dimensions, and yet unwilling to give up her freedom. And all the while she felt Tweety become more greedily alive, growing fuller and more magnificent in flesh.

Oversoul Seven experienced Lydia's and Tweety's feelings at the same time, and he'd been trying to get through to Lydia since Tweety first fell down in the snow, only Lydia had been too distracted to listen. "Lydia," he said, "you have to enter fully into your experience, which *is* Tweety's. Stop feeling sorry for yourself. Look at the backyard as Tweety does, with wonder, and your wonder will lead you where you want to go."

But Tweety had made it to the door. Bianka let her in, and now Tweety sat inside by the wood stove, where the hot breath of the fire rushed out at her when Bianka opened the oven door to keep her daughter warm as she took off her wet clothes. Lydia, exhausted, found herself as fascinated and frightened by the fire as Tweety was; and she tried to hold on, and not lose herself in the heat of Tweety's intense concentration.

Tweety felt heavy, bulky, and unpredictable.

Bianka said, "Now we'll take your leggings off."

"Look, sweetheart," Josef said. His voice, always loud, thundered in Tweety's ears. She started to scowl, but Josef held out a piece of bread and jam, and even if it was loud, his voice was yellow and warm and heavy like honey.

"You're trying to bribe her for a kiss," Bianka said.

"You bribe me," Josef answered, grinning. "And not with bread and jam either."

"Stop it now. This isn't the time," Bianka said, blushing and partly angry, because sometimes he just knew too much when you didn't want him to.

While Bianka and Josef laughed, and Tweety began chattering agreeably enough as her snow clothes were removed, Lydia nearly panicked. She'd forgotten herself again, hypnotized by the domestic scene, the warm kitchen, the adults . . . The adults! Oh God, she'd done it again, she realized—fallen naturally into Tweety's psychological world.

"That *is* the idea, after all," Oversoul Seven said, finally getting through to her. "I've been trying to talk to you. It's time now."

"It's time now? For what?" Lydia asked mentally. Then she thought: Of *course*. It really was time. Tweety's clothes were off now. Bianka was rubbing her skin with a towel that had been heated in the oven. The pleasant sensations made Tweety squeal.

"It's time to forget, just for a while," Seven said. "Time to give your new self a chance. You've helped Tweety all you can for now."

"Papa's little darling," Josef exclaimed, coming nearer, with his big face close to hers; brown moustache bristling.

Lydia felt all life calling. The wood in the stove crackled, it seemed, as no other kindling wood ever had. Josef gave Tweety the bread and jam, and the texture and taste was brand-new in the universe, a sensual wonder. All life and reality suddenly seemed concentrated in that warm immediate kitchen.

Inside herself, Lydia sobbed, with nostalgia for the future *and* the past.

"I'll be with you," Oversoul Seven said. He was a point of light on the windowpane.

Mentally Lydia muttered, "A lot of good that will do. I'll forget you too, won't I?"

"She looks like you, Bianka," Josef's voice warmly thundered. He stared, grinning, into Tweety's face.

And Lydia for a moment stared back. She thought that he'd already forgotten that they had chosen to be father and daughter; that . . .

"How strange she looks sometimes," Bianka cried, worried.

And Lydia looked out of the child's eyes, through the unsteamed portion of the kitchen window, seeing the seventeenth-century fields covered with snow; the past come alive, and turning into the present.

"But it isn't the past, of course," Oversoul Seven said. "And I'm so proud of you."

"The time *is* now, isn't it?" she said. "I wish there was some way that you could give Tweety some of the knowledge that I've picked up along the way. Or the knowledge that *you've* picked up. Like a built-in set of instructions or . . ." She paused, dizzy. She could feel herself becoming Tweety even more completely. It was difficult to concentrate. "Seven, it *will* be all right, won't it?" she called, for Oversoul Seven seemed to be disappearing into a kind of psychological distance, while she, as Tweety, impatiently wiggled as Bianka dressed her in warm clothes.

"It will be fine," Seven called back. "I promise. And I promise that I'll give Tweety some kind of 'instruction book' for her new life. And what you've learned will be a part of her heritage, too." In his pride in Lydia and his desire to help her, and in his exuberance, Seven shouted, "I'll think of something terrific."

Bianka stared. "Tweety looks different now. Look at her." She wiped her hands on her apron and looked closely into Tweety's face. "She seems more *here!*" she cried.

"More where?" Josef laughed. "She's my girl."

"She's more *here* now," Bianka muttered to herself. She stood watching as Josef swung Tweety over his shoulders, and singing a ballad, carried her into the other room.

"It will be just fine, dear Lydia," Seven whispered.

"Whee," cried Tweety.

Oversoul Seven felt like crying. He felt like laughing.

"Good-bye for a while, dear Lydia. And hello, dear Tweety," he said. But Seven suddenly felt himself being drawn away; something was happening, some important psychological readjustment...

Before he could wonder about it, Seven found himself back with Cyprus. Jeffery and Ram-Ram still sat talking and sipping drinks.

"No time has passed here," Cyprus said. "But Lydia's forgetting is letting Jeffery—"

"Remember," Oversoul Seven finished. "Of course."

"What is it?" Ram-Ram asked, leaping to his feet. "You look as if you've seen a ghost."

"Maybe a figurative one," Jeffery said mysteriously. "No, I'm all right. I just remembered something, though. Now it seems impossible that I'd ever forgotten it." Then, irritably, "And stop looking at me with that fake kind-old-psychologist smile, will you?"

"Yes, yes. All right," Ram-Ram said, unoffended.

"You may or may not know that my middle initial is W for William," Jeffery said. He stood up, almost groggily. It was hard for him to talk. "Well, just now, just this minute,

235

mind you, I remembered that I used to identify myself as Will for, I don't know, several years. I even signed my name as William, not Jeffery. This was at a time when I was feeling quite despondent, really. Yet for years, all that slipped from my mind. Only earlier today I remembered an... what shall I call it?... almost-suicide attempt. One day I played around with the idea anyway, standing dangerously close to a cliff edge. And I never was sure what happened... a lapse of memory... but I didn't jump. And I just this moment remembered, after that day I never thought of myself as Will again. And until now, I'd completely forgotten that I ever had."

"You'd better sit down," Ram-Ram said anxiously.

But Jeffery paced the floor excitedly, calling over his shoulder, "But that was a kind of psychic suicide, wasn't it?"

"I suppose it *could* be called that," Ram-Ram said cautiously.

"You know damn well it could," Jeffery said. He was so agitated that Ram-Ram patted him on the shoulder, but Jeffery pulled away.

"I don't need any sympathy now," he said. "Suddenly, as I remembered the name thing, I had the oddest feeling. I feel more *here,* more me, as if I've resurrected portions of myself."

"Suddenly you make me feel quite envious," Ram-Ram said. "I could have written your book when I was your age, or my version of it. But I didn't, of course."

"I didn't say I had a book," Jeffery exclaimed.

"My first guess was a scientific treatise of some sort," Ram-Ram said, as if he hadn't been interrupted, "but afterward I realized that a different kind of manuscript must be involved. In any case, I had my chance and muffed it. But now it's almost as if I went back in time and changed a version of *me,* by helping you."

"I'm not any version of you," Jeffery shouted.

"Of course you're not. You're too literal-minded," Ram-

Ram said. "Still, your future will be more like the future I might have had..."

Oversoul Seven was having difficulties following the conversation. For one thing, he was losing his focus on earth time, so that objects appeared and disappeared according to when they had existed, or would exist, in any given space; and particularly in the space that was Jeffery's living room. He heard Jeffery's voice, but sometimes it was speaking yesterday, sometimes tomorrow, and Oversoul Seven couldn't find a proper present at all.

Beside him, Cyprus waited. "You're too far to the left of today," she said.

Seven called somewhat anxiously, "I can't seem to find any today to start with."

"*Any* time is a present time if you're there. Stop where things seem to be 'right now,' and call that today."

"All right, if you say so," Seven whispered. "But now it's a different present than it was before. I got confused; or I *get* confused. I mean, you're in a different present time than I am."

"No matter," she said. "I'm on a platform above time. And theoretically, you should be, too. But tell me *when* you are."

"I'm to the left of time from your viewpoint, uh, I think," came Seven's hasty reply.

"All right; that's Jeffery's past. Now back up a bit further."

Seven was growing dizzy. Chairs and tables changed their positions according to their locations at any given time. Jeffery's figure appeared at the window; then, at the door. Ram-Ram disappeared entirely. The living room flickered bright, then dark, as nights and days flashed by.

"*Now*," Cyprus directed.

Seven tried to stop things as quickly as he could. Then he grinned. It was Jeffery's room at night, before... before what? For he saw himself and Cyprus, both in adult male images, out on Jeffery's patio.

"That image suits me rather well," he said to the Cyprus on the platform above time.

"Shush. Listen and watch," she said.

"I think I have it all straight," said the earlier image of Seven who stood with the male Cyprus.

"All *what* straight?" asked the "present" Seven.

"Will you just listen?" said the Cyprus out of time, while the Cyprus of the past, standing with the past Seven, said, "I think you're very wise. After tonight, you'll completely forget that Jeffery is one of your personalities living in time. That way you can look at him more objectively, since you seem to be having trouble relating to him properly."

"So that's it!" shouted the present Seven, and suddenly it all came back to him, just as the past Seven said, "Right. I agree. We'll both appear to him in his dream state, and cleverly lead him out of the depression he's been in since his wife left him. Some psychologist; he doesn't even recognize his own depression."

Cyprus on the platform above time said, "And Lydia and Jeffery can help each other, as each looks for a meaning to existence . . ."

And the past Seven cried, "And we'll stimulate Jeffery's creative abilities, which he's buried for so long, and rearouse the young Will with all the dissatisfactions he feels, so that Jeffery can recognize them and deal with his problems . . ."

"Exactly," both Cypruses said.

"While Lydia rediscovers the joys of earth life, also helping Jeffery revive his own love of life."

"Exactly," both Cypruses replied.

And as both Cypruses and both Sevens spoke at once, time thickened; Jeffery's living room had two levels of time, simultaneously: In one, the earlier Cyprus and Seven in the male images were just entering the room from the patio and arousing Jeffery as he lay on the couch. The wind tugged at the geranium pot on the patio which would shortly fall over, alarming Jeffery.

In the second level of time—in their present—Ram-Ram

and Jeffery still sat talking. "Yes, yes, yes," Ram-Ram was saying. "I could almost have done an automatic manuscript myself; and someday you'll have to show me yours."

"Do you feel that we aren't alone?" Jeffery asked suddenly.

Ram-Ram smiled and shrugged. "I've been staring at the ceiling all the time we've been talking. Drawn to it. See those two lights up there, by the corner? Reflections most likely, but..."

Jeffery looked. At the same time, though he saw nothing extraordinary, he felt an extraordinary yearning that made him say, "Do you believe in the soul? I mean, as a psychological entity?"

(And as Jeffery asked the question, in time's vast depth, Tweety looked out the window of her childhood room at the stars, and thought that the starlight formed a familiar yet strange image, as if looking out, she was looking inside her own mind.

(And in the vast reaches of Jeffery's consciousness, Will walked up mental steps to the threshold of Jeffery's growing understanding.)

Ram-Ram said comfortably, "More to the point, since you asked, do you?"

"I believe in...something," Jeffery said. "But there's some writing I have to do just now. I don't mean to cut our conversation short, but there's something I must finish."

"I thought there might be," Ram-Ram said.

Then Jeffery wrote this chapter and the previous one. He wrote all night, no longer astonished as his own experience wound through the narrative and was reshaped, turned endwise and sidewards, focused and unfocused, his and yet more than his . . . and . . . Will's.

And then, after a brief sleep, he continued.

Chapter Twenty-eight

Oversoul Seven Keeps His Promise to Lydia and Begins Tweety's Education

Oversoul Seven said, "I'm going to start Tweety on Sumari right away and really give her an excellent education, because I promised Lydia that I would. Besides, I've thought of a terrific idea."

"First, you'll have to explain what Sumari means," Cyprus replied.

"No problem," Seven said. "I'll tell Tweety that Sumari means many things, but we'll be using it as the name for the inner lands of the self." He paused expectantly and said, "Well, aren't you a bit curious about my brilliant idea?"

"I'm waiting for you to tell me," she said, again looking nowhere in particular.

"You probably know already," he said reproachfully.

"No. I know you like to surprise me..."

"Well, what do you think of *Seven's Little Book?*" Seven asked, unable to keep the secret any longer. "It will be a book just for Tweety—not a physical book, of course, but a dream book. I'll read some to her each night when she's asleep. I'm going to start with Sumari Geography; you know, the inner lands of the self and their, uh, subjective locations. Well, what do you think?"

"Truly inspired," Cyprus said. Her woman teacher image positively glowed, and Seven's fourteen-year-old male form glittered happily around the edges.

"Lydia wrote books, you know," he said. "So I thought it would really be fitting to do a book for *her;* I mean, for Tweety. It will have all the important things about life in it. And because it will be a dream book, her subconscious will, uh, lap it up like cream."

Cyprus started laughing. Lost in her humor, she forgot to hold her image, so that she started changing from a woman into a man and back again so quickly and in such hilarious fashion that Seven's head was almost spinning. "Stop that," he said indignantly.

"Oh, Seven, I was laughing *with* you, not at you," Cyprus said.

"Well, I wasn't laughing," Seven said glumly. "You just made me remember something that I forgot to put in the book. How am I going to explain that we aren't really male or female? I'll have to do a book on Sumari Sex, but maybe I should wait until Tweety is older."

"You'll work it out," Cyprus replied. "Are you going to show me the book now?" She turned into a male image, tall, brown-skinned, with thick black hair, just for the change, and to take Seven's mind away from the earnestness that seemed to possess it since he began talking about the book.

"Good form; Indian," Seven said automatically. "No, you can watch me read the book's first installment to Tweety, though, and check my bedside manner. But I don't want to show you the whole book yet. I *do* like to surprise you.

241

And it's a little book, after all." He started grinning and turned into the image of an Indian guru, saying in mock-intense tones, "This will be a sacred book, containing the knowledge of the ages!" Then he stared at Cyprus hypnotically, materialized a turban around his head, with a gigantic jewel in the center. "How's this for my book-session attire?"

"Awful. You'd scare Tweety to death," Cyprus said, laughing, so Seven turned into a twelve-year-old guru, with a robe the color of brown fall leaves, and a face the same color only faintly tinged with gold, and deep soft eyes the shade of tree bark. "Now that's excellent," Cyprus said. "And it fits you, somehow. You should wear that image more often."

But Seven was already brooding again, and his whole image blurred a bit. "This is my first real creative endeavor in the line of multidimensional art per se, and I also hope to submit it as a thesis to meet my own educational requirements. So I certainly want it to be good. It'll be around for ages, influencing all kinds of people beside Tweety, because transdimensional art transcends so many realities." His eyes suddenly glowed. "Still," he said, "maybe there'll be other-world translations, so I should give the title special care too. *Seven's Little Book* was my first choice. But maybe I should give it a more formal title like, *The Beginner's Course in Sumari: A Preparation for Creaturehood*.

"Don't get carried away," Cyprus said.

"You're just jealous," Seven said, grinning. "Well, maybe I am a bit overly enthusiastic. But I really *am* excited. I'm trying to give Tweety all the important information she needs to start a new life, and yet it must be simple enough for a child to understand. And I think I've done it. So, are you ready? This is the first installment."

Cyprus nodded, and in less than a moment she and Seven sat by Tweety's bedside. The child was sleeping soundly. Oversoul Seven arranged the mental pages of the book in their proper order, and began to read:

Sumari Geography

Sumari cities are states of mind. They are quite as real as physical cities, more real, if the truth be known, and they have their own boundaries, cultures, crafts, and trades. Some people are travelers, visiting one city after another, and sometimes even living in two cities at once, for in the Sumari cities, moods and thoughts are like streets, alleys, or wide boulevards, all existing together and intersecting.

So, two Sumari cities can become one all of a sudden, without bothering the inhabitants at all, who are simply aware of the added richness of their surroundings, and an astonishing freshness of experience that they hadn't noticed before. In other words, the boundaries can shift and change constantly, with streets and paths always appearing and disappearing.

A Sumari city can suddenly become very small also, with dark hills springing up closely about it, shutting out the sunshine and hemming in the shops until it seems that the city has no room in which to grow.

Now, each person alive really lives in a Sumari city, or in several at the same time, no matter where he or she lives in the world outside. And all of the real work and creativity takes place first in these inner Sumari landscapes. People visit them at night when they're asleep in the outside world, but even when they're awake outside, some part of them is always aware of their citizenship in the inside world.

Of course, a whole Sumari reality is involved, with its own mental continents, countries, oceans, and deserts that are inner counterparts of the world outside. Only, the Sumari world is there . . . or here . . . all the time. I mean, you live in it whether you're alive or dead in outside terms. So it's very durable, and forms the physical world that you're beginning to know. But the Sumari world is more responsive, and changeable, because—well, everything moves by thought and feeling. And as you'll soon discover, people's feelings change all the time.

So, worried people all together in one inner city might make a mountain tower above them, dark and threatening, so that everyone stops what they're doing to look up at it, and worry some more. But their worrying just makes the mountain higher, and darker, and more threatening. But even then, some wise child or man or woman will say, sooner or later, "Our worrying only makes the mountain grow more frightening. So let's unworry it away. Let's ignore it, and see what happens." And if enough people listen and follow those suggestions, then in a twinkling the mountain disappears, and the city is free of it.

And when those same people are awake in the outside world, they'll remember what they learned, and realize that their thoughts and feelings cause their physical experience too. Or at the very least, they'll realize that worrying can turn into a mountain of trouble. In the outside world, of course, mountains stay around much longer and there are happy mountains too, in any case. But the inner bothersome ones don't have to grow at all.

All adventures and explorations really take people into inner landscapes where they can make their own underground caverns and woody paths and oceans to sail across. Then the people experience it all top-side, so to speak. People are always creating the physical world too, you see, materializing it in space and time in the richness of its seasons. And to do that is a magnificent adventure.

Most Sumari cities are the most brilliant, splendid places imaginable, and their light and creativity shines from the inner landscape to the outside one, so that the physical world is always illuminated; and each physical city always has some joy and vitality shining through, no matter what may be happening there.

Each person is unique. So are you. You have so many aspects of yourself that you create physical lives in which you can focus on particular abilities, and fulfill and enjoy them. In so doing, you help yourself and others too, and add to the richness of being. But that's a subject for later on.

Oversoul Seven paused. In the distance somewhere he heard Cyprus say, "That last part was far too complicated for Tweety. Besides, nobody wants to be read to all night, Seven. More important, though, there's something quite vital that you forgot."

Seven frowned briefly. He'd thought that everything was going very well, though it was true that he became so involved with his reading that he'd almost completely forgotten Tweety. In fact, where was she? Her body lay serenely on the bed, but Tweety had wandered off somewhere; her spirit was gone. As usual, Cyprus was right.

Somewhat disappointed, Seven mentally searched the house and grounds and finally he found Tweety, out of body, playing in the snow. Seven shook his head. She'd probably been there for some time, and he hadn't noticed. Worse, she hadn't heard a thing he'd read.

"There you are," she said, grinning up at him and grabbing at his turban with pudgy jam-stained dream hands. A beautifully hallucinated jam jar was beside her, and she'd even hallucinated her brown coat and leggings so that she looked like a small bear at the jam jar. Snowflakes were falling. Tweety looked so triumphant that Seven knew she thought she'd pulled something over on someone.

"Why the jam?" he asked, squatting down beside her with his twelve-year-old guru image.

Her brown eyes turned angry and belligerent. Seven made the jam jar dance in the air and turn over several times until she started laughing and clapping her hands. Then he asked, "Why the jam? I know, but I want you to tell me."

She glowered for a moment, but he was her very own friend; no one, she knew, saw him but her. So she smiled, brilliantly this time, and opened her mind to him the way he'd taught her. Seven saw her then, earlier that day, in a rage, screaming for bread and jam. Bianka was busy and sent her out of the kitchen. So straightaway, after bed, Tweety rushed outside all by herself, down the stairs and out—something she wasn't allowed to do when she was awake—and she took the hallucinated jar of jam. (Killing two birds at once, Seven told Cyprus later.)

But Seven said nothing. He turned himself into a snowman for her while she tired herself out racing around him. Then she followed him upstairs to bed and he read her the material on Sumari Geography that she hadn't heard before. This time, though, he kept watch on her, and read more slowly so that she could ask questions.

Cyprus returned, looking like the ancient yet ever-young woman. "You *are* going to tell her how to keep in touch with her life, aren't you?" she asked. "And certainly you intend to discuss magic and Sumari Time . . ."

"Hello," Tweety said, matter-of-factly. She'd met Cyprus before, under these same circumstances.

"Of course," Seven said to Cyprus. "Don't rush me. Those subjects are in other chapters."

Looking nowhere in particular again, Cyprus said, "Seven, I have a suggestion. Actually your little book could help many people, not just children. Let's publish it in the Appendix of Jeffery's book. That way, people can read it themselves when they're awake."

Seven was so pleased that he couldn't maintain himself. He took three images at once, all of them dancing. "What do you think of that, Tweety? Your little book will be read around the world," he said.

But Tweety was really fast asleep this time, spirit and all.

"Your *Little Book* can follow the Afterword and Jeffery's notes," Cyprus said.

"Afterword?" Seven asked.

And Cyprus said, "The gods still have a word or two to say on their own behalf, so they're inspiring Jeffery to write an Afterword for them."

Afterword of the Gods

"Is anyone looking?" Zeus asked.

"Verily, no," Christ answered.

"Are you positive?"

"Would the Son of God lie? Aren't I omnipotent?" Christ asked. "Aren't you?"

"Oh, Jesus!" Zeus thundered.

The two of them sat momentarily alone, in the green wooden rocking chairs on the porch of the old gods' rest home. Silence settled gently about them, but a very peculiar silence indeed, one so vital that within it all probable sounds seemed ready to emerge. Yet even Zeus's voice, thundering, made no sound that anyone human could hear, because it was sounding on the other side of silence. And in the same way, Christ and Zeus rocked contentedly in *their* godly dimension, invisibly, on the other side of light where no one, including Oversoul Seven, could ever find them.

"It's always ever so much more peaceful after the visitors

leave," Hera exclaimed. She came out onto the porch and peered into the divine distance. "I see our own world is back, thank heavens." She sat down and began to rock so that her orange taffeta gown went swish, swish, swish, with a sound that no one could hear, of course, but the gods.

"Just like the swish, swish, swish of Mohammed's sword," Christ said. He made the sign of the cross with wrinkled fingers, then sprang to his feet, his gray curls bobbing. "Well, the charade is over, at any rate," he said, and then in a voice even louder than Zeus's, he shouted: "Alee alee in free! You can all come out now."

As Christ spoke, a variety of developments happened simultaneously. Hera, Zeus, and Christ were instantly rejuvenated: The flush of a thousand births turned their skin from paper-brittle gray to an idealized, glowing texture impossible to describe. Christ stood as a young man, each hair on his head and beard a crisp, lively brown. Zeus, with new powerful thighs and black beard, was anywhere from sixty to a hundred, yet with such an ancient youthfulness that his vitality was literally of divine proportions. Hera was also magnificently old and young at once, a mother goddess of such stature that Christ called out ecstatically, "Hail, mother of God."

"Why, bless you, my son," Hera cried, laughing, and she turned into the Virgin Mother for him.

"It won't make any difference that the charade is over," Zeus shouted. "Whatever guise people put us in is deceptive, and I'm tired of playing roles. Where's poor Mohammed? Someone should tell him he can put down that damn sword now. And poor Buddha; they *are* turning him into a mess of jelly, when you come right down to it."

But Christ yelled boisterously, "What difference does it make? That doesn't change *us*. But you're right; let's get about our godly business. These roles *are* hampering."

This time, all together, Hera, Christ, and Zeus shouted, "Alee alee in free! You can all come out now."

Zeus shouted, even more loudly, "Let the charade be over," and instantly a gigantic flash of divine lightning struck at the gods' rest home, coming down from a sky literally infinite, that no spaceship could ever find. And, as the lightning struck, sudden tumult began with such a riotous roar that all possible sounds did seem to be sounded, though again, these were inaudible, rising up on the other side of silence that divides worlds.

And, as the lightning hit, the thousands of gargoyles that decorated the gods' rest home began to move. Laughing stone heads grew fleshy; entwined stone limbs stretched. Angel wings of plaster began to beat. The statues, the wooden carvings of Mohammed's men, the bust of Zoroaster, and each and every gargoyle above the window casings and around the pillars moved, stirred, and rose to jump, fly, or leap to the garden, so that the building itself dissolved into the forms of all the gods who had formed it. There were future gods and old ones, probable gods, aunt and uncle gods, animal and bird gods, each shining and unique with its own image.

"What an edifice that was!" Christ said, as one by one the gods turned from plaster or wood or stone, edging or turret decoration or whatever, into living forms and dropped down beside him.

"Nectar for everyone," Zeus shouted; and in vast good humor he added, "Or Christ, do you want wine and fish?"

"Laugh all you want," Christ said. "You can play Christ next time. I'm sick of roles that include crucifixions. The goddesses will be back in style with humanity soon, and I'm going to be one of those for a change."

"That's the trouble. We *do* have to change with the times," Mohammed said. He came running lightly up from the back garden, heaving his sword into the grass. "Buddha was always smartest there," he said. "He was always so ambiguous..."

The divine conversations went on as the gods lounged

on the sunny green grass, sipping nectar; and each image was spectacular in proportion. The Virgin Mary's voice rose, "It's too bad, though; the Crucifixion story ruined the whole thing as far as I was concerned. Yet the people always insist that the gods be killed in these dramas in one way or another."

"Come now, it's all over," Christ said snappishly. "I admit it got on my nerves too, but if that's the kind of symbols people need, that's the kind they get. And besides, they *are* learning."

The Virgin Mary turned back into Hera and joined the group just as Pegasus came in for a landing and began to nibble delicately at the grass. Looking up, he said indulgently, "Why such squabbles? There'll be new gods before long. It's in the air."

"Well, I hope they're better than the old variety," Zeus said. "It's not creative at all to be stuck in the same old roles. Maybe the new gods will have more sense, so that we can really make something out of them. Christ didn't grow at all, for example. Neither did I, for that matter. But a new magnificent god role that we could really sink our teeth into . . . now, wouldn't that be something?"

"Wouldn't it? Wouldn't it?" The question was taken up by all of the assembled gods; wonderingly, yearningly.

"Impossible, I suppose," murmured Pegasus, sadly.

Hera said, "We can't force people to recognize us as we are."

"Sometimes I think it would serve them right if we could," Zeus said, laughing.

"But if they *could* perceive us apart from the roles . . ." Christ said dreamily. "I mean, if we didn't have to conform to their ideas about us! But if we don't conform, they don't perceive us at all. And all in all, each of us had some excellent qualities. The trouble is that people insist on their idea of specifics, I suppose. To imagine us as superhuman, in terms of their species alone, is understandable enough at their level. But to define us by their ideas of sexuality or race is ridiculous even by their standards."

"They're really quite unbelievable," Buddha said, arriving late as usual. He looked like an Indian guru, a situation he remedied at once by turning into a tree. Quarrelsomely he said, "They twist around everything a god says. If only they could perceive us as we really are..."

"Just what I was saying," Christ said triumphantly. "But it's a lost cause, I'm afraid."

"Except for nature," Zeus replied. "And *that's* my favorite materialization."

"Mine, too. Let's not forget that," Mohammed cried.

"It's ever so much more rewarding and creative," Pegasus agreed.

"But why *isn't* nature enough for them?" Buddha asked. "They keep misquoting me as saying that nature is unsavory; or that the point of earth life is to get over it, like a disease. And then they rant about annihilating desire, and I never said a thing like that."

Hera turned into the Virgin and said, "I probably understand humans better than any of you, and my miraculous conception told the whole tale. They just don't trust nature. They don't like the death part and they've never been able to see beyond it, really; it obsesses them. All of nature shouts of new births, yet humans have the greatest difficulty imagining any divinity in nature. I don't understand how they can be that way, but they are."

"They don't see any divinity in themselves, either," Zeus said. "At least the Olympian gods were in and out of nature—and human nature—all the time. But Christ was born into nature just once, and yanked out fast."

"Well, let's get back to ourselves," Christ said. "Everyone's gone. No need to keep up these roles."

"Still, they *could* hold such promise..." Hera said nostalgically, just as she and all of the other gods dispensed with their images and with the personalities that went with them. Their individual awarenesses mixed and merged one with the other, swept through the others, psychologically romped and whirled through mental universes unending.

"It's time for our 'nightly check,'" came the unspoken, on-the-other-side-of-silence, multimillion thought. And each divine awareness turned its attention toward the earth, seeing it and all of its parts, down to the tiniest particle; merging with the mountains, sky, seas; rushing gloriously into each living thing, exulting in the cozy preciseness of earth time.

The gods dived exuberantly into the earth, minus images: growing up as trees in a million backyards, as fish in the oceans, as people and insects and animals. They merged with the twilight that came in through Jeffery's window, flowing through the pages of the manuscript of this book that sat on the table. And the gods continued to give life, form, and substance to the earth.

Jeffery's Closing Notes

         It is with mixed feelings of exhaustion, triumph, and misgivings that I close this manuscript with these few notes. Anyone who reads this book can easily trace the development of my own involvement, until I, myself, became a character in its bizarre narrative. For me now, the division between reality and fantasy exists no longer: That is, I realize that to some extent each of us deals with varying kinds of reality. Perhaps each of us also has a younger, unresolved self wandering the wild reaches of the psyche, but in any case . . . and despite the oddness of therapeutic measures, I feel whole for the first time in many years.

    This doesn't mean that I have accepted Oversoul Seven as my psychological guide *per se*, but I do believe that he represents those more creative and expansive aspects of the psyche that most of us ignore. Would that ever-enthusiastic imaginative portion of the psyche then take such steps as this automatic manuscript to bring itself to conscious awareness? In my case, at least, the answer must be yes. Moreover, there can be no doubt of the devotion that such a mission implies, as this usually unconscious level of the self surfaces, and acts as a teacher for the conscious mind.

There are still many unresolved questions, some mundane and some quite mysterious. What will I do now? I have no idea, except that I'll no longer stay in the confines of my academic field, but roam more adventurously elsewhere into other investigations that I hope will please the curious Will, who still wonders about the meaning of existence.

I was astonished at Oversoul Seven's announcement of a little book for Tweety. "For God's sake," I thought, "the book is writing a book." Without explaining its origin, though, I intend to send it to Sarah for her child (she delivered a son about the same time Tweety was born) and to read it as well to any possible children of my own. The simplicity of the material is most deceptive, and had I read such prose as a boy, perhaps Will would have found more joy in life, and we would not have needed to stand on the precipice of psychological duplicity, contemplating a double suicide. For it now comes to me clearly that any suicide involves the death of thousands, those born or unborn; the slaying of probable selves who might have sprung otherwise from the points of our lives. And even if we continued to exist, we would have altered our own relationship with ourselves, perhaps... who knows?... becoming probable versions actualized in other worlds than those *we* know.

Obviously, I had become a stranger to myself before this manuscript began. I isolated my younger questioning self; buried the questions, for that matter; denied the dissatisfaction that was meant to lead to creative solutions. If I had not saved Will, in my past, would I have committed suicide in my present? Or wouldn't that present have existed to begin with, since, as Will, I would have died years ago? Or because my present *did* exist, was it a foregone conclusion that Will wouldn't commit suicide? I don't believe so. I think that I had gone as far as I could in time without Will, though, and that he was so despondent not only because of the problems that existed in the past, but also because I'd kept him apart in a psychological limbo that lacked all give-and-take or chance for fulfillment. So for him, time had stopped, then. And when I went back to save him, I started time up again, which meant that he had to jump or not jump.

As I read *Seven's Little Book*, I could feel Will reading it too, and I felt as if a new memory for both of us were being formed; a memory of having read the same material somewhere as a child; and in the strangest fashion as I read of Seven's nightly book sessions with Tweety, I saw my own childhood bedroom transposed in my mind over Tweety's. And Oversoul Seven was reading to *me* as well. Embarrassing confession!—but as I typed the material of the little book, a part of my mind went open and transparent, childlike; and was refreshed. The *Little Book* is being included in full, rather as an appendix to this manuscript, as Cyprus suggested to Seven in the last chapter.

Yet the *Little Book* is more than an appendix by far, and if there are mathematical and scientific formulas, perhaps there are psychological or psychic ones as well. If so, then *Seven's Little Book* presents one such formula by which life can be experienced more fully. Before I began these adventures, I would have been appalled by such a statement, of course.

About Lydia, who always remained a character in a book to me, I'm less sure, except that I began to realize, long before the manuscript itself told me, that her pilgrimage was for me also—and, of course, for Will—who visited the Virgin in that ludicrous scene before the nightmare sequence that I so frighteningly shared. I felt, without wanting to admit it, that Lydia's dilemma to be born or not born paralleled my own psychological state, even when I hid my depression from myself.

So, in a most unobjective fashion, I feel that in this case at least, fictional characters and real ones helped each other, interacted, and formed some kind of interdimensional series of events almost impossible to describe. I must state my belief that Cyprus and Oversoul Seven are real, then . . . fictionally real . . . and their reality may straddle such simple definitions.

Ram-Ram the godologist presents a problem. I have no idea if he is an independent personality of some kind, purely a fictional character, or a composite. He could somehow represent the futility of applying Freudian principles to religion, for example; or he could symbolize a portion of Ram-Ram Brail's deep distrust of religion and certain tenets of psychology as well.

I personally found the material on the gods fascinating, simply because it brought home one vital issue. To search for the gods in conventional terms is a useless pursuit, for most often our vision of the gods all but disappears in our ideas *of what they must be,* or what they must be like. The strange production of this book itself gives me a nebulous "feel" for the kind of creativity that any divinity must possess; a vast gestalt of being that could scarcely be contained in any of our conventional godly tales. I see now that in the past I equated God with the images organized religion had of Him, and recognizing their spiritual poverty, I cast out all thoughts of divinity altogether.

Evolution's "chance universe" was no solution to the origin of life either, however, though I trusted *that* more than a capricious god. But many questions concerning the existence of divinity still remain.

The most difficult and still unresolved question remaining regards the status of Ram-Ram, who I assure you is a very real person with a traceable history. The interview as re-corded in Chapter Twenty-eight was the last one we had. I never saw him again, and he left no forwarding address. By all reasons of logic, Ram-Ram cannot be a future self of mine, since his history exists in my present and well into the past. So, in those terms, I can't grow into who he is. Yet I am certain that Ram-Ram is a different person now than he was before these adventures began; as I am, of course. It wouldn't surprise me to find myself in my future growing into the *kind* of man he would be, had he in *his* younger years written this automatic manuscript instead of me.

As to whether or not Cyprus and Oversoul Seven are independent entities or personifications arising from highly creative elements of my own psyche, I have no answer. It's possible, I suppose, that some unforeseen future events might shed light on that basic question. Perhaps I will be suddenly urged once again to write down words not my own, pro-ducing a script that lives now only in probability. Or perhaps this book was a one-time boost, arising in response to my problems; in which case I suppose I shall never feel that bizarre and fascinating rush of creativity again. Or perhaps in a few months, I may look back and find the entire episode unbelievable. If so, I shall be far poorer than I am now.

The patients in the mental institution were quite real, of course. I personally met Queen Alice and the girl who thought she was Christ. It wouldn't surprise me terribly if in the future some odd manuscript of Queen Alice's came to light, perhaps prepared with Ram-Ram's assistance.

So *this* manuscript raises more questions than it answers, which is really the whole point of it, I imagine. Most cer-tainly I will live the rest of my life examining reality in the light of what is written here.

Epilogue

Seven said, confused, "I *do* understand that Jeffery did write the book. But from another perspective, you and I both know that Jeffery's a character in a book, too."

"Precisely," Cyprus answered.

Seven was quiet for a moment, pondering. He really didn't want to say what was on his mind, but Cyprus said, "And . . . ?"

"Well," Oversoul Seven said, "what bothers me is this: We both know that from still another perspective, we're characters in a book, too."

"Precisely," Cyprus answered, smiling.

"But we *know* that we exist!" Seven shouted. He was beyond exasperation.

258

"Then what are you so concerned about?" Cyprus asked. "We created the book that we're in. We created ourselves, and a dazzling reality that *does* exist. We create the physical world in which the books have meaning."

And Seven cried, "I'll never get to Oversoul Eight stage if I have to understand all that first."

Oversoul Seven's Little Book
An Appendix

And Oversoul Seven sat by Tweety's bedside
each night, reading from the special book he'd written
just for her. But he also knew that it was written for all
children, those young in years, and those hidden within
adults. He also knew that the book would automatically
rearouse the children within the adults so that they could
be comforted in the present for the misunderstandings of
the past.

He said to Cyprus, "And my little book *is* magical. That's
the beauty of it! Who ever really understands what I'm
saying *will* have a charmed life. In fact, I have a whole
chapter on that alone..."

So Seven read to Tweety, a bit at a time...

The Charmed Life

Each life is charmed (Seven said), yours and everyone else's, and you must never forget it. The instant you're born, you're charmed, because life itself is a charm. Each being is charmed into existence in whatever reality it finds itself, and given everything it needs to operate in the environment. Your body is charmed, too: It's a magic part of everything else; springing up from all the things you see about you. Atoms and molecules go singing through the miraculous air, forming themselves into rocks and trees and dogs and cats and people, too. You *are* magic. You charm the air so that it thickens into your body wherever you are.

When you want to move, you think the air ahead of you into becoming your body, and the air behind you then stops being your body ... all very magical indeed. You move your arm just one inch to the right, and the air to the left one inch stops being part of your arm. But it all happens so quickly, your snatching of the air and making it turn into your body, that you never notice it at all, and take it quite for granted. Which is why it works so well, you see.

But your life *is* charmed. And there is a secret, a very simple one. Really, it's not a secret. But you have to remember that your life is charmed. People who forget can't use their magic nearly as well as they did before, and they have a tendency to get angry at those who can. So, often, they pretend that no magic exists at all. Then they evolve great philosophies to prove it, which is itself magical, of course. But they can't see that, because they're so convinced that magic doesn't exist.

And many people forget how simple and natural magic is, so they evolve long theories, and methods that are supposed to make it work, when you and I know, and everyone else *really* knows, that magic happens by itself, because that's what magic is.

But people are also very creative...magic again!...so they make up gods of this and that, and realms and spheres, and maps to chart out in advance where magic might be taking them so they don't get surprised, which is silly because magic goes where it wants to, which is everywhere. And when you try to map it out in advance, you really cut yourself short.

Because a characteristic of magic is that it automatically turns into whatever you want it to be. You create your own reality with it, so whatever maps you make are real. And if you forget what magic is, then you're liable to think that your map is the only real one, and all others are false. You get in a terrible bind, fighting over which way is right, which road or map, while all the time magic is what makes the maps. And a great variety of maps can appear in the twinkling of an eye!

Particularly when you grow up, many people will tell you that there is no magic. If you believe them, then you'll forget too, and you'll act as if you aren't charmed and bring unmagic into your life...which is magic too, you see, but magic that doesn't know itself. Then you'll create things that go with unmagic, like sorrow or sickness, and you'll have to deal with them at that level until you remember that your life is charmed again.

So in the meantime you'll feel nasty and unloved and angry, way beyond what is natural, and have to worry about sad or fearful emotions and what to do with them, when magically, you'd know: They'd just come and go exuberantly like summer storms. But anger and hate and sorrow are all magic too, and left alone, they'd lead you back to the knowledge that your life is charmed. Because hate is love looking for itself everyplace but where love is; and love is what you feel for yourself when you know that you are where you're supposed to be in the universe, and that you're lovely just because you are, and, of course, charmed.

Not only that, but you're also the magic maker; the inner living part of you that forms your life. But consciously you have to know this, accept and acknowledge it, and let the magic of yourself happen. That way, you're directing the magic of yourself.

But it's even more fun just to let the magic happen as it wants to, because it's your magic, and that way it keeps telling you more and more about your magical self. Then the magic flows through you with unimpeded delight. If you keep saying, "I want it this way and no other," then you may be limiting your physical experience, because there's no doubt that your inner magical self knows more about your potentials than you do. And it will tell you quite clearly, if you only listen.

To many adults, all of this sounds too simple and unintellectual, because unfortunately many of them think that the mind is just something to say "no" with, and to keep out magic. Nothing could be further from the truth.

But if you use your mind to say no to magic, then it's like closing doors to your own charmed existence, and refusing to use the full power of your life.

Everyone works with magic, whether they realize it or not. Beliefs are magic, too, you see. Many people think that one particular belief makes everything right; or makes magic happen. And as long as they believe that, they're all right for a while. But if they start doubting that belief, and don't find another one to replace it, then they think that they've lost their magic, or that life has. Instead, of course, the magic is there all along.

But people love systems, so they use all kinds of beliefs . . . some of them quite handy . . . as aids. And they travel through belief systems, sometimes going to considerable trouble to do so, when all they really have to remember is that they are magic themselves, and their lives are charmed without their having to do anything about it at all.

And your conscious mind is magic, too. Its workings are mysterious and complicated, and simple and clear at once, like air is. Your conscious mind looks out through your eyes, and knows parcels of air as its body, and smiles through cheeks and skin the same way that the moon shines through the wide skin of the heavens. See how clear and mysterious it all is? So, in a way, it's silly for the conscious mind to question magic, because—well, it's so magical itself.

But systems of magic are silly, too, and all of them are really based upon doubt. Magic is considered so tenuous that someone has to be at it all the time, making spells or paying someone else to do it. And the spells all have to be done just right, so people concentrate on how to do this spell or another. This gets very complicated, and many adult books deal with the subject.

But everything is a spell. Your words and thoughts are spells. Science is just another system that tries to discover what certain spells cause certain effects. Usually, of course, scientists don't understand magic any more than priests do; and they all get caught up in their own complicated methods.

There isn't much basic difference between muttering a lot of different phrases or drawing magic circles to protect yourself against illness, and taking handfuls of pills given to you by doctors. Both methods work if you believe in them, though the practitioners of one method will never agree that the other way works at all, of course. And unfortunately, neither side *really* understands magic, which is behind all of the spells and methods and formulas.

Spells work if you believe in them; only you don't need spells at all. Everything happens by itself. You happen by yourself, so does the world. And the principle behind it all is magic. And magic is the beingness within and behind all things.

The Body and Creaturehood

Within your creaturehood, you have all kinds of freedom. And all of the freedom you can ever enjoy in your lifetime must come through your creaturehood. Some people spend a good deal of time trying to ignore their own bodies, or trying to pretend that they only have minds, or that minds alone are important. Some people even try to ignore their bodies almost entirely in an effort to be more spiritual, or to be "better" people, which is like a bird trying to fly better than any other bird alive . . . all the time refusing to use its wings, or pretending that they weren't there. He'd never get off the ground. A bird would never think of such foolishness, of course, and often other creatures are smarter than people.

In fact, whenever you're in trouble, it's a good idea to watch the animals, for they bask in their freedom and don't worry about their limitations. A cat or dog can teach you a lot. A cat really enjoys its catness, just as you should enjoy your creaturehood. Even a fly buzzing around the ceiling loves its own reality and is free in it. If it stopped to wonder whether or not it could really fly—well, it would fall down in a minute or never go fast enough to outwit your mother's flyswatter.

So, trying to be religious or "good" or "better" by ignoring your body doesn't make much sense either.

Actually, each person has a private kingdom for his or her very own, because your body is the one part of earth that is really yours, that no one can take away during your lifetime. It's the part of earth, moving and alive, that belongs to you and nobody else. In a way, it's your portion of the planet, sprung up in a living, moving statue of earth-stuff, for you and no one else. So how you treat your body is important.

You just don't live *in* it, either. You live *through* it; there's a difference. You flow through it, moving in all of its parts. The body is your own magic country. Your conscious mind is like a monarch. Now, a good king or queen is loving and gives the people freedom to move about the country. In this case, your own feelings and thoughts and desires are like the people in *your* kingdom. So you should

265

treat your own feelings graciously, and you and your kingdom will flourish. Some monarchs are dictators, setting up all kinds of impossible laws and taboos, because they're really afraid of the people who make up their own kingdom.

If you're a good king or queen, you'll realize that your kingdom is a good one, and you won't be afraid of your own people... your thoughts and feelings and desires... but will encourage them. And you and your body will have all the freedom necessary to flourish and grow.

The Power and a Special Sumari Song

Now, here's a Sumari song, to help you remember that your existence is a charmed one. A Sumari song is one that speaks to your ordinary self and to your magical self at once. It's a charmed song, of course. But it isn't a spell or a sign or even a symbol, because all *those* things can be very tricky indeed. For example, if you believe that your magic comes from a medal or a cross or a necklace, and you lose your luckpiece, then you're in trouble, and you think that your magic is gone. Then you *can* spend a lifetime trying to find it.

And if you think that spells make magic, then you aren't secure either, because you might forget the words to the spell, since no one is infallible. Besides, people who believe in spells guard them very jealously, and often think that they alone have "the power," and if you want to learn their methods, then you must endure trials to prove your courage. And, of course, you must promise to follow the rules, and prove that you are worthy of "the power." Again, all of this is very silly because flowers and birds and frogs have the power too, and without having to prove themselves to anyone, or pass any tests.

So the Sumari song is just a reminder. It's been translated

from an inner language into one that you can understand, but the magic is still in it. It will jog your memory when you're in danger of forgetting that your life is charmed. Of course, you might forget the song. But even then, you'd only lose a valuable reminder—which would be a pity— but you wouldn't believe that your magic had gone with your memory. Still, I hope that you'll always remember that your life is charmed, and that your magic is you; and you don't have to prove anything to yourself or anyone else to get it!

Here is the Sumari Song:

> My mind is like a frog
> On a lily pad,
> Knowing, alone,
> But never lonely.
>
> My mind is green
> And glowing,
> Leaping without slipping
> From lily-pad-thought
> To thought.
>
> My mind sits smiling
> On the pond of my being,
> In morning and evening,
> Always knowing the time,
> Yet not needing
> A clock.

Sumari Time

There are special moments that are open channels in which a different kind of time emerges; an inside-Sumari kind of non-time. And in that time, everything is miraculous. One hour of it is worth—well, days of ordinary minutes. In Sumari time, you can learn something in a twinkling that might otherwise take years, and insights spring up, brilliant as fresh fruit, for the picking.

This Sumari time is the special heart of time, and contains its real meaning. Again, it's really a non-time, always new and shiny, and it contains secrets that are secrets only because so few people realize that this glittering time exists, and right in the middle of the regular time that they know.

Now, in earth time, so many minutes add up to so many hours, and when you're living in that framework alone, then so much time is needed to get things done. But inspiration is quite different. It seeks out those special moments when magic leaps from one world to the other with such ease.

And each person has his or her own key to Sumari time. All you have to do is use it. You can write or paint or learn things or solve problems or just be supremely happy ten times as well in one hour of Sumari time as you can in ten regular hours.

Of course, Sumari and earth time coincide, which is tricky, I admit. And earth time springs out of Sumari time, but people divide up usual time so much that they never realize that time is really whole.

So, Sumari time is whole time, since we're using the term "time" at all. Later we'll dispense with it entirely. But right now the trick is to recognize Sumari time and use it.

If time were a fruit, then Sumari time would be its nectar and essence, and if time were a holiday, then Sumari time would be Christmas.

When most people bump into a corner of Sumari time, they're delighted, but they don't know how to find it again, when it's there all the while.

Stacks and stacks of the wrong kind of hours won't give you even one minute of good Sumari time, though. Because in a strange way, a Sumari hour is the other side of an earth hour. I mean, all of a sudden, for example, 11 o'clock becomes transparent; it is what it is, on top, but it's something else too, underneath. And you can peer through—well, time itself.

The Beginning

It's deceptive to say that thus and so "happened in the beginning," or that "in the beginning was the word," or whatever, because there was no official Beginning when God suddenly came parading out of nothingness, bearing the ingredients of mountains, oceans, and land, and trailing sky banners proclaiming the opening of the universe, or the creation of life from a sea of gasses.

There are multitudinous beginnings. "The Beginning" is only the one you came in on, so to speak, which is rather like coming into a dream in the middle and wondering what happened earlier. In dreams, everything really happens at once, even though there seems to be a beginning and ending . . . the past and present and future merge . . . and the universe is like that in a way. You're bound to wonder what went on or how long it's all been going on, not realizing that in a manner of speaking, it just started when you got there. And in another way, it really isn't there at all.

If you dream that you're in a jungle, for instance, no vines or tangled undergrowth climb up the bedpost, and no exotic animals prowl between the window and the door. Yet the jungle certainly seems real. Where did it come from, or when did it begin? The universe is like the dream jungle. It exists quite properly, yet in the most profound way it makes no sense to ask when it began. It begins each day, each moment, at each point of our contact with it. The gods exist in the same manner, like a giant species of consciousness, striding psychological paths of vast proportions that never really physically appear in the world at all.

The gods and the universe really begin everyplace and

everywhere at once, at every point. Our psychological reality rises from an inner inconceivable divine mind that's invisible to us, since we are It, earthized, individualized. We're the gods in camouflage.

On Methods

("This small chapter is very important," Oversoul Seven said, "so do pay attention, Tweety, and anyone else who might be listening.")

The whole thing about techniques is the idea that you need certain methods to make things *work* for you, when all you have to do is let things alone: Then they "work" for you automatically. If you forget that fact, then you'll always be looking for better and better methods...which will never really work...because Nature and your own nature work best when left alone.

If you're going to study such issues at all, then look for what you do right, and you'll always find that in those areas you let yourself alone and do what comes naturally, because you are inclined in that direction.

When you concentrate on what's wrong, you almost always try too hard, look for methods that will work better than the ones you're using now... when the truth is that the methods themselves stand in the way, whatever they are. Because Nature doesn't use methods. It "works" because it is what it is.

Methods presuppose the opposite, in whatever area of your concern. They show your belief that nature doesn't work right on its own.